The Donors

Fabio A. Bordino

Edited by Rob Harman

ISBN: 978-1-9162711-0-4

First published 2019

Disclaimer

The Donors is a work of fiction. The characters within this book are not representative of any person, alive or dead, and are purely fictional constructs.

In fondest memory of absent family and friends.

In loving tribute to my Father, Kat and two Evelyns,
without whom none of this would have been possible.

Further thanks to Eagle, Sibbo, Chris B, Tony 'Montana'
Elwell, Marcus G, Reece Jackson, Sally Kirkup, two Cliffs
and a Dougie Nuisance!
Also to JH and HH (remains a contender!)
and the Hebert family- long may they quiz.

And deepest apologies to the many, many
not mentioned since that list would become
another book in itself.

And last but by no means least a very special thanks to Mary
Rose C. Barrera-
The greatest typist in Capiz!

Foreward by Walter Herzagovia for 'The Donors'

 You actually have the temerity to ask *me* to define for *you* what amounts to a documentary?! Why, *I*, Walter, Maestro Herzagovia, the foremost leader of this sacred medium, *am* the very embodiment of what is known to us as *the documentary*, nothing less and very much *more* besides! How would you have me define myself?! Ha! I evade definition even within my *own* very broad terms!

And so you request an introduction for your own production? Having been subjected to the footage, and having suffered the transcript, I was heartened only by the possibility these characters you have woefully chronicled are fictional, *but no!* It was my sad realization to surmise these sub-normal dregs are actual walking and (unfortunately) talking people! Judge not, a wiser man *even* than *I* said, *but come on?!* I would have tenderness, even pity, for such wretched creatures where it not for the horror and disgust they provoke within me. *What* on Earth where you thinking?!

As the leading documentaerilist of our age I could advise you to make some other approach, find completely different Subjects even, but alas you have made your own very messy, soiled, *depraved* bed! I take leave of your contagious petri dish

Werner Herzog was unavailable.

Contents

Episode One:

Robby – Adult filmmaker

'He who makes a beast of himself gets rid of the pain of being a man.' – Dr. Samuel L. Johnson.

'Welcome to my cock.' – Dr. Robby Strauss.

You can learn a *lot* about someone from their lavatory. More about this later. When I return from the bathroom belonging to Robby Strauss, I find him sitting behind his desk, beckoning me to take a chair opposite him. It might seem *overly* elaborate me relating such seemingly insignificant aspects so I shall explain: I am loath to omit even the *slightest* detail in this transcript should I need to rely upon a particular fact which might have later resonance.

'Can we just have a brief introduction please?' I ask, once I've set up my camera and when *eventually* Stan, my soundman, lets me know his readings are correct.

'Hi, I'm Robby Strauss,' the Subject of my documentary states, 'and I'm a Captain of Industry in the Adult Entertainment Business. Welcome to my cock, *sorry*, my *World*.'

I should at this point make clear that I am not making a film about - as Mr. Strauss defines- "the Adult Entertainment Business" , nor am I documenting *specifically* the man sitting opposite me: the fact is that Robby is a window into a *broader* project I'm currently conducting. Stan appears to be trying to tell me something but I frown to indicate I will not cut filming since Strauss continues in his flow. 'So Alfie, *what's* it all about?'

'My name *isn't* Alfie,' I tell Robby. 'As I mentioned before, I am *Fabio* and this is Stan.'

'Sorry,' he replies, 'just my little joke. It's a reference, by the way. Perhaps I shouldn't have delved into profundity quite so early in the morning?' This, I suspect, is an allusion I might have to investigate *later*. I choose not to ask him to expand upon this since it seems an unnecessary digression. In the brief time I've known Mr. Strauss I've observed that he takes *very few* points of discussion seriously. The e-mails and phone calls prior to us meeting today had contained a series of obscure references and baffling "jokes". Subsequently, he'd greeted us at the front door wearing what I'd initially speculated to be a novelty fancy dress outfit. It only became apparent later though that this garish garb is his everyday attire.

'I'm intending to make a documentary about your brother,' I tell him, repeating what I'd stated in *all* our correspondence.

'That doesn't *exactly* narrow it down,' Strauss replies with a wink and mischievous smile. 'I have six brothers.' I suspect he's attempting to play another jest at my expense so I feel now is the time to give you, *dear reader*, a bit of back story concerning the Strauss family.

Around half a century ago -somewhere in the South-East of England- a twenty-seven year old woman named Mary Strauss (nee O'Grady) gave birth to Sextuplets, an extremely rare phenomenon my dictionary defines as "*six* children born to the same mother at once." To avoid further digression I shall specify more upon this miraculous multi-birth at some *later* point hence.

'I'm referring specifically to your youngest brother, Roland,' I inform Robby, who subsequently looks crestfallen. This is possibly due to having been reminded of the perilous plight of his younger brother whom, I should mention, is not one of the Sextuplets but born several years later. This is not an altogether unmitigated tragedy however since it might later serve for the dramatic benefit of my documentary.

'It's about Roland?' Mr. Strauss asks, possibly still stunned as a result of not yet able to come to terms with his brother's ill-turn of health.

'Yes,' I reply, 'was this *not* all fully explained in my brief?'

'Ah yes, good old Rolly-polly. Get well soon bruv, and all that.'

'The donation of a kidney would very likely save his life,' I state clearly, to deter from further digression. I notice my current Subject has a distracting habit of flicking and grooming his dark - very likely dyed- ponytail.

'Well, us Strauss brothers are a tight lit group. We'll all band together to get him through this. *All* for one, and united we fall, and never the twain.'

'So that's a "*yes*" then?' I find it best to remind this person the precise reason we sense him to be a suitable Subject for our documentary and, quite possibly a book tie-in also. 'We can chronicle you donating one of your kidneys to your brother?'

'That bit was probably a typo from my Secretary.' At this point I feel I should reiterate my point but Mr. Strauss carries on regardless, 'Let's not jump to any hasty preconceived conclusions-that's the *first* rule written in stone at Documentary School, I'm *sure* you'll agree? I feel there could be some *mutually* beneficial aspects to this film you're attempting to make'.

'How so?' I ask, genuinely perplexed.

'Have we actually started *yet?*' This seems to be a rhetorical question because he ploughs on with his increasingly excitable gush. 'I suppose there's no harm in you giving a background story to my *dearest* of dear brothers. Indeed, it would give weight and gravitas to your, hitherto, modest little production, forgive me for mentioning?'

'*Modest?*' I echo but he persists breathlessly, as though his very life depended upon it.

'I can make it *less* modest, give it depth *and* breathe, perhaps even give a little publicity, sorry, back story, to my unique, thriving adult film production company. And if I help young Roland then so much the better still.'

'First and foremost,' I sternly reply, 'as a film-maker I aim to maintain as *much* of an *objective* eye as possible, and this eye is trained upon this search, *first and foremost*, for a *suitable* donor for your brother'.

'That would be great,' Strauss responds but I sense he's been wounded by my justified abruptness. His previous smile has become a grimace, his tone receding from enthusiasm to halting, even spasmodic, grunting. His words now begin to escape from him like low, groaning intonations somewhere between agony and ecstasy, as though casting some dark, guttural spell. 'That would be good…very good…*very…very good!'* This builds to a frenzied crescendo where he eventually exhales in what appears to be an expiring breathe, before slumping forward upon his desk as though altogether shuffling off his Mortal Coil! I consider leaning forward to administer help -or to call the Emergency Services at the very least- when something *even* stranger occurs: a figure, as yet previously unnoticed by myself, emerges from under the desk. To my complete astonishment I observe this to be a brunette in her mid-to-late twenties. Her lipstick is smudged. This female then climbs to her feet to reveal an outfit that certain people (more judgmental than I) might classify as "*slutty.*"

'Sorry, *where a*re my manners?' I turn back to the desk to see that Robby Strauss has been miraculously reclaimed from the jaws of Death. He becomes re-animated once more. 'This is my wife Scarlett, or "Scarlett Hotlips" as she's known in the Industry.'

'Pleased to *eat* you!' they chorus together as though this were rehearsed, or part of a regular ritual. I give Stan a quizzical look. His response is merely a baffled shrug. He *later* claims he'd only had a fleeting glimpse of Scarlett entering the room whilst I was in the bathroom and, preoccupied with his duties, *presumed* she'd made a speedy exit as opposed to slipping beneath the desk.

'How did you two meet?' I enquire.

'It was something like what you've just witnessed,' Robby shoots back with a guffaw, which earns him a playful slap on the arm from his wife. 'But seriously, I put an advert in the lonely-hearts column of the local newspaper.'

'You *did?*' My incredulous tone is mirroring Scarlett's now perplexed expression.

'Yes,' Strauss continues, 'it went something along the lines of "Arts loving pervert seeks needy nutter for mutually assured destruction." Remember that, love?'

'He's a total liar,' Scarlett counters, 'we met in Florence.'

'Florence in Italy,' I probe, 'home of the Renaissance?'

'Florence, the swingers club in Stockport,' she replies earnestly.

'I was the last man standing,' Robby declares with puffed-up pride, 'and she was the last woman…*laying down.*'

'Well, I couldn't sit down for nearly a week,' Scarlett elaborates, 'that's when I *know* I've had a good night out.'

'Darling,' Strauss says tenderly whilst guiding his wife out of the room, 'make our guests a cup of tea? After washing your hands and brushing your teeth, *of course.'*

Robby is giving a guided tour of his home which also serves, I'm informed, as both his business premises and occasional studio. He points to a row of framed photographs stretching out along the whole length of the wall, mostly featuring images of himself. Stan and I are then led to a doorway at the end of the corridor.

'And now to a less glamorous place, the nuts and bolts, in a sense.' We go inside this room to observe a series of tables, each one piled high with dvds, vhs tapes, explicit promotion material and other assorted, less recognizable paraphernalia.

'This is my distribution depot, the brain of my business, *as it were.'*

'Is there *still* a market for videotapes?' I ask upon noticing the boxes in this format are thick with dust.

'This is the essential place where my product is released back into the wild,' Strauss replies, as though in response to a completely different question. 'Imagine, *if you will,* not quite all these items are wholly glamorous. I'm honest if nothing else, perhaps not *all* of these are amazing movie Stars, some might even be *mere* timid office clerk types.' It takes me awhile to process the fact that he has personalized his produce, referring to them as *Human* Entities! 'But they have all set off on a perilous mission, a tumultuous odyssey, *a baptism of fire!'* His declamations become increasingly passionate. 'And all *this* conveniently leads me to a most pertinent question to my detractors-who suffers the most, a young Starlet, one of my so called *"victims"*, who has been mercilessly subjected to glamorous Showbiz events and the torments of exotic locations travelled to, occasionally, on *first* class, or the oppressed wage slave who helplessly sees themselves parceled and packaged off to some bleak, windowless office somewhere in the backside of beyond?' Robby puffs himself up for his exhorting crescendo, and in doing so knocks over a pile of DVDs, which are subsequently strewn across the dirt-coloured shag pile carpet like lifeless birds shot out of the sky. 'Anonymous questionnaires prove me right *yet again*-I thank you!'

'That camera needs to be turned *off*,' the Manager of the adult bookshop sternly insists.

'But I didn't get your message,' Robby replies. It had been *his* idea to film this visit to a retail outlet which stocks a selection of his titles.

'Look mate, it's not my fault you've had a wasted journey,' the man behind the counter continues. He's tall, thick-set, about the same age as Robby. 'You shouldn't have presumed we'd re-order.'

'Mine are bestselling titles,' my Subject protests, 'I'm not selling baked beans here!'

'New titles come out quicker than you can blink, pal.' The Manager's tone is dismissive. 'The punter is always wanting the very best quality item. So, *how*'s your product performing elsewhere in the market place?'

'I *can't* believe I'm being scrutinized about my Master Craftsmanship by some mere *shop assistant!*' Strauss counters.

'You're right pal,' the man replies whilst emerging from behind the counter.

'Yes, I am!' Robby is now less self-assured however, and finds himself backing off with the shop-keeper's approach.

'Your product ain't beans because people *like* beans!' My Subject is then all but chased out of the premises. Then the man turns to address my camera directly, 'I *won't* be giving my consent for this filming. I *know* my rights that you can't broadcast *any* of this without my signed consent. You'd best leave too.' I shall have to consort with a copyright Lawyer to see if there is *any* way around this.

'When one tires of the smoke,' Robby issues with theatrical flourish, 'and yearns for something of natural beauty, then one heads for the countryside to replenish, to recharge, to heal.' He and Scarlett are embracing on the back set of my car. There had been no need for the production vehicle today. Stan, my sound-recordist (fully insured as standard practice dictates, of course) is driving. I'm in the passenger seat, filming the couple seated behind me as the green landscape flashes past. This can serve as part of a montage for voiceovers within my film.

'The sat-nav says to take the next left,' Stan says, 'but I seem to recall another route.' This minutia will be edited out of the final cut, of course, though I retain it within my transcript to remind my Employee how in future to follow my plans *to the letter.*

'That's rather poetical,' I compliment Robby: there's no harm flattering a Subject to help them open up about themselves; later I'll approach Scarlett- currently nodding off to sleep- with a similar conceit.

'You *know* that I'm a poet,' he responds, 'we emulate a return to Eden.'

'Are you religious?' I quiz.

'*Tis* but an *anal*ogy- I sense a beautiful location for my Magnus-Opus-son.'

'Your *Magnum Opus?*' Perhaps I shouldn't have corrected him? I am an observer; *merely* a camera.

'As I said,' Strauss retorts with a fleeting frown before getting back into his flow, 'it will simply be known as "Eden-garden of Erotica"!'

'I think this is where we're supposed to be?' Stan rather prosaically interjects whilst pulling up along a lay-by.

'*Hark!*' Robby exclaims, '*All* of creation, man and woman, fauna and flora, beasts of the field coupling wildly!'

'Perhaps we should have carried straight on?' Stan drones in his joy-killing monotone.

'*Not* all together with each other, of course,' my Subject continues. 'It *must* be noted that I'm not the purveyor of any of that dodgy interspecies bestiality stuff. My artistic vision is one of utilizing the sexual energy of Nature, all of Creation as a consolidated, single convulsive Entity of compulsive ecstasy, copulating with itself.'

'What, like wanking?' Scarlett says, alerting us that she's just woken up.

'It is my divine mission to *re*-eroticize Nature in order to restore Paradise on Earth in *all* her sexual splendor,' Strauss expands.

'Lucky her!' his wife concludes. 'Are we there yet?'

'Here we are,' Robby announces to Stan and myself as we return from a staff meeting where I've been forced to admonish my careless Colleague. From Strauss's demeanour you'd imagine he was referring to something wholly commonplace but to my amazement I'm confronted with the sight of Scarlett, blindfolded, gagged and tied up against a tree. She's wearing only the briefest of underwear.

'What's happening, Robby?' I ask, genuinely perplexed.

'This is for a proposed series I'm planning,' he replies in a matter-of-fact tone, 'the working title is "point-of-view pervert," you know, one handed filming-*get it?!*' Then he bursts out laughing as though I should recall some specific point of reference. 'Let's walk and talk'. Strauss proceeds to lead us deeper into the woods to an area where the trees and foliage becomes more conspicuous still.

'Are we just going to leave her there?' Stan is already unheeding of the brief given him just moments earlier to consult with our Subject *only* should it concern some *essential* technical matter.

'I approach all my movies like a method actor', Robby muses as we trudge onward.

'How so?' The increasingly dense forest now obscures our view of Scarlett.

'I'll be playing a role, such as poacher or game-keeper, perhaps pervy Lord of the Manor, or maybe just some dodgy passing dogger.'

'Which role exactly?' Mrs. Strauss has now completely disappeared from view.

'We'll decide that on this nice little stroll. It will help me get into character.'

'Do you know where we're going?' Stan asks, again clearly in breach of my own Modus Operandi.

'Let's just look at it as an odyssey,' Robby replies, 'an *erotic* odyssey.'

'Are we lost?' I enquire. There seems nothing familiar about the current vista. We've double-backed upon ourselves in the hope of retracing a pathway or lane we'd been along earlier, alas with no success.

'I sense we're not so very far now.' I detect mild alarm within Robby as he leads us through a copse which resembles countless other similar growths on our bizarre meander. 'This will help her to get into her role.'

'Do you suppose your wife will be ok tied up and vulnerable like that?' For this further intrusion I shall have to again reprimand Stan later!

'Robby', I say, trying to steer this project back on course, 'how did you get into sex movies?'

'As a school-leaver I visited the careers section of my local job centre,' he replies whilst guiding us along yet another path that looks much the same as a dozen previous ones already traipsed along, 'you know, where they ask you your interests to see if there's a suitable apprenticeship they can put you on.'

'How did that go?' Just at that moment I surmise a more reliable route back though remain silent in order to allow Robby to elaborate upon his chosen path in Life.

'I told them I like sex, and that I also like the movies, so they suggested I should make *sex movies.*'

'They *did*?' I suspect Stan's taking Mr. Strauss wholly at face value; I might be forced to *soon* look for a replacement Assistant.

'They *did* indeed,' Robby exclaims triumphantly. 'And the rest, as they say, is History. Live the dream-Kerching*! That's* my special mantra.'

'I know,' I agree, 'you said that in the car on the way here. Several times.'

'My brother advised me to select a personal mantra.'

'Which one?' It must be remembered he has *six* brothers in total.

'Billy, the lifestyle coach.' I recall this particular sibling from my production notes but was led to believe he's merely a motor mechanic? 'We should head back now. I'm sure Scarlett has gotten into her role by now.'

The next half an hour can serve in the final cut as a montage: Robby disappears into some bushes; he re-emerges again, this time from a hedge elsewhere; he slips and accidently unearths a nearby sapling; our Subject cursing the cruel indifference of Nature; latterly strolling along down yet another pathway even *after* I insist it's another wrong turn.

'This certainly *looks* familiar,' Strauss calls out at last from behind a hillock. There's a raucous noise I suspect to be the machinations of a chainsaw cutting through wood. This gets louder and more persistent. Eventually it becomes likely we're approaching whoever is wielding such an abrasive work tool. Or perhaps *they* are approaching *us?* 'Do you imagine it might be like that movie?'

'*Which* movie?' I've been aware for some time of a correct route back to Scarlett but had decided instead to concentrate on Robby's reactions to having lost his wife in the woods.

'We'd have to change the name for copyright reasons, of course- we could call it "The Wimbledon Common chainsaw massacre"!' I'm suddenly visited by a horrific vision of Scarlett getting dismembered by a maniacal tree surgeon! I now regret not guiding Strauss straight back to his wife earlier. Eventually the chainsaw falls silent.

'*This* pathway looks familiar,' I say whilst leading us back along a now certain pathway.

It's another ten minutes before we finally catch sight of Scarlett. She's in exactly the same position as had been left, still firmly secured against the same tree. But her lower underwear is now down around her ankles.

'The chainsaw was a nice touch,' Scarlett says after Robby removes the gag from her mouth.

'It *was?*' He's looking directly into my camera, a baffled expression upon his face.

'*What* gave you the idea to roleplay as a randy gardener?' she asks, once relieved of her blindfold.

'Just a whim,' he replies, suddenly sheepish and averting the scrutiny of my lens.

I make allusions to Homer on our way home: such as the possibility we'd *likewise* been waylaid by our own Calypso; or that we ourselves had become lotus eaters; and that it was likely that Scarlett could be perceived as a modern day Penelope, kept waiting and almost snatched away *altogether* during her husband's absence. Robby glares back at me. Maybe he doesn't want his wife to know the *full* extent of our *own* meandering odyssey? Perhaps his earlier point of reference had not even been about Homer *at all*? I suggest we should find some modern-day equivalent of our homecoming to Ithaca but am merely met with a blank stare. We drop Mr. and Mrs. Strauss back at their abode just as the sun is setting.

'See you tomorrow, you old Homer,' Robby says whilst climbing out of my vehicle: it seems my Classical allusions were *not* altogether lost on him *after all*.

'What have we here?' Strauss says, once more behind the desk in his home office. He's opening some letters. 'It's not quite all e-mails these days, there's still some old-school types like myself out there who use handwritten correspondence.'

'Is that in keeping with the Obscene Publications Act?' I ask, observing the sexually graphic material he sifts through.

'This is merely my bi-monthly Adult Newsletter a few of us in the Industry decided to keep running to let the distributors know we're all *still* in business.'

'How actually do you still remain in business? *Surely* you must have been affected by so much free porn available on the internet with just a few clicks of a mouse?' I have this information *only* on account of a reliable source of mine.

'It keeps me posted about my competition,' Robby says, either not hearing me or choosing not to answer. 'Here we go: a list of new releases; "Raped by a Sumo… Part 6"-good to see my old mate Chas "Chunky" Harris still in business; a new edition to the series "Ganged by Niggaz-part 7".'

'Is *that* title not a little bit racist?'

'Apparently not,' he replies. 'Something to do with the spelling, and the film-maker is "appropriating the bitches," or something to that effect.'

'The *film-maker*?' Do these pornographers actually imagine that term can be applied to *them?!* 'Is *this* really what constitutes a film-maker?'

'Yeah,' Strauss responds without pause before showing me the brochure in all its explicit brazenness. 'Another old pal of mine Winston "Chalky" Jones, or "Jamal" as he now likes to be known.'

'Do these people *really* define themselves as film-makers?' I reiterate, but my question remains unanswered when Robby's landline rings.

'That will be the phone,' he smirks though forsakes answering it, instead letting it go to answerphone message which declares, 'I would come to the phone right now only I'm busy getting sucked off on my yacht! Leave a message and I'll get right back to you.'

'You still have that same message?' I ask as Robby bursts out laughing: does this amuse him *quite* to this extent *every* single time somebody calls?

'I *should* change it I suppose,' he replies, once having dried his eyes. 'Mum isn't very impressed by it.' I'm then compelled to ask about his Mother but am cut short by an angry voice bellowing out from the speaker.

'Robert! *What* have I told you about that muggy message?! Are you there?! Pay me back that loan I made to you or you *won't* be seeing me!'

'Who was that?' I enquire once the Caller has cut contact.

'Just my brother,' comes a limp reply.

'Which one?' I'm once more thwarted, this time by the doorbell.

'Excuse me?' Then Robby is dashing to the front door and, after a cursory glance through the spyglass, opens it to reveal a tall, extravagantly dressed black man. 'Did anybody order a pimp?'

'Hey Robby,' this man whoops, 'they told me you would be a *funny* guy.'

'You must be Hung Hawkins?' my Subject grunts before beckoning him to enter.

'No, I'm the pizza delivery guy,' Hawkins replies whilst stepping into the house.

'Are you the rent-a-cock -*yes or no?!*' Strauss's tone is suddenly abrupt, impatient, aggressive even.

'*Yes*, that's my stage name,' the man replies timidly, 'I was only kidding.'

'I make the jokes around here, donkey dick!' Robby's brow then unfurrows, his characteristic smile returns. 'Get ready quick 'cos your co-star is already ready.'

'Is it Scarlett?' Hawkins asks, his eyes lighting up.

'Yep, but you know what she's like-the meter is running!'

'How did the shoot go?' I'm with Robby in the park later that afternoon. He's feeding the ducks at the edge of lake. Even though I had not been discouraged from observing the filming I'd made myself scarce on account of it being a bit *too* early in the day to witness a full-blown live sex-scene!

'I *thought* you might have stayed?' Strauss is giving me a quizzical look.

'Does jealousy ever came into it?'

'Into *what?*' he replies but does not wait for further explanation. 'Scarlett is my muse. Besides, it's just business.

Will you be staying for lunch? She should have started cooking by now.' I'm amazed how casual he is about other men having sex with his wife. I make a mental note to investigate the concept of cuckoldry, and those who practice it.

'Is Scarlett your soulmate?'

'Of course,' he replies without a beat.

'Robby, you strike me as somebody who lives very much in the senses.'

'Well, Life *isn't* a rehearsal, Fabrice.' I consider correcting his mispronouncing of my name though refrain in case it might halt his flow. 'I believe we have to get as much mileage out of these mortal coils before forced to embark on the stumbling shuffle towards decrepitude.'

'That's very profound- Shakespeare perchance?'

'Not right *here* in the park,' he replies with a smirk. 'Later on, *if* you ask nicely.'

'That's if you *do* make old bones, of course?' Perhaps he's misinterpreted my allusion?

'This is why I live my life largely and loudly,' Strauss says as he tosses the last of the bread to the noisome, avaricious ducks. 'To drown out the din of lives unlived.'

'Sounds Checkhovian.'

'Just mild asthma,' Robby wheezes back with such earnestness that I'm certain it's a reference to the aforementioned great Russian storyteller's tale about a disillusioned man delivering a digressive lecture about smoking.

'What of the Life after this one?'

'After performing? I suppose I could concentrate on distribution.'

'No,' I counter, sensing that his points of citation have become too dense, 'I meant *after* having shuffled off this mortal coil?'

'*Oh*- the great unknown country no traveller returns from?...Blame your package tour operator!'

'You mean reincarnation?'

'I feel rather optimistic about reincarnation,' Robby replies as we head back to his house. 'This revelation came to me one day, *just-like-that!* It was like De-ja-vu *all over again*. An epiphany not unlike the one I'd had upon discovering the internet provides something *other* than pornography.'

'Are you not concerned you might return as a snail, or a fly?' There's no harm playing Devil's Advocate at this point.

'I've lived a good Life. Good karma and all that, innit! I'm fairly certain that in the next Life I shall be coming back as *me!* Know what I mean? *Ker-ching*! Live the dream!' He's still laughing as we cross the threshold of his abode.

'Scarlett!' Robby calls out as we search his home at length for some trace of her. I reason that perhaps she's merely popped to a nearby shop to purchase some extra ingredients for our lunch. 'Doubtful,' he replies, 'we're having a microwave-ready meal. And she *never* leaves the front door open- she's been kidnapped!'

'*Surely* not?' I rationalize, although make a mental note this would make for some agreeably dramatic material. 'Let's just attempt to stay calm and conduct a full and methodical search of the entire house. Do you have many enemies?' I then recall the ominous phone call earlier which he'd claimed to have been from one of his brothers.

'He *wouldn't* have?!' Strauss gasps, seemingly reading my mind. He opens a wardrobe. 'Her clothes are still there,' is his reply to my reasoning that perhaps she'd *merely* just left him. Then he goes to a further wardrobe door and flings it open. The sight meeting us is as peculiar as *any* I've previously witnessed: a woman has been blindfolded and gagged; her wrists are suspended above her, secured by handcuffs around a high clothes rail.

'You arsehole!' Scarlett explodes once Robby has removed the gag and blindfold.

'Sorry sweetheart,' he replies whilst unfastening the cuffs, 'me and Fabrice got chatting and I lost *all* recollection of time.'

'Get me out of *here*, you prick!' Her eyes are ablaze with ferocity.

'Calm down, love- you know how easily distracted I get.'

'Distracted?!'

Let's not get physical again,' he bleats whilst jumping for cover.

'Telling a woman to calm down usually has a counter-productive effect,' Robby says as we're about to eat. He occasionally dabs his cut lip with a paper tissue. '*I*, of *all* people, should know *this* by now.'

'How's lunch?' Scarlett asks. There's a flinty look in her eye which unnerves me.

'Interesting flavours, darling,' Strauss replies whilst tucking into the meal. 'I'm sensing parsley...maybe oregano?...I don't think you've included turmeric or chilli?...*Possibly* basil?...I'm getting something else...*Oh*, it's pubes *again*, isn't it?!' His face falls as he picks a curly hair from between his teeth before turning to me, 'You might want that readymade meal, Fabrice?'

'Well, here we are on the road again,' Robby is picking me up in his car from my production office.

'No Scarlett today?' I enquire while climbing into the vehicle. I'm already filming.

'She's had to visit her mum for a few days,' comes the reply as we speed away. 'I thought you might like to accompany me on a new and concerted sales drive?'

'*New*? How so?'

'I thought it the right time to distribute some of the product myself, as well as publicize my new titles'. I'm tempted to mention that I'd already accompanied him previously on such a mission, which had proven fruitless. 'Memo to myself, publicize my new titles.' I'm curious why Robby has repeated himself then turn to notice he's speaking into a recording device. 'I should explain-this is a work tool. Note for Fabrizio, rather than for my own Dictaphone.'

'Point *noted*', I tell him as we join the motorway.

'Memo to myself.' Strauss is again speaking into his voice recorder. 'Cyril from "sexy lady" will have my new titles but only at a ten percent reduction. A dilemma to sleep upon.'

'Robby, am I to presume that Cyril is the manager of that shop?'

'Well, it can't be claimed that he's named the premises after himself. Not least since he's certainly a contender for the Industry's *least* convincing cross dresser!'

'Maybe I should accompany you on your next sales drive?' Perhaps there might be a possible side-project, depicting other people within the Industry; this is my *own*, albeit mental, note to myself.

'Note to Self,' Robby issues, disregarding my question in favour of the device he's sprouted a dozen or more inanities into earlier, 'must shag some famous women. Perhaps target more *mature* Candidates to ensure more likelihood of success and subsequent gratitude?'

Strauss returns to the car, still clutching the full cardboard box he'd taken to another shop only a minute previously. I'd been told to remain in the vehicle in *no* uncertain terms.

'Memo to myself…' Robby's speaking into his machine for the umpteenth time today. We're parked in a lay-by. It seems he's suffering from stress. ' Memo to myself …idea for a book, film or perhaps *even* a musical: story about a man who harnesses sexual power over women all over the World by discovering the secret to finding their lost pet cats…Further memo to Self- help the woman at number forty nine to find her lost cat. *Further,* further memo: invent convincing alibi to Scarlett, *should* she return, to explain this absence, perhaps confect a fictional darts night? *Further,* further *additional* memo; swot up on the rules of darts to avoid getting caught out!'

'Are you alright, Robby?' I call out after he's vacated the vehicle. He neglects to answer whilst pacing up and down, perilously close to the traffic hurtling by. 'I have a paper bag you might want to blow into? That *usually* helps with hyperventilation.'

'Memo to myself…' my Subject announces when eventually climbing back behind the wheel. He seems calmer but I'm concerned he might pull the car out into incoming traffic. 'Memo to self- others do *not* have the power to harm you!…Further memo to myself- create a drug powerful enough to convince hostile shit-bags to co-operate with *me!*'

Strauss later composes himself to attempt one more delivery but this *also* does not go well. He emerges from this newest shop *in less than a minute*, shadowed all the way back to the vehicle.

'Something you need to learn, Fabrizio, is that *every* story is told twice- first as comedy, then again as tragedy,' I'm told once we're back on the road again.

'Surely it's the *other* way round?' Seemingly in response to my dispute he slams on the brakes of the car and swerves onto the hard shoulder. He then reaches into the breast pocket of his knee length black leather coat ("the uniform of the pornographer" -confided to me in a lighter moment) to pull something out in a sudden, *violent* motion. I fear for my own safety before realizing it's not a weapon but merely his over-used Dictaphone.

'Memo to Self, make certain people very, *very* sorry for their actions! Further memo to myself- to achieve this compile a "*shit*" list. Then add names to it. This will be your "*shit list*"!'

'Robby,' I say at last, once his moment of rage has passed, 'I'm getting the impression that perhaps something is troubling you- is there *anything* at all I can do to help you?'

'Tell me about darts!'

'*What?!*' Is this a trap?

'The rules concerning the game of darts,' he elaborates. What can all of *this* possibly mean?

'Good morning!' Strauss is greeting me at the front door of his home. We haven't seen each other in almost a week. 'Please come in?' I gesticulate to my camera. He responds with a mime I take as consent to be filmed.

'Was that the front door?' a familiar female voice resonates from the living room. I hear the clip-clop of high-heels before observing Scarlett walk into shot just as I've activated my video camera. 'Why are you standing in the hallway? You might as well *come* in and make yourself at home?'

'I hate it when we ain't getting on,' Robby says a minute later whilst cuddling his wife on the sofa in the front room.

'Me too,' Scarlett replies warmly, 'I've got something for you.'

'Making-up sex?' Then she's leading him by the hand out of the room towards the staircase. She's soon virtually dragging him upstairs. I sense it my professional duty to follow, albeit at a discreet distance. I catch sight of them again at the top of the stairs but they disappear from view once more, this time behind a door I presume to be their bedroom. I hear squeals and giggles, and soon surmise the portal has been left ajar. Out of only *vocational* curiosity I peer into this space, holding out my camera at arms length, the lens being the Observer rather than *I, physically,* myself. In the monitor -which had been extended at the side of my recording device- I witness that the Couple are now positioned upon a sprawling bed. Several implements I *suspect* to be sex toys (along with other erotic paraphernalia) are splayed out around them. I soon hear a buzzing followed by a clicking sound which gives me recourse to recall their strange tryst with handcuffs in the woods. A clanking effect is then heard, *heard* being the operative word since my view of these *exact* events is restricted, and so this puts me in mind of the rattling of metal chains. I'm about to call out to them- to make my excuses to leave- when I hear Robby call out *"yes."* He then repeats this word over and over again as though intoning some mysterious spell. Slapping noises- possibly impactions between two forms- become louder and more frequent. There are more buzzing effects, louder, increasingly persistent, these eventually resemble an industrial work tool rather than a mere love aide.

'No…no!…*no-no-no*!' Strauss is then crying out in replacement to his previous calls in the affirmative. 'Please, not *that* way! Please not *without* the lube!!' Soon it sounds as though he's sobbing. 'Not *there*! Please, I beg you! NOT THERE!'

'You can always bite the pillow,' comes Scarlett's scornful response. Her husband's subsequent screams almost blow the speakers on my video camera. I'm beginning to suspect this form of *"making-up sex"* hasn't gone *precisely* to his desired expectations?

'You *didn't* leave us then?' Robby asks upon entering the front room. I had relocated here once his screams had subsided, when silence suggested his suffering was no more- either as a result of his wife relenting in this torment or by his *actual* demise. Apparently he still lives. His bondage-themed death would *however* have served as a dramatic denouement for my Project.

'I thought you might have wanted *some* privacy?' Strauss is wearing his obligatory dressing gown, his flushed face almost matching that gaudy garment. It takes him much effort, and with clear *visible* pain, to only partially sit down opposite me as best he can.

'I'm sure he got it *all!*' Scarlett says upon entering the room. She's wearing a vividly-hued robe similar to his, and sits upon the arm of the chair where he hovers. There's an uncanny glow about her.

'I really want you to make an *extra* effort with that shoot tomorrow,' Robby tells her, 'if you make a good impression then they'll ask you back for *more* work.'

'Is Scarlett *not* an exclusive Performer for you then?' I enquire.

'*What* are you talking about?' she shoots back. I'm about to attempt to explain myself in a clearer, more *concise* way before realizing she'd been replying to her husband. 'I *always* make the fucking effort!'

'Well, you can't rest of your laurels, my love,' he retorts, 'there are a dozen *younger* Models lying in wait to steal that crown away from you.' My own personal memo to myself: it is peculiar that Scarlett defines herself as a *Model;* almost as bizarre as Robby's delusion that he's a *real* Film-maker; and still he persists; 'You will need to give two hundred percent effort if you are to remain on top!'

'Is there such a thing as *two hundred* percent?' Mrs. Strauss is quite correct in *this* matter, *at least*.

'All well you being a smart-arse but what if you lose your edge? We have to be Performers always, at *all* times. Even when we are clothed. Dress to impress, I mean- *why* do you think I dress the way I do?'

'I don't know,' Scarlett replies, 'maybe you did something really bad in a previous life?'

'I can't believe *this,'* Strauss growls, 'you actually have the temerity to lecture me on style and dress sense?!'

'You and any type of sense *at all* are strangers, mate,' she chortles back, 'you are stylish dress kryptonite!'

'Fabrice,' he erupts, turning to me in what I suspect is an appeal for support, 'you can look through my wardrobe to see that she's talking bollocks.'

'Actually Robby,' I cut him short, 'my name is *Fabio*- why is that *so* hard for you to remember?'

'Look through his wardrobe, indeed,' Scarlett scoffs, 'he wears shirts *even* Nelson Mandela would refuse to be buried in!' I shall have to research to see if this is factual, rather than *merely* a racist comment.

'What a disgraceful slur!' my Subject bellows back: it seems he might have a political conscience *after all.* 'You mean he *would* be seen dead in one of my shirts?! Well, let's contact him now to ask the man *himself!'* It now becomes apparent that Strauss does *not* follow Current Affairs. Then a broad smile spreads across his face. 'I get *it* now'. But *does* he? Perhaps he was only feigning ignorance? *'Dead!'*

'Indeed,' I lament, 'the world is a far dimmer, poorer place for the tragic loss of such a great Statesman and-'

'Deceased!' Robby cuts in. 'Brown bread! Your mooey is temporarily demised!' I'm confused now: surely Nelson Mandela was a representative of the A.N.C. which is still - to the best of my knowledge- very much thriving?

'You keep my minky out of this!' Scarlett hisses.

'A bit hard 'cos it's your livelihood, love,' he retorts: could we be at cross purposes?

'I'm not *even* close to my period, you prize plum!'

'Best not be,' he counters with a wink to my camera, 'or otherwise it will be an altogether *different* shoot! It would become a *period* piece! Certainly a lot of bloodshed- *know* what I mean?!'

'*I know* when I'm due on my menstrual cycle,' she spits with disdain.

'You are absolutely right, my love, please forgive my ignorance for presuming all this is down to moon madness?' His tone has become tender but I observe a familiar glint in his eye. 'Silly me for forgetting that you're a *full-time* mentalist!' Scarlett's full-throated response is less intelligible. I take this as a cue to go out into the back garden to make a business phone call.

'Is that somebody screaming?' my potentially new work Colleague asks from the other end of the line.

'We all have our own individual ways of conducting business matters,' I reply.

'Most witty, very droll,' I'm told by this person named Troy, whom I'm now seriously considering to employ as my *new* Sound Recordist to replace the inefficient and intrusive Stan.

'I hate it when we row, babe,' Strauss tells Scarlett when I return to the front living room. They're cuddled up together on the sofa: had there been *ample* time to have *"making-up"* sex?!

'Me too, honey- have you forgotten what tonight is?'

'Chilli con carnie night?'

'*No silly*,' she affectionately chides him, 'it's role-play Wednesday.'

'Oh yes, *how* could I forget?' Robby looks a little daunted: perhaps he's concerned about his failing memory? I myself have been witness to him losing his wife in the woods; and again mislaying her *even* within the confines of their *own* bedroom wardrobe! 'So what have you got in mind?'

'*Tonight* Matthew, you will play the *Milkman!*' Scarlett's comment perplexes me, not least since -according to my production notes- "Matthew" is the name of one of his brothers: could this be a Freudian slip where she's unconsciously revealed she'd prefer to be in a relationship with one of his siblings rather than *him?* Perhaps this has come as a terrible surprise to Robby because he's then bundling me out of the room and towards the front door: will this lead to yet *another* domestic crisis? I find myself waiting for an answer on the doorstep *outside*.

'What's happening, Robby?' His rotund form returns to the frosted glass at the front door. 'Have you been angered by your wife's unconscious desire for one of your brothers?'

'One of my *brothers?!*' he responds incredulously as he steps out of the house. The front door slams shut after him. '*What* are you talking about?! Are you a *complete* nutter?!' This comment is deeply ironic, not least since Strauss is now naked apart from wearing an official-looking cap upon his head. It's now completely dark outside. I've been rendered genuinely speechless by these bizarre developments. But this is true to the form since I'm merely here to observe. And film. Observing *is* filming. And filming, in an even *greater* sense, *is* observing. I *observe* Robby knocking on the front door.

'*Who* is it?' Scarlett asks from inside. Obscured by the frosted glass, she now resembles a crudely pixilated digital image.

'It's your friendly neighborhood milkman, darling,' he replies, winking to my camera, 'I've come to give you a *very* special delivery!'

'No milk today, thank you!' Scarlett breezily retorts before her form recedes from view.

'I said I've come with your *special* delivery!' Robby yells at her through the letter box then pounds upon the front door knocker, which is fashioned in the form of a busty female. 'It's your randy milkman with a special treat…Don't fuck around Scarlett-*let me in!*'

'You're breaking character,' she calls out from somewhere inside. In response he hammers on the wooden frame of the door, and then upon the glass with such force I feel the pane is about to smash and shower us both with shattered glass! A series of lights from the neighboring houses now begin to come on. It seems this situation has become a public disturbance. I decide to film in long shot, choosing to capture this drama whilst avoiding becoming part of it *myself*.

'You've had your fun, Scarlett,' Strauss shouts to the bedroom window above. Her form now resides there, resembling a shrouded phantom through the net curtains. 'Let me *in*… I'll catch my bloody death of cold out here!' he bleats pathetically. 'It's bloody freezing! I do hope you know this is *upping* the stakes, my pet…Do you *really* imagine you can harm me this way?!' He's then attempting every form of appeal to be let back inside the house, from pleading to begging to outright threats. 'You'll *really* have to try harder than *that*, bitch!'

'It seems she's not *really* trying at all, Robby, it would appear *no* effort is being made in the slightest,' I tell him. 'Do you supposed she's gone to bed?' He turns to me, his face like thunder. Suddenly a flashing blue light spills out from somewhere and Strauss, possibly suspecting this to be the arrival of police car, dives into a garden bush for cover. I retire to the comfort and warmth of my production vehicle parked just a short distance away, from where I can film any further developments.

'She's a card, *isn't* she.' I have Robby's face in extreme close-up. This is an hour or so after he's been locked out of his home. Scarlett has still not allowed him entry. Strauss is no longer wearing the milkman's cap upon his head. 'Me and her have had some giggles over the years. There's not many like her, *bless her.*'

'So you wouldn't say that you are stuck in a morbid relationship, where it would seem the mutual purpose is merely to destroy each other?'

'*What* are you like?!' Robby is grinning but there is no longer mirth within his eyes. '*Where do you get your funny ideas from?!*' He seems to be attempting to convince himself rather than me. 'Show me a couple who don't *ever* have their ups and down and I'll show you a pair of corpses.' Suddenly I'm revisited by a recent nightmare experienced shortly after the episode where Strauss had lost Scarlett in the woods: I recall a horrifying image of her still tied up against that same tree, getting *eaten alive* by foxes!

'These are *not* just little tiffs.'

'*All* regular couples play these type of pranks on each other,' he replies with an unpersuasive smirk.

'*You* are just a *regula*r couple?!' I quiz him incredulously.

'*Of course* we are,' he shoots back. 'Once you take away the hardcore pornography, the playtime with numerous other participants, the Law-flaunting exhibitionism, the odd bondage misadventure, the infrequent sexual injuries, the group sex, the prolonged list that, only on a *superficial* level, looks as though it runs the full gamut of every conceivable erotic possibility, *along with only the occasional mildly apocalyptic domestic row*, then we're as boring and run-of-the-mill as any couple you could ever *hope* to find. You've seen our lives with all the regular, mundane concerns that preoccupy other ordinary folk, *surely?'*

'But what of *this?'*

'This is nothing,' he scoffs, "it's all but a little bit of fun, and even if it hasn't been "one up the bum*" this* time then at least we 're keeping the love alive.'

'What precisely is "love" to you?'

'We're not *just* a loving couple,' Robby elaborates, 'we're best friends too. We share *all* the same natural, *and unnatural*, interests. There's so much *more* me and Scarlett share, and have in common, than that which is *immediately* apparent. And *all that* amounts to a proper, loving, caring and sharing, *completely* fulfilling relationship.' I zoom back out of close-up to reveal that he's now utilized the milkman's hat to conceal his privates.

A noise wakes me. I look outside to observe a wheelie bin by the side of the house. It's rocking back and forth as though guided by some giant invisible hand. This wobbling continues with yet more vigour. *What* could be causing this? The motion of this waste receptacle becomes increasingly violent til eventually it tips over entirely, thus falling on its side. The lid flips open and, to my amazement, Robby climbs out from it. It appears that whilst I was sleeping he'd found refuge within this refuse container. I see that he's appropriated a bin liner as a garment - a singlet of sorts- after having made holes for his arms and legs to sprout out from. It then becomes apparent that it hadn't occurred to him to ask for solace within my vehicle. It would, *of course*, have seemed intrusive of me to make this offer myself. Strauss is now stretching out his limbs as though the cold has affected him in some way. Then he approaches the front door again, once more to rap upon it. I see a light come on upstairs then shadows shift, which leads me to suspect some activity is occurring within. Robby has his back to me so I can't see *precisely* what he's doing but it looks as though he's attempting to insert something through the letterbox.

'Is that *you?*' I hear Scarlett call out from inside.

'Who else?!' he replies, then something else which is less cogent to me: 'Well, it's *cold* out here!' She seems to relent, and so opens the door but then he's yelping in pain and desperate to disengage *whatever* he'd inserted through the letterbox. Eventually Strauss is allowed through the front door. No further noise comes, which leads me to believe the conflict between this couple is now at an end. It's nearly dawn. I decide to drive home to get some further rest before commencement

of this fine new day which, I suspect, shall be offering some fresh developments yet.

At this point I should explain progress made during the break in filming, which has now amounted to almost a week. During this interval -between Scarlett leaving to visit her mother and her delayed return- I use the time to research Robby's family more thoroughly. As I've mentioned previously, Roland (the brother in need) is the *sole* Strauss sibling not to have been part of the preceding Sextuplets. Furthermore, Robby is not the only brother to have found fame *beyond* inclusion within this multi-birth. Douglas has also had some additional exposure in the slightly more respectable medium of the Music Industry, albeit with what proved to be a *very* short-lived career.

There are three other brothers, Kevin, Billy and Peter, who appear to have commonplace jobs (as painter-decorator, motor mechanic and security guard respectively) and whose early fame did *not* infect them with the urge to remain in the Public Eye.

There is one more member of this brood, Matthew, whose slender social media profile defines him as a property developer. I've tried to find out more about this particular brother, alas with *little* success for the time being. I may be forced at some later point to throw my net out further as concerns getting an angle on him. And so my judgment remains on hold concerning this *specific* member of the Strauss Clan, who appears to be so *entirely* different from the rest.

'And so we begin,' Robby announces upon impacting a rounded mallet against a giant bronze gong amidst his front room. This resonates with the gentle Far Eastern music which seeps from an unseen speaker somewhere. He has appropriated the dress of what he's defined as *"Samurai leisure wear."* In addition to wearing his obligatory robe, Strauss has applied eye-liner which he *insists* gives him an authentic Oriental look, but which I imagine *in actuality* is borderline racist, and apt to cause broad offense. His mullet is tried up high upon his head in a "man-bun," and skewered with what I suspect to be one of Scarlett's knitting needles. He resembles a half-hearted Sumo from one of his own tasteless movies. Incense swirls around Strauss's broad form as he declares, 'In ancient Japan there was a prohibition on conventional weapons so man was forced to fight fellow man with either farming implement or the open hand.' He's addressing a collection of a dozen or so men who'd arrived ahead of me. I suspect those present have *not* been summoned here under the pretense to learn about Martial Arts: they all wear dressing gowns but not of a conformity: I'm visually assailed by a frayed, stained selection of beiges, muddy tartans, assorted greys and a chocolate brown which likely masks a myriad of sins. 'Out of this auspicious Age the Samurai rose, and distinguished themselves as brave and noble warriors. It was they who maintained Law, Order and Honour above all else, a loss of which would have dire, *drastic* consequences upon their Society.'

'What's all *this* about?' a bored looking middle-aged man stage-whispers to a spotty Youth to his side. 'I didn't know this would be a bloody *history lesson!*'

'I expect it's all background guff,' this person replies in a surprisingly well-spoken accent, 'to get us into the mood.'

'A faithless woman would be given a *unique* punishment,' Robby continues after shushing the chatter amongst the ranks. 'Buried deep up to her neck she would be subjected to the time-honoured ritual of bu-ka-kee.'

'*What's that?*' a man in a corner asks in a broad Birmingham accent.

' Bukkake- basically some dirty bird gets a massive amount of Harry Monk all over her face,' Robby replies in a matter-of- fact tone that breaks character. 'That's where you lot come in…or rather, *on…literally*.' With a dramatic swoop Strauss pulls a nearby sheet aside to expose something I'd previously suspected simply to be a cover for furniture, or possibly a bust or statue. A gasp subsequently resonates around the room. At first I imagine this object to be a mere mannequin but eventually it exhales, therefore revealing itself to be a living, *breathing* entity.

'I'm glad it's a *woman* this time,' a mature man with a Northern burr wheezes. I look closer to see that this figure is wearing Scarlett's dressing gown. Here's where the similarity ends because this is a *considerably* older female for whom even a thick layer of cosmetics cannot transform into anything resembling even a *remotely* accurate picture of Youth. She has the same ridiculous hairstyle as Robby, though I suspect in her case this is a wig.

'Harry Monk?' asks a mature, diminutive male of South-Asian appearance. 'Was he not a jazz man?'

'It's *all* about the jazz!' Gareth, an Essex-based male in his twenties, exudes with a guffaw. 'Porridge straight from the pistol-she'll be *saturated* in the stuff!'

'She's a little old,' comes another, less enthusiastic voice, which prompts a scowl from our Host.

'I was hoping it would be *Scarlett,*' an obese man with a West Country twang laments.

'Numbers one to four, advance and disrobe,' Strauss exclaims, once more back into his role as Bushido pedagogue. I'm startled by the sight of these men getting naked: their ages and appearance are varied: broad; thin; dark; pasty. I will, *of course*, need to pixelate both their genitals and faces for the final cut. *None* present -*needless to say*- confirm to the Classical physique associated with *conventional* beauty. 'The rest of you get warmed up,' Robby instructs while setting up his video camera. 'No budget for a fluffer so prime your *own* popcorn.'

Over the next hour I find myself filming Strauss more than the events he's "directing," not least because the whole scene is soon resembling some *especially* squalid episode from 'Dante's Inferno,' which would have found itself excised and banished to the *darkest* depths of the Vatican's most notorious Archives.

'Come on Brenda, sweetheart,' my Subject appeals to his current female performer, 'that cock won't suck *itself!*'

'Give us a chance!' she croaks back before being presented with yet another unappealing member. 'I'm gonna need a fag break soon!'

'Put that gob to better use, the best part of a blow job is the two minutes of silence,' Robby tells her before collectively addressing the performers. 'Number six, stand back now, yep, and *you,* you've already served her your penile-paste so go freshen up and try again soon… You! You've lost your number! Just get in closer so she won't spill a drop of your love lava… Dear me, she's *swimming* in the stuff. Have you got your water wings, love? You're really drunk on it now, ain't you just! Darlin'-you're a *proper* little spunk-aholic!' It is at *this* point that I have to retire to take stock of the situation and get some much-needed fresh air: the chance now comes where I can muse upon Robby Strauss's bathroom as I'd earlier made mention of; it has the perpetual scent of disinfectant; or at least it *did have* before being assailed by my vomit!

'You, the black fella who looks like…No, you-Trevor McDonald!' Robby is still ordering about his performers when I return from my spew-fest. They in turn, are increasingly resembling extras from an *especially* harrowing apocalyptic zombie movie: *surely* the highly respected Broadcaster and Knight of the Realm Sir Trevor wouldn't be taking part in such a lurid activity?! It would be preferable he were dead and in his grave rather than resort to *this!* 'It ain't working out, old son, so step back,' Strauss insists. 'You too, John Major. Let the Fred West lookalike have a go at her- shagging her *rather* than killing her, of course!'

Robby sits alone in his office. All his extras from Hell have finally left. He'd had to pay Brenda extra for helping him clear up the considerable mess afterwards.

'It didn't *quite* end up the way I'd envisioned,' Strauss confides. 'Have you ever tried directing two dozen wanking idiots?' Then a familiar smile creeps over his chubby features. 'Sorry Fabio, I forgot you'd done some work in TV Commercials, and on a *certain* soap opera that shall remain nameless.' He then whistles the theme tune to that specific television program he'd alluded to: it seems he's done considerable homework on me; but just *how* has he been privy to such information? 'Needless to say, *none* of today's so called performers are going to get their deposits back.'

'You *don't* pay them?'

'*Are you nuts?!*' his tone is incredulous. 'The days of paying male performers is done. Been and done and *long gone*. You want that I should say to some mug, "here mate, shag this beautiful woman *and* I'll pay you too"?! Brenda is not a great example but surely you get my drift? No fucking way, pal, now *they* can pay me. And some of them can't even keep it up! Well, I suppose I can sell the footage as a charity sex event, you know, give your donations *generously* etc. A sort of wank-athon, you get the picture?' Unfortunately I've *already* been given a very vivid, *very* disturbing picture of all *that!*

Sensing another dramatic situation is soon to occur I remain with Strauss until Scarlett returns home. He goes to the front door to greet her. His attempt at a kiss is spurned as she pushes past him to enter the front room.

'The place was quite a mess but I cleared up,' he proudly tells her as she plonks herself down to sprawl out across the sofa. I notice she's entered bare-footed. 'Just let me know when you want dinner…How did you get on with your shoot?… For what it's worth, mine didn't go *too* well…What's *this*-a sponsored sulk?'

'I lost a shoe heel and broke a nail,' Scarlett replies listlessly at last. I'm suddenly haunted by an *especially* horrifying image from the bukkake scene earlier: one of the participants, having found a pair of Mrs. Strauss's Footwear- and apparently harboring a fetish- had transferred his affections *towards them*; the said shoes had subsequently been defiled! Robby had told me he'd have to find replacements for these items since *no* amount of cleaning product could possibly remove the incriminating stains and resulting odour from them.

'Don't worry, baby,' Robby says soothingly, 'one day I'll open us up a combination nail bar/shoe re-heeling shop…I suppose I'll have to cut keys there too…Why is that?'

'Why is *what?!*' Scarlett's eyes narrow. I observe that her mascara has run.

'The fact that shoe menders also cut keys,' he blithely replies.

'*What* are you actually on about?' she asks caustically. '*What* precisely is the matter with you?!'

'What's up, baby?'

'*Don't* baby *me!*' she barks back. '*Seriously*, you *really* need to get yourself some *professional medical help*!'

'I would do,' he replies, suddenly sombre and seemingly introspective. But then he looks directly into the lens of my camera, which subsequently appears to energize him. A familiar flash of mischief lights up his visage, 'I *would* get some medical help but…I'm having *far too much* fun! Living the dream-*Ker-ching*!' He then explodes into laughter.

'You pointless prick!' she retorts scornfully whilst exiting the room.

'It really is *that* time,' Robby whispers to me once he imagines Scarlett is out of earshot. 'Yes sir, rag-week has *officially* begun.'

'Oh, *there* are my shoes,' Scarlett calls out from the bedroom. Suddenly Strauss looks *stricken* with terror. 'What's that stuff on them?' we hear her enquire. The subsequent scream emitted is *truly* ear-piercing. Robby jumps up as Scarlett re-enters the room, cursing him in a horrific rage that culminates with an attack upon his person with those sperm-soiled stilettos.

Over the following several weeks - once it becomes clear Scarlett has left him *for good*-I am witness to a genuine and unprecedented crisis of confidence within Robby Strauss. This depression is to linger so long that I'm forced into getting in contact with several of his brothers as both substitute donors and replacement Subjects for my filming project. Then, after a lengthy period of inactivity, I again hear back from Robby whom (in his *own* words) has at last *'snapped out of it'*. The possibility that he'd gotten wind of my alternative plans has not escaped me, and so to make my position stronger I get him to sign release forms at the *first* possible opportunity to legitimize and use the existing footage in *any* way I choose.

'Right,' Robby says once these preliminaries are out of the way, 'I have a shoot today.'

'This sounds like the *old* Robby,' I reply by way of encouragement.

'*Oh yes!*' he cheerfully responds. 'A promising young debutante by the name of Emily. I've got good vibes from her.

Now then, check for work tools: stills camera-check; video camera-check…'

'Will you be using your Dictaphone?'

'No, I'll be using my finger like everybody else,' Robby whoops back.' 'Keep it clean-*you!*..Oh, and pass me my script please?' I hand him back the betting slip which he'd asked me to hold while signing my filming release forms: just three lines amount to this *"script,"*; 'blow job,' 'shag' and 'facial cum.'

'Perhaps it's a mere delay?' We're sitting motionless in Strauss's car. I have seen the whole gamut of emotions flash across his chubby features in the past hour: everything from jaunty expectation to trepidation; boredom to frustration; despondency to snappy irritability.

'Looks like we've been stood up my old mate,' he eventually sighs. '*Someone* is well and truly pulling our plonkers here.'

'Is it worth trying her mobile phone again?' I suggest, even though he's *already* sent a dozen texts and fruitless calls to the young woman he's expecting to meet.

'This bird I'm suppose to be meeting might not even exist,' Robby laments at last.

'How so?'

'It might *even* have been Scarlett masquerading as a potential new Starlet in the email correspondence, using fake pictures and disguising her voice over the phone.' This possibility had already occurred to me but I'd allowed Strauss to come to this very probable conclusion *himself.*

'*Why* precisely would she do that, Robby?'

'She'd do anything to destroy both me and herself,' he replies sadly.

'Destroy herself? *Surely* not?'

'I'm sensing that she's in cohorts.'

'Where's that?'

'In conspiracy with my competitors,' he explains before reaching for his Dictaphone. 'Memo to myself, here is advice to aspiring celebrities- to attain success con people into liking you even when persuading them to buy products from you that they *don't* really need.'

'Reading the trade newspapers, Robby?' I ask, once back at his home.

'The lonely hearts columns, *believe it or not*,' he replies from the sanctuary of his sofa. 'Let's see what we have here… "single mother seeks holiday romance in her high-rise".'

'*Surely* that's not a genuine advertisement?'

' Here's another,' Strauss carries on regardless, ' "Mature lady, hubby preferred my hair blue but *that's* gone now-hubby, *rather than* the hair. So come on, boys - give this vintage model a test run. Upholstery a bit worn but the headlights are still showing no signs of dipping-basically *goes like the clappers!*" Sounds *quite* a woman.'

'What would your ideal woman be like, Robby?'

'I think my perfect woman would be an amalgamation of *all* my previous loves,' he replies without pause. 'A single consolidated embodiment of quality components carefully selected to be conjoined. I'd choose an ex-girlfriend called Gloria for cuddles, well, at a time before her glands made her slightly *too* cuddly. Into this equation, this *cunt cocktail* as it were, I'd add little Sammi for her sweetness and optimism. Then Lady Diana for-'

'Would *anything* of Scarlett be within this idealized woman of yours?'

'Yes, for her depraved mind, *of course*, I'd be hoping to edit out some of her foibles, naturally.'

'But this is all *just* supposition,' I tell him. '*Surely* such a configuration is *not* scientifically possible?'

'On the contrary, Fabio, there's actually *already* been some highly advanced scientific developments that have made initial progress in creating this idealized feminine hybrid, this perfect *Frankenfuck* .'

'*There has?!*'

'Indeed, a certain Dr. Steve Martin of the University of Hollywood is developing this plan for my flawless female *as we speak.*'

'*Dr. Steve Martin?*' I question with skepticism. '*Surely not the comedian?*'

'He's more a Professor actually,' Strauss elaborates, 'they don't call him "The man with two brains" *for nothing!*'

Following this particular encounter we didn't hear from Robby for several weeks hence. Phone calls and emails would remain unanswered. It even got to the point where- for all his *previous* enthusiasm- Mr. Strauss no longer seemed to want to be the Subject of my documentary. This would lead *us* to the conclusion he was now even *less* likely to be a kidney donor for his *increasingly* ailing brother Roland. Eventually Robby *did* reply to our series of messages, and even agreed to *meet* with us (myself, my sound recordist Stan, and a new production assistant named Troy, a young recent graduate I'm intending to employ full-time, should the situation demand) in a public park where I'd previously engaged with him earlier in our acquaintance.

'Hi,' Robby calls out from a bench we'd sat upon the preceding month, 'I've asked you here specifically today, to specifically tell you something specific that for me, *specifically*, has the *greatest*…importance.'

'Can you be more specific?' I enquire.

'Ok,' Robby replies, his face falling, 'I *won't* be able to be a kidney donor for my brother Roland.'

'May *we* ask *why?*'

'What is this *"we"* all of a sudden?' he retorts. 'Why *only now* bring some back-up?'

'This is my production team, Robby,' I calmly tell him, 'can you at least explain *why* you've changed your mind concerning donating a kidney?'

'Lose your crew and I will tell you.'

'We'll not be far away,' Stan tells me whilst strolling off, gesturing for Troy to follow.

'This is *not* very easy for me to tell you this,' Strauss says, once he imagines we're out of earshot of my employees: the actuality is that I'm wearing a tiny button-hole microphone so Stan will pick up this *whole* conversation in its *entirety.* 'The fact is I've succumbed to a *certain* illness which would make it impossible for me to supply *any* of my organs.'

'You mean you've succumbed to-'

'That fly in the ointment within my industry,' he sighs, 'that *most* unfortunate of occupational hazards.'

'But *what* of Scarlett? Has *she* been health tested?'

'Scarlett tested *negative,* though I suspect that was for an I.Q. test. So anyway, *this is goodbye.'* I attempt to ask several more questions but he's already walking away.

We continue to follow Strauss's movements from a discreet distance, and without his knowledge, *as far as we could tell.* You might ask us *why* we continued this pursuit, the reason being because we, *as film-makers*, are *greatly* dissatisfied with the *dubious* excuse given to us, *not least* since he appears to be carrying on with his life *in much the same way*!

'You've been caught out!' Robby calls out to us whilst emerging from a non-descript building identifying itself as a photographic studio.

'Au Cointreau,' I correct him, *'we've* caught *you* out!'

'We've *already* said our goodbyes,' he bristles back whilst barging by.

'It seems that it's *business as usual*, Mr. Strauss,' I put to him as he makes a scramble towards his car. 'Wouldn't you admit that it is *very* irresponsible of you to continue in your line of work, considering your medical condition? *Are your co-performers aware of that?'*

'This really is goodbye!' Robby bellows out the window of his vehicle during his hasty departure. We're compelled to follow.

'Good afternoon, Mr. Strauss.'

'You have become a proper nuisance!' He's just emerged from the sexual health facility within a hospital.

'Mr. Strauss, we *don't* believe you've been *entirely* truthful with us.'

'*Truth?* You're *not* entitled to the truth, you parasites,' he exclaims whilst pushing past us to get to the car park. 'You've done *nothing but* exploit my well-meaning exhibitionism-now go point that thing *at somebody else!*'

'*We* believe you have just received test results which give you a *full* bill of good health,' I cry out as we continue to give chase. 'You are giving us *every* impression that you're *nothing* more than a deeply selfish opportunist who *only* sought to publicize your own *failing* business under the *pretense* of helping your increasingly ailing brother Roland.'

'Go pester one of my other five brothers to be your fucking donor!' Robby blurts back before halting to stand his ground. This gives our camera ample opportunity to peer directly into his *unvarnished* soul. '*Go sniff round Kevin's paint pots!*' he rants. 'Go ask Dougie the *singer for a fucking kidney!*'

'We might just do that,' I calmly reply.

'Go stick your nose in *Matthew's* business!' my former subject yells whilst resuming flight towards his vehicle. 'I *dare* you to do that and see what happens…*See what happens!*'

There is clearly *no further need* to pursue Robby Strauss. It seems several *more* promising possibilities have suddenly presented themselves to us. *Our* quest continues.

Episode Two:

Kevin, Master craftsman

'You blocks, you stones, you worse than senseless things'
Shakespeare.

As a result of no answer at the front door my sound recordist Stan and I stroll around to the back of the house. This place, which I've been *led* to believe is the location for our filming today, resides at the end of a row of near identical properties. Beyond the side gate, *left ajar,* we observe a silhouette projected against the back wall. Is this a greeting stage-managed *specifically* for us? This shadow then proceeds to move and sway before going through other strange activities not *immediately* obvious to us.

'Those sounds', Stan remarks whilst setting up his audio-recording equipment, 'they resemble percussion instruments, the light brush against drums.' Since my Assistant is the authority on this *particular* subject I decide that his prognosis would be more accurate than mine, and so I'm forced to take his word for this.

The dark outline on the wall seems to nod in confirmation, as though *beckoning* us to advance further to see if this projection corresponds with the person it *supposedly* belongs to. At first we fail to see an actual person, which leads me to imagine this figure is acting *independently* to *any* sort of human endeavour. Soon *however* a broad-shouldered man in early middle-aged sits up to reveal he'd moved position since our initial recognition of his presence. He has his back to us, and seems occupied in what *resembles* the playing of drums, complete with matching audibility. With our advance we notice a radio blurting out a pop tune, to which this person appears to be accompanying. He then becomes aware of our presence, and turns to face us. A slow, deliberate smile creeps across his face. My first impression is that I *already* know this person.

'*Surely* it's Robby?' The semblance to his brother is uncanny.

'We're often mistaken for each other,' this man replies. '*All* of us brothers are.' It's only now that I can see this person identifying himself as Kevin is attempting to beat off dry clumps of paint from a pair of broad brushes against a colour-bespattered row of sealed tins.

'Not a drummer, then?' Stan asks, seemingly disappointed.

'Dougie is the musical one,' Kevin replies as he discards

his clotted brushes to approach us and firmly shake me by the hand. '*That's* if you can call it that. You must be Fabio?'

'Indeed,' I reply once he releases me from his vice-like grip. 'And this is Stan.' It is now my sound-recordist's turn to have his palm crushed.

'How does this work then?' Strauss asks, refreshingly sounding the *exact* opposite of his *all*-knowing brother, Robby.

Over the next hour of getting to know this new sibling I'm to discover he has his own *very* unique form of confidence. I could try to explain but I sense it would be better if you'd find out for yourselves during the following transcript.

'I'm Kevin,' this new Subject states once he's aware the recording equipment is rolling. 'It seems fickle fate has blown you in my direction.' He's staring directly at the lens, not my favoured position for a Subject but I let him continue with the introduction we'd earlier agreed upon. I *could* use this as a voiceover for the final cut.

'What is it you do for a living, Kevin?'

'I'm the Master Craftsman of the family,' he beams. This is *immediately* deviating from our emails and phone calls prior to this physical meeting.

'You told us you're a painter and decorator?' I'm *already* sensing there will have to be *much* editing ahead.

'Well, there was *only* the briefest of telephone calls,' Kevin retorts. 'Perhaps some lack of connect occurred, *mixed* messages, and all that?'

'Do you feel your wife might offer an interesting *further* dimension to our project?' It was with her that I'd had *initial* contact.

'*Not likely!*' he guffaws. 'Glenda would chat your hind legs off- I doubt if you'd want an *endlessly* talking head.' Perhaps I've sounded suspicious of his motives because he's then shifting tone. '*Look,* the best way you can get to know me, discover me as a *true* Subject, is to came with me to work. Is that your van outside?'

We decline Kevin's request to use our production vehicle but instead tell him we can document his progress from the back of his *own* van, a battered vehicle that has clearly seen better days. He seems unreceptive to this, even after I explain at length how we *must* avoid manipulating him in *any* conceivable way.

'Here we are,' Kevin says as we pull up outside a block of flats barely a few hundred yards away from the initial location.

'The job is *here?*' My tone might have sounded doubtful on account that we could have walked here just as effectively.

'No, we're picking up my workmate, Geordie.'

'He's from Newcastle?'

'*Somewhere* like that. Poor old Geordie, he recently lost his wife.'

'She died?'

'Nah, she left him, just upped and buggered off! And she used the *strangest* of female reasons, saying it was for the ridiculous notion that he was coming out with me to the pub most evenings. Just proves women will use *any* excuse to dump some poor loser when they tire of them.'

'I imagine so.' I'm sensing there could possibly be *another* side to this story?

'But I've helped him get through it,' Strauss says proudly, 'I was there always for him even if *she* wasn't- he had a lucky escape, really.'

'How so?'

'She looks like Peter Lorre,' he replies sadly. 'A young Peter perhaps, but *certainly* a Peter Lorre-lookalike *all the same*.'

'So you felt they had *no* future together?'

'Are you *joking?!*' Kevin shoots back, as though I've said the *most* outrageous thing he was likely to hear. 'Her mother looks like late period Charles Laughton so *you* work it out!' I try to reason with him that -in our now *thankfully* less patriarchal society- women should no longer be judged on their appearance *alone*. Strauss is then laughing but I imagine he eventually infers the poignancy of my words because he falls silent awhile, adopting a more sober expression.'I'll be there for my *dear* old mate. I'll be kind, understanding and sensitive. He's *really* been through it.' Just then a tall, lean figure in a woolen hat appears on the balcony at the first floor of the flats. This person sees us then looks startled before disappearing back behind the door he'd only just emerged from. *'Fucking tit!'* Kevin bellows out his window, 'Come on, Geordie, you fucking twat! Get your finger out of your arse!'

This man emerges again then dashes to the stairwell. He soon reappears at the ground floor entrance to hurry along to the van, *heralded all the way* by Kevin's horn and verbal abuse. Suddenly this individual halts just short of the vehicle, seemingly alarmed by the presence of my camera. 'The people at the dole won't get to see this, *will they?'*

'*Nah,*' Strauss counters whilst pushing the passenger door open for his work colleague, 'they've been programmed only to watch Jeremy Kyle for benefit fraudsters. Here, Geordie, *what's* that on your shoe?' The man looks confused then flips up his heel, looking down behind him to inspect his sole. '*Hello sailor!*' Kevin yells out before dissolving into a fit of raucous laughter. 'Magic! Works *every* time!'

Some time later we're driving along the South Circular, near Clapham Common. Strauss slows the vehicle to observe a mature man painting a fence. 'You've missed a bit!' he shouts out- startling this person and making him spill paint over himself- before accelerating away and exploding with laughter once more.

Less than a mile later Geordie's expression is pained. 'Pull over man.' he groans.

'Why?' Kevin asks. 'You want a go at poor workmanship shaming?'

'No, I do *not,*' he yodels back in a strangulated North-East falsetto, 'I need to pee!'

'We're nearly there.'

'I'm *bursting,* man,' Geordie whimpers, 'it was all that tea I was drinking waiting *for you's!*'

We're waiting for Geordie. He's urinating behind a tree whilst bleating that *this* couldn't possibly be of any interest to the documentary. At least I *suspect* that's what he's *trying* to say in his broad dialect, which makes it extremely difficult to understand almost *everything* coming out of his mouth.

'It's only really out of *pity* why I employ him,' Strauss says whilst watching his work Colleague complete his task in hand, 'it's *hardly* for his tepid work.'

'He's not a master craftsman like you?' I'm responding in reference to a claim he'd made for *himself* earlier.

'*Hardly!*' he scoffs. 'You see, Geordie has had a series of crises.'

'You mentioned earlier.'

'Something is missing within his *mental* make-up.'

'A *congenital* disorder?'

'Not precisely *there,* as you saw *yourself* when his tackle was out! No, what Geordie is specifically suffering from is that his *posterior-elbow differential awareness* is faulty.'

'That's a medical diagnosis?'

'Yes, in layman's terms he *doesn't know his arse from his elbow*. Still, I find it in my all-too heavy heart to save him from starving.'

'*Starving?*' Geordie enquires, having returned to the van at last. 'Not me, man, I had *more* than enough time to eat waiting for *you*.'

'You're projecting again, Geordie,' Kevin replies in a superior tone, 'you'd be late for your own funeral, mate.'

Ten minutes later Strauss pulls up outside a row of shops.

'Is this where your job is, Kevin?'

'First things *first,*' he replies. 'A good Empire-building breakfast first. *Or Salmonella?* It's a toss-up between the two, really.' Visiting a workman's café was *not* on my list of expectations but I follow out of *professional* curiosity. 'Good morning, young Mark,' Kevin says, startling the middle-aged man behind the counter.

'Oh, it's *you*,' the man identified as Mark replies listlessly. 'Where's Tweedledee?'

'He's parking the van. As you know, it *may* take some time.'

'What can I get you?'

'I'll have a watery egg, burnt sausage, fatty bacon and cold beans.'

'Your *usual* then,' Mark groans, gazing directly and agonizingly into my camera as though Death himself would be more welcome here than Kevin.

'I have to get up very early in the morning to catch *you* out!'

'Either that or use *more* than one joke *per lifetime*,' Mark replies before disappearing into the kitchen.

'And a couple of bacon rolls for Ron,' Strauss calls out after him. I ask who this person *"Ron"* is but the question is in vain because when I turn back he's already seated and subjecting the other patrons of this establishment to his *unique* take on banter. 'Give us those bacon rolls to go,' he requests whilst finishing his own breakfast.

'Help yourself to some take-out sandwich bags,' a tired-looking, elderly waitress croaks back from the counter. Strauss picks up a thin transparent bag then goes through a bizarre ritual in an attempt to open it. I suspect that is more of his *supposed* humour. The waitress ends this laborious struggle by helping him. She places the rolls into the bag but by some clumsy contrivance -possibly due to Kevin's overzealous rush to contain them- the food items fall to the floor.

'Five second rule,' my Subject says as he retrieves the rolls, brushing them with his fingers and blowing upon them before receiving more help to *re*-bag them. 'Sub standard merchandise.'

'What is?' Geordie enquires as he enters the cafe.

'Never you mind,' Kevin replies, 'I've got you a couple of rolls.'

'But I've *already* eaten.'

'Have them for Ron.' Again I ponder who this elusive Ron is. As Strauss is leaving he trips and stumbles against a potted plant positioned by one of the dining tables outside.

'Hey Mark,' he calls out to the Owner who is stepping out for a tobacco roll-up, 'Claims Direct!'

'Only *you* could trip up on that!'

'It's a health and safety nightmare,' Kevin bleats back whilst surveying the streets for his vehicle.

'It's called *"class",*' Mark replies. 'If you don't like it you are more than welcome to take your custom to Joe Sad's café down the road.'

'I prefer it *here* at the Ritz,' Strauss retorts once Geordie has guided him in the direction of the works van. I have to look back at the sign above the café's entrance, and am confused to see it's *not* called 'The Ritz'.

We're now at a client's residence. They themselves are not home. I begin filming Kevin, who is assessing the work to be done on the ground floor.

'Upstairs is a bit *manky,*' Geordie says while coming down the staircase.

'Knock up some filler, son.' There is something of the patronizing patriarch about Strauss even though both men are of a similar age. I mostly refrain from filming the prosaic nature of these particular chores, choosing instead to document only the occasional shot. This can serve as a montage later *if* needs must.

Latterly Kevin is descending a ladder after having painted a ceiling. I cough to alert him he's on course for stepping backwards down onto an open tin of paint.

'See, I *told you* I'm an Artisan,' he boasts, suddenly aware my camera, 'I see myself as continuing the craftsmanship of William Morris, Dulex and Mr. I.C.I.'

'*Stop!*' I say as he resumes his way down the ladder.

'How *can* I?' he replies, regardless of my warning. 'Like those illustrious men I am the *Master* of the brush and roller.' It's at *this* point he treads fully down into the pot of paint, which *entirely* swallows his whole foot, and even envelopes the bottoms of his overalls. He pulls his foot out to reveal that the whole region halfway up to his calf is now a glistering *expanse* of white.

'*What* you want to do *that* for?' Geordie asks when he returns from having filled the rotten window sills with polyfilla. For some reason best known to himself Kevin is then applying paint to the wall with his foot.

'Why's he doing that?' I ask his work Colleague.

'No doubt he'll have *some* excuse,' Geordie shrugs before attending to some other task.

'*Why* are you painting with your foot?'

'It might *look* like that to the *uneducated* eye,' Strauss replies, 'but this is *in fact* my very own technique which is now *universally* recognized. You might not want to film this *precise* practice just yet because I'm *still* in the process of getting it patented.'

'It's *not* just a case of you trying to get excess paint off your shoe?' Geordie remarks with a wink.

'The *Advanced* Strauss technique, *of course*,' Kevin retorts, though his voice is trailing off, 'an applied cohesion to maximize…*application*.'

I have joined the two painter-decorators for a post-work drink for purely professional reasons. I decline in drinking alcohol. They, *however*, have no such inhibitions. Strauss's mobile phone has been constantly ringing. He neglects to answer it even after checking the caller's identity.

'Who's that who keeps calling you?'

'Who do you think?'

'You really *should* answer it,' Geordie tells him. He's also in the process of getting drunk but displays an earnestness which is in deep contrast to his Workmate's belligerence. 'You told her you'd be home for dinner'.

'Hark, the girl guide *here*.' The phone continues to ring and, with his Colleague's further appeals, Kevin groans theatrically before eventually answering it. 'Hello love…Yes Glenda, my phone has been playing up…Yes…*Listen,* I forget my door keys'.

'They are right *there* on the table,' Geordie interjects.

'That's *me* knocking on the back door,' Strauss says after shushing his Workmate and winking at me, 'can't you hear me?…*What do you mean you can't hear me?!…* I'm waking up the *whole* neighborhood…Well, you'll just *have to* get out of your bath then…*hurry!'* He cuts the call and explodes with laughter. Geordie looks on with contempt. Kevin is oblivious to this however and reminds me that it's my turn to buy the drinks *even though* I've been refraining from consuming alcohol.

We're travelling in the film production vehicle. Half an hour before I was due to meet Kevin this morning he'd called to say his works van had broken down, and was *unable* to tell me *when* it would be fixed.

'We've got a bit of a job today,' he tells me from the front passenger seat.

'How so?' I enquire from the back of *my* vehicle. Geordie Gordon and I have been relegated here after Strauss had called out *"shotgun,"* some practice he'd insisted was *essential* for filming.

'We're painting a certain notorious public convenience,' he replies while gesturing to Stan -my sound recordist who doubles as my driver- to take the next left.

'Notorious, how?' a wide-eyed Gordon asks.

'It's become a *cottaging* site.'

When did it become a cottage?' Geordie responds. 'What, *like,* become residential? I *thought* we were painting a park toilet today?'

'He's *pretending* he doesn't know what the name of a pick-up place for gay males is called,' Strauss tells me. 'In reality he's known as *"Geordie of Gender confusion central".'*

'I'm fed up of telling you, I'm *not* a Geordie- I'm from *Sunderland!'*

'Whatever,' Kevin counters, a now familiar glint is in his eye. *'So the rest of that applies* then?'

'A pick-up place for gay fellas, like? Aye man, *yous' having us on?!'*

'I've heard this somewhere,' I contribute, though instantly regret this since I'm *merely* here to observe and document.

'Well, you do the *inside,'* Geordie tells his Workmate, 'I'm for the *outside.'*

'Are you *out* then?' Kevin is smirking. Perhaps this is a private joke between them?

'Aye man, you *mutton*, like?' Geordie responds, possibly also in code. 'You'll be painting inside with all *your* gay mates whilst I'll be outside.'

'*So you are admitting you are out?*' The sly grin is never far from Strauss's lips.

'Whatever, 'ya daft cockney shite!' It seems Geordie is challenging his Colleague's authority. '*You* know *all* the terms- it must be a London thing.' This is the first time I've witnessed this man from the North East clearly asserting himself. And the first time I see a look of self-satisfaction upon his face. The rest if the journey is in silence. I *imagine* that *both* men are claiming a victory in this war of words. We arrive eventually at the public toilets within a park somewhere in South-West London.

Kevin is painting a wall adjacent to a row of cubicles. Standing nearby is a smartly dressed man in his late twenties. He's been here for some time, neglecting to use the conveniences and *seemingly* studying Strauss's progress. I'm momentarily distracted by the sound of a cubicle door being unlocked then opened from within. I turn but fail to see the Occupant, who slams the door shut as though either to avert attention or -in some peculiar sense- attract it.

'Sorry mate, you're going to have to move.' I turn to see Kevin speaking to the young man. 'I've got to paint this place.'

'I'm waiting for…' This person seems reluctant to move. 'I'm waiting…for …*my son*. He's not very well.'

'What's up with him,' Strauss asks, 'apart from him being *fictional?*' And yet there clearly *is* somebody inside the cubicle.

'Will you be *very* long?' There's agitation in his tone.

'Look mate, I don't care what you get up to,' Kevin tells

him, 'I just need you to move so I can paint.' The man is refusing to stand elsewhere for same reason. He stubbornly remains in the same position and petulantly folds his arms. In an act that comes as *extremely* unexpected, Strauss proceeds to paint over the man's shoes. This person falls silent, uttering no further word as his smart ox-blood brogues are appropriated with a thick layer of gun-metal grey. Once the task is fully completed he nods stoically to both Kevin and I before leaving in a manner far *more* subdued than previously.

'What's *that?*' Strauss asks the occupier of the cubicle, a bearded man in late middle age, as he's leaving. There's some confusion here on account of the other, *previous* inhabitant of the toilets *claiming* to be waiting for his *son.*

'A glory hole,' this older male replies with a mischievous wink and leer, 'you *had* your chance!'

'I'm all out of filler,' Kevin says once the elderly man has departed. He then produces a marker pen from his overalls, steps into the cubicle and proceeds to write on the wall, *"For sexy fun call Gordon,"* before adding the digits of a mobile phone number. As we leave he's chuckling to himself. I sense this shall create *some* situation later.

On the way back to my production vehicle- where Geordie and Stan have returned to retrieve respective work supplies- Strauss's mobile phone is ringing again.

'Hello Glenda!' I cannot *distinctly* hear what his wife is saying but her tone is fast and anxious. 'What do you want *me* to do about it?' he eventually asks. 'I'm at work…Well, you'll have to do your *own* food shopping…You lazy cow!' Kevin's voice gets louder to combat the tirade emanating from his phone. 'I'm *not* the one who put your leg in plaster-*you're* the one who *insists* on leaping down the stairs like Batgirl with big, wet, slippery feet… Listen, go bore the Samaritans… I'm not surprised they disconnected their call with you…Oh *really*, well here's a question for *you*-what's good looking and hangs up?' It's at this point he cuts the call. On the way home he elaborates on the context of this conversation: Glenda had broken a leg whilst charging down the stairs at home *in response* to the prank call he had played upon her that he'd been locked out. As Strauss relays this story, punctuated with much giggling, I notice Geordie glowering.

'You'll lose that girl,' he says at last whilst they're eating a packed lunch prepared by Glenda.

'Are you trying to cheer me up?' Kevin growls. 'We'd better start on the pavilion and complete it so we can get out of here before the traffic gets heavy.'

'It'll be a push,' Geordie counters as they rise from the brick wall they've been sitting on to approach the locality of their final job at this location, 'it's dead *manky.*'

'Nothing a bit of filler won't cure.'

'What are our lives *but* filler?'

'That's very deep for *you*, Geordie.'

'I'm from *Sunderland*,' he snaps back. 'I'm tired of telling you- in the ten years I've known you why can't you get *even that* right? I'm a Mackem, man. And my name is *not* Geordie, it's *Gordon!*'

'Here, we did a few jobs in his neck of the woods,' Kevin projects to my camera once the dust of quarrelling has settled.

'Aye, the Gateshead bridge,' his work Colleague elaborates.

'*Before* it fell down.'

'It *never* did!' Geordie, or rather Gordon, as I should now *correctly* address him, responds.

'I jest,' Strauss replies, 'we *always* apply pride in the job.'

'Aye, that we *do.*' Gordon has a far-away look in his eye. 'No stone unturned, no surface uncovered, no hole…'

'*Unfilled!*' Kevin helpfully interjects. 'Indeed, there's something Zen in what we do'.

'*Zen?!*' Gordon shoots back, a sudden look of distaste upon his face. 'I'm C. of E., pal. Let's just pack up our gear and get out of here before we get *all* the traffic.'When they get up to leave -with them walking ahead of me- I see that both their backs and posteriors are covered in green paint.

'You *can't* sit on the upholstery of my production vehicle like *that,*' I inform them. They're initially confused.

'What's that on your arse and back, Geordie?' Strauss asks as he dabs at wet paint on his colleague's behind. 'You could have told me you'd painted the bench *before* we were sitting on it?'

'Defective paint, Kevin,' Gordon limply replies. I explain to them certain *conditions* concerning the offer of a lift home. They obediently sit on their dust sheets in the back of my vehicle, glumly gazing out at the road ahead, and mostly unresponsive to my questions about *what precisely* constitutes the quality levels of house paint.

'Hello…You want *what?!*' Gordon is responding to an unknown caller who has rung his mobile phone. 'You want *Roger?*…No Roger here, chum…You want Roger to do *what?!*…

To get *Rogered?!*...Oh, he's gone. Well, I'm fucked if I know what *all* that was about!' the man from Sunderland declares. Kevin is standing behind with his back to us. His shoulders are quaking with some task I'm unable to behold. We're now in a pub garden. Strauss eventually turns back to me and I see that he's painted both his and Gordon's work overalls with white emulsion in an attempt to neutralize the green paint they'd sat upon.

'That's *just* plain stupid, Kev!' Gordon erupts once he notices this.

'I'm just tidying up your mess, Geordie- *the story of my life.*'

'But it's just *more* wet paint,' he groans whilst attempting to put his work outfit back on, 'I thought you were going to get it off with white spirit?'

'*More* effective this way.' Strauss sees that his work Colleague still has some green paint on his hand and so retouches it with his brush. Gordon is then cursing him again but Kevin ignores this in order to answer his mobile phone. 'Now *what,* Glenda?!...I'm *still* working!...Every spare moment is with the film crew...Yeah, *it is* about my brother Roland but...Well, maybe I'm *not the one* who refuses to listen...Well, give Roland my dinner *then*...He couldn't possibly get any more ill so *you may as well!*' He cuts the call, and so I take this as a cue to address the subject of his brother.

'Kevin, we need to talk about-'

'*What* exactly is your agenda?' He sounds agitated.

'My agenda is to be as good and competent a documentary film-maker as possible! And *what's yours?*'

'A couple more pints, might as well get a few shots in too.'

'Have you given *any* more thought concerning the plight of your brother?' I enquire after my expensive visit to the bar.

'His *what?*' For some reason Strauss has repositioned us close to a speaker which blasts out loud music from a jukebox which he'd earlier induced me to feed.

'His health struggle,' I reiterate, 'his search for a kidney *donor.*'

'*Obviously* Roland is in our thoughts,' Kevin replies whilst placing a coin down upon the nearby pool table.

'Have you given any more thought to perhaps donating one of your *own* kidneys?' I'm forced to raise my voice since I'm now in competition with the Sex Pistols.

'Geordie,' he roars, seemingly not having heard what I've said, 'are you going to buy a round at last, *or are you going to ponce off me for the rest of your life?*'

I've been forced to put my foot down with Strauss the following morning. Shortly before expecting to be picked up again I'd called him to say my production vehicle is *no longer* available, and that I'm deeply displeased he and his work colleague had left paint marks on the upholstery. I'm alarmed that he takes all this in his stride, and even *more* discomforted when he turns up at my production office an hour later, his work van suddenly and *miraculously* restored to its former functionality.

'*What* can I do for you, Kevin?' I ask him upon arrival.

'I feel we got off on the wrong foot. I'd be ready to talk now. But come to work with me so we can kill two birds with one stone?'

I'm still trying to work out *precisely* what he'd meant by *that* on our subsequent journey. Gordon has not accompanied us on this occasion. Eventually we arrive at a shabby-looking bungalow which looks at odds with the more well-tended houses surrounding it.

'Where's Gordon?'

'He's here, around the back. I got him to dig the hole first.' Strauss is smiling. This unnerves me in a way I'm unable to articulate. 'Come on, unless you want to sit in my van *all* day?' I follow him through a crumbling wooden doorway, and immediately lay eyes upon the hole he'd mentioned. Goosebumps assail my spine as I note it resembles a freshly-dug cemetery plot! '*Poor* Geordie.' My pulse quickens and my mouth becomes dry.

'Why? What's happened?!'

'Poor stupid Northern bugger,' Kevin elaborates, his tone tender and all the *more* chilling for that. Then he nods to a corner of the overgrown garden where a gangling form is poring over an ungainly concertina of crumpled paper.

'Is that a map, *Gordon?'* The relief is *evident* in my voice.

'It might as well be,' the Sunderland man huffs back in frustration. 'Its coded instructions that is baffling the shit out of us.' I approach smiling as I realize it's nothing more sinister than an assembly manual for a garden shed.

'It can't be *so* very hard?'

'Geordie can't read,' Strauss replies, which helps explain the hold he has over his Colleague.

'It's *all* fucking pictures!' Gordon blurts back.

'Here, I've done some filming myself.' Kevin has that

characteristic smirk upon his face once more. He then shows me footage on his mobile phone of Gordon trying to assemble the wooden components in every variation, *all* without success. 'We can use it for your documentary, speed it up to fast-forward and put the Benny Hill theme tune to soundtrack it.' I thank him for his suggestion but explain this isn't *quite* what I have in mind for my production.

'It's clear to see,' Gordon cries out, 'it's not *even* the right fucking instruction manual.' I suddenly suspect I've been brought here under false pretenses, and that there's an *ulterior* motive at hand.

'Why *exactly* was that hole dug?' I'm fearful what the reply might be.

'Ducks,' Kevin says, and I comply since I imagine this to be an instruction. 'Fucking duck pond.'

'*But why?*' I ask, once I've recovered my composure.

'Crazy old lady who gave us the job,' Strauss elaborates. 'She *claims* her son was planning to assemble this pile of old wood but I'm not sure he *even* exists. Here Fabio, have you ever put together a garden shed?' Eventually Kevin takes to the lengths of wood with a saw.

'You're *not* a carpenter,' Gordon tells him, to which he replies that he can turn his hand to *any* trade.

'You *shouldn't* have left it like that,' Gordon says on our journey to another job. I regret not travelling in my production vehicle today since I feel there's very little at present to film. I had asked Kevin to drop me off at my production office but he'd said his next job wouldn't take *very* long, adding that he'd be able to deliver me home *before* traffic congestion was to commence.

'Left it like *what?*' Strauss enquires.

'In bits, man. *It's a disgrace!*'

'Her *son* can complete the job. The deposit *only* amounted to a day's work, *anyhow.*'

'We're *not so far* from my production office,' I tell Kevin but he seems preoccupied with taking a diversion to a dual carriageway.

'We're *just* picking up some supplies.' We're joining the motorway services just off the M25. Strauss drives towards a lorry which is parked away from a cluster of other vehicles. Suddenly a police car parks alongside the rig we're heading towards. My Subject looks alarmed when *another* Constabulary vehicle pulls up nearby. Just before he makes a U-turn I see several uniformed police officers speaking to a man I suspect to be the driver of the lorry.

'Wrong turn,' Kevin says whilst steering us back to the motorway. 'We'll *have to* go visit Desmond.'

Desmond -I subsequently learn- is a Shopkeeper. Gordon is indulging him in conversation inside his hardware premises. For some unknown reason Strauss has neglected to join us and *instead* has entered the venue through a *back* entrance.

'I see you are still *well*-stocked, Desmond,' Gordon remarks.

'There's no point being *under* stocked,' the aged man replies tiredly.

'Here Desmond, *did you know* that paint is edible? It's *true*, man.' I follow the Northerner's line of vision to observe that Kevin has now reappeared at the back of the shop. He takes two large tins of paint from a shelf before exiting the way he'd come: perhaps he has a standing credit account?

'Is that one of Kevin's facts?' Desmond asks. 'Is he *not* with you today?'Suddenly Gordon says he must go, bids the shopkeeper goodbye then gesticulates for me to join him in an *abrupt* departure.

We're in the pub once more. Kevin had emphatically explained that the roads would be gridlocked with traffic, and that we're best to remain here until the rush hour (several hours in fact) eases off. Gordon's phone is ringing. Strauss is smirking, as though he's *already* aware whom the Caller is.

'Good afternoon,' the North-Easterner says by way of a warm-hearted yodel…'Oh, aye, the advertisement?…*Frottage?*'

"Rubbing down,' Kevin enlightens him, winking at me for some reason.

'Rubbing down, indeed,' Gordon continues, 'with sandpaper…No sir, *not* painful at all…*Rimming?*'

'Another term for skimming,' Strauss translates.

'Of course, sir, that's *all* part of the service.' It's at *this* point that Kevin chokes on his beer. 'Can do, Sir,' Gordon proceeds, straining to hear over the raucous noise his Workmate is making. 'Yes, it *is* hard…*to hear*…Try me later in a more *accommodating* reception area, Sir?…My pleasure. Bye for now.'

'A fair bit of *interest* from the advert then?' Strauss remarks once he's dried his eyes and regained his composure.

'From what I heard *in spite of* your racket,' Gordon replies. I hadn't precisely heard what this potential Customer had been saying but I'd inferred that their tone was somewhat strangulated. 'There was *another* call earlier whilst I was waiting for you, with a list of requests, to which the client sounded very excited at the prospect of a satisfying job. I told him *we aim to please* then he sounded *very* relieved, saying *he was sure he'd found the right guys to get him sorted out, at long last.'* Kevin begins coughing again, thankfully covering his mouth this time. His eyes are streaming once more. He only finds respite when his own mobile phone rings, forcing him to adopt a more sombre tone. Soon this conversation with the Caller, whose identity is *not* immediately apparent, degenerates into a heated -though incoherent- rant.

'Never mind,' Strauss - strangely calm again- says after this call, '*only* the wife.'

'I can't help noticing, Kevin,' I boldly venture, '*quite* how much time you *do* spend in pubs.'

'*Who exactly* are you?' he suddenly demands, staring me directly in the eye. I attempt to explain that I'm *merely* a documentary film-maker trying my best to get an *objective* account of proceedings but he cuts me off. '*A marriage councillor?'* His tone becomes chilly. 'Here's a little known *fact* for you-did you know that paint is edible?' I mention that I'd heard *something* to this affect somewhere, though dispute it's wholly factual. He persists however, once more disregarding what I have to say. 'Don't worry about that nonsense.'

'*What* nonsense?' I reply, sensing he's at last urging me to contribute to the conversation.

'About all the lead said to be in paint- my wife had a craving for paint during her pregnancy.'

'*She did?'* Gordon asks tentatively.

'Yes, she *did*. Not *just* eating little bits of paint but whole *swathes* of the stuff, lumps of it, fucking *mounds* of it!'

'Did it *not* affect your bairn's brain?' The colour has suddenly become drained from the Northerner's face.

'What do *you* think, Geordie? You know him-*what would you say?*' I recall now from my production notes that Kevin's son is currently incarcerated within a young offender's institution.

'He's a canny lad,' Gordon replies gingerly before excusing himself to go to the gent's toilet.

'He'll be working for me soon,' Strauss calls out after him, *'replacing you!'*

I find myself *again* accompanying this curious pair the following day as they're starting another new job with *yet another* uninitiated Client. I'm beginning to discover that, for *all* their new customers, *none* have asked them to return other than to *rectify* their shoddy workmanship. My initial objective was to investigate the possibility of Kevin Strauss donating one of his supposed healthy kidneys to his brother, Roland, but this seems to have been put on a back burner for the moment since my current *full-time* activity has become merely to witness the next series of disasters, which no doubt *shall shortly* be presenting themselves to me.

'We'll need a *lot* of filler,' Kevin calls out to Gordon whom, *unseen by him*, is already committed to this very task.

'I'm knocking it out,' he sighs.

'I'll say,' Strauss replies, once more looking straight into the lens of my camera, 'he's always *knocking one out!*' He then proceeds to demonstrate what's known as the "Wanker" sign.

'Do you know that "knocking one out" on the job is in strict breach of the painter and decorator's code?'

'Aye,' Gordon grunts back, 'I'll be knocking *you* out in a minute!' I sense this banter is becoming a trifle wearing on the man from the North-East.

An hour later I'm observing Strauss making a hole in a wall with an electric drill. After this he fits another, *bigger* drill bit to make the existing hole larger.

'What are you doing, Kevin?'

'You'll see,' he replies before picking on even longer, broader metal utensil to make the hole in the wall *greater still*. 'I see you, you Herbert, *you!*'

'What the fuck are you doing?' Gordon yells from the next room. I get a good camera angle of the taller man through the now fist-sized gap in the dividing wall between the rooms.

'A serving hatch.'

'They've *already* got a fucking serving hatch,' Gordon bellows back, 'downstairs!' This is a fair point since we are in fact *upstairs* within this premises, and such a device is traditionally utilized between a kitchen and dining area, both of which - more often than not- are found within a conventional household on the *ground floor.*

'Maybe they are kinky and want a glory hole?' Kevin replies with a sardonic smirk. At this point he has to jump aside because Gordon has thrown something at him. Then the Northerner is attempting to thrust his hand through the hole in an attempt to grab hold of Strauss, who antagonizes him *further* by telling him to *"knock another one out."* Soon it becomes apparent the man from Sunderland's hand is wedged within this hole in the wall. I offer advice for him to free himself but he seems unresponsive. I then *consider* advising that he should have addressed his complaints directly to his Colleague by *simply* moving through existing doorways in the traditional way, though decide against this when his wails of anguish grow *louder still.*

Another hour has passed. Kevin *did* eventually help release Gordon from the hole within the wall but only *after* reassurance that his temper has abated. Gordon's hand is now grazed but this does not stop him completing a task he's more comfortable with, painting a wall. Eventually he places his brush down on a nearby window ledge to have a smoke. It is *then* I notice that Strauss, having shared the same pot, has dripped paint all over his Colleague's phone. There is *no little amount*; it is in abundance, and enough to warrant it's been done willfully for mischievous, nay, *malicious* effect rather than by mere carelessness. As Gordon is finishing his roll-up his mobile begins to ring. Seemingly distracted he *unwittingly* answers it.

'Good afternoon,' he says before realizing his ear, and *most* of the side of his head, is now covered with paint. '*Oh fuck*!... Hang on, Sir...No, *not you*...I had something in me ear...What d'ye mean *"oh kinky'?!*...Fuck right off, man!' Gordon terminates the call after this bizarre misunderstanding. He wipes paint from his ear whilst glaring at Kevin.

'*You've* probably lost us another good customer there!' Subsequently the man from Sunderland takes Strauss's mobile phone and deftly drops, then pushes it deep into the open paint pot nearby. Its black shape is almost entirely enveloped within the white emulsion.

As Gordon finishes painting the room Kevin is *still* struggling to wipe his phone clean. A ring tone sounds off. He looks incredulously to his communication device before realizing this originates from his *Workmate's* phone. Gordon calmly answers it then hands it to his Colleague.

'Hello Glenda,' Strauss replies gingerly to his wife's enquiry, 'I *know* my phone's not working…An accident…Yes, *even I* have accidents occasionally…I *don't* know…Glenda, I don't know if I will be home for dinner…Oh, *whatever!*'

With the work completed Kevin sits on a sofa in the living room, which is now freshly wall-papered. He's looking extremely pleased with himself.

'I've done *my* bit,' he says, stretching his legs out upon a coffee table before him, 'but Geordie's lagging behind so it might take *some time yet.*' It's at *this* point I became aware of a vague rattling noise which gradually becomes louder and more urgent as the Subject of my documentary becomes *increasingly* self-aggrandizing. 'There you are, I told you *nobody* can wallpaper like me- another first-class job indeed! A Masterclass, as it were!' The rattling becomes increasingly noisy, and for some reason the paper on the wall behind Kevin begins to ripple and quaver as though pulsing *with a life of its own*. He obliviously continues with his self-praise, 'In fact, you *should* have filmed it.'

'I had some technical issues to attend to, Kevin.' *What's* that noise?

'*Your* loss, Fabio,' he persists, 'you could have released the footage as a "how to" instruction video guide, and use the James Bond tune *"Nobody does it better."* No, perhaps…'

'Yes, perhaps you're being a bit *too* immodest? *What is that racket?*'

'You're right,' he surges on, unheeding of both my questions and the *increasing* audio disturbance. 'The tune *"Simply the best"* would be more appropriate. Well, the work speaks for *itself*'.

'Indeed,' I reply whilst watching the wallpaper begin to split. The crescendo of the rattling is joined by a cacophony of tearing noises.

'I'm not *just* the best,' Kevin insists, *'I'm better even than that!'* At this *precise* moment the wall behind him parts as though it's a river breaking its banks. Bursting through is not water but instead the blinding light of a low sun streaming in through the *kitchen* window.

'I told you, man!' Gordon exclaims as his head pops out through the tatters of the wallpaper. 'They *already* had a sodding serving hatch- how could you *not* have noticed that?!' Kevin continues to feign nonchalance.

'You fit?' Strauss asks as he's packing up the work utensils.

'Job's a good 'un,' Gordon replies whilst looking fondly on the corrections he *alone* has ratified. I walk out ahead of them to the vehicle then hear the front door slamming behind me. Another sound, like the fluttering of wings comes, and I find myself lingering as the two men pass me by to go to the van. Out of curiosity I head back to the bay window to peer into the front room. The mystery of this additional sound is *solved* when I see that a roll of wallpaper has become dislodged from the wall. It now sprawls out over itself like a curled length of scroll. It was *quite possibly* the slamming of the front door which had prised it away from the wall.

'Are you coming?' Strauss calls out from the van. '*Or do you want to stand there forever more?*'

We stop at a pub on our way home. I'm told by my Colleagues it will serve as a place for them to relieve themselves after having been stuck in traffic for so long. Gordon wastes no time in ordering drinks from the bar. I resist the offer of alcohol, though am hardly surprised when a member of staff places *three* pints of lager before us. Kevin is spending so long in the men's toilets I feel compelled to investigate. I find him standing at the urinal, watching my entrance in the nearby mirror. Just as I'm about to conclude he'd been taking the world's longest pee I see something in his hand. *Thankfully* it's one of his paint brushes. He then resumes the act of dabbling at the walls with this brush, which is *still* loaded with paint. With both of us having completed our tasks in hand, I exit after Strauss courteously holds the door open for me. A large man - earlier identified as the Pub manager - approaches.

'Kevin, have you been unlawfully painting my walls *again?*'

'Here's a little known *fact* for you,' Strauss pontificates at the bar, 'a man can survive several weeks on just eating paint *alone.* There's yet *another* paint-based fact for you.'

'Have you tried this yourself?'

'Gordon has,' he replies as his Colleague returns from the toilet, 'I don't suppose it did him *much* harm.' Then a doubtful look comes over him. 'In fact, *don't* try it-it could have a *very* adverse effect upon you'.

'*What's that?*' Gordon enquires.

'*Same again, thanks*,' Kevin replies before calling out, 'three more beers please, Mr. Barkeep.'

It seems churlish not to partake so in the interests of good will I *accept* a drink with my Colleagues. I sense Strauss is about to spill some interesting revelation just before his newly purchased phone begins to ring.

'Hello?' He remains silent awhile so I surmise it's a call from a Client *rather* than his wife. 'That's correct, sir,' he says at last, 'if you want a really *decent* and thorough and professional job then I'll have to charge extra for the *Dutch finish*…Yes, it utilizes a double Swede.'

'*Double Swede?*' I echo. Gordon merely shrugs in response.

'Yes sir,' Kevin continues, 'only a Renaissance coating will get you a grade four…Because I *won't* lower my standards to a grade three…It's a *trade term*, sir, anyhow, to clarify things I wouldn't be able to do any *less* of a service on *vocational* grounds. It also happens to be a question of *conscience* …Let me clarify, sir, any *less* effort would result in marital disappointment, domestic gloom, family quarrels, a decline in health for all, and quite possibly *even a bereavement!*'

'Is this a sales pitch?' I ask Gordon, who in response merely shrugs. He shrugs a lot. He is certainly one of Life's *shruggers*.

'*Why* would you take the chance, Sir?' Strauss persists. 'Well, *what* price would sound fair to you, sir?…I'm afraid you would *only* get a H-block beige effort for that amount, sir…For the amount I'm quoting, for the standard of work you *would* require, squire, we'd *have to* use *special* brushes…Yes, made from the hair of a special pony that resides only on Easter island, sir…the name of the *pony?*'

'Unicorn hair,' Gordon blurts out, imagining he's helping with the sales pitch.

'No sir, he meant *Sable*…hello sir?…Sir?' Kevin is then glaring at Gordon. '*Unicorn* hair?!'

'Sorry Kev,' the North-Easterner laments, 'I always get those and sable ponies mixed up. Did the client hang up?'

'*Course* he hang up, you plum-*you're a fucking unicorn yourself!*'

'Well, it makes as *much* sense as the bollocks you were on about!' I'm inclined to agree with Gordon, though hold my silence for *professional* reasons.

I find myself in Kevin's works van yet again the following morning on our way to yet *another* job. I'm persevering with my Subject since I sense I'm about to make a breakthrough *of sorts*. He slows the vehicle to observe a familiar-looking elderly man painting a fence then yells out that he's missed a bit before bursting out laughing and accelerating off: am I suffering a bout of *de ja vu?*

As we're pulling up outside a semi detached house -the location of today's job-Gordon's mobile phone rings out.

'*Another* number I *don't* know,' the Northerner grumbles.

'Well, answer it then,' Kevin hisses to him. 'I'm sick of *you* losing us customers!'

'Hello?' Gordon responds to his caller. 'That's correct sir, the advert I left…*Where?*…Surely some mistake, *surely* you meant from our newspaper advert?…Yes sir, there are *two* of us, in fact…Of course, *satisfaction guaranteed.*' He makes an aside to Strauss, 'What's *feltching?*'

'Covering *every* surface,' comes a giggly reply, 'skirting boards *and all.*'

'Of course, sir', Gordon affirms to his Caller, 'we *always* do that…Oh yes, it *can* be messy but we *always* clean up well afterwards…Yes sir, we will *indeed* clean up any shite left after the job…Certainly sir, I'll get my partner to call you back on this number with a price quote…Certainly sir, speak, to you soon. Bye for now.' He turns to Kevin who- for some reason- had been chortling during the *entire* course of that conversation. '*What* the hell is the matter with you?! You'd *better* straighten up when you call him back with the prices for what he's *expecting* from us!'

We climb out of the van. Both men proceed to take a ladder and paint pots from the back of the vehicle. They transport these to the house where the work shall commence. I notice a stray dog approaching then sniffing around the back of the van where the doors have been left open. I call out to alert Strauss of this canine visitor *after* it jumps into his van but he's preoccupied with a further discussion with his Workmate, which soon degenerates into *another* quarrel. The dog appears to be spending *considerable* time inside the back of the van so I *myself* investigate. It's then I see that this errant hound is - as Kevin would say- *"laying some cable."* I hiss at the offending cur in an attempt to shoo it away out but it leaves only *after* having defecated over *most* of the work tools! Eventually Strauss returns. I inform him that his vehicle has been *defiled* but he's still too busy yelling at Gordon to heed my words. He grabs hold of the said soiled items yet remains oblivious to the abhorrent mess, which is now upon his hands! Whilst emerging from the back of the vehicle these excrement-stained tools slip from his grasp.

'Here, you *lazy* Northern bastard! Get out here *now!*' Gordon is not immediately responsive so Kevin goes to put his fingers to his lips to whistle for his attention. I alert him to *not by any means* do this act but it's *too* late and his soiled fingers are *already* in his mouth! For the next few minutes Strauss is busy vomiting into the nearest drain.

'Did you eat something iffy?' Gordon enquires when he *eventually* returns.

I'm filming the man from Sunderland descending a ladder. This looks strange on account of his long, thin legs which give him the semblance of a spider. His heel accidently clips a paint roller tray, which had been precariously propped up upon a tin of paint. He then looks alarmed, prompting me to pan towards the cause of this. I see that Kevin is now wearing a strange sort of hat. It soon becomes clear *though* that this is *not* some zany form of headwear but rather the *paint tray*, which has landed upside-down upon his cranium. Extended streaks of paint are streaming down his face like long white strands of hair. Gordon is then profusely apologizing, lifting the tray from Kevin's head and *attempting* to wipe away the glossy locks of emulsion now coating his grimacing visage. Strauss seems ungrateful to his friend's attempt to clean him up because he then slaps his hand away before finding voice to air his *deepest* displeasure- *the air subsequently turns blue.*

The atmosphere in the van on the way home is frosty to say the least. Kevin has managed to remove the majority of the paint from his hair and face but there's still something of a ghost about him. Gordon's earlier offer to clean him up with white spirit had been *wisely* declined.

'I *said* I'm sorry,' Gordon says at last.

'Poke it!'

'It were *nowt* but an accident.'

'There is a school of thought,' Strauss replies, 'that subscribes to the theory that there is *no* such thing as an accident.'

'I'll make it up to you,' Gordon offers.

'How?'

'I'll buy you a pint…*or a few*… That's if I can have a sub till pay day?…*When* is pay day by the way?' It seems *inevitable* we end up at a pub again.

'Go get them in,' Strauss says, handing Gordon money to buy the drinks. I go to follow him inside to the bar but remain stationary on account of Kevin taking out his new mobile phone. He seems oblivious to my presence. *'Hi fellas, it's me again,'* he says into the phone, confounding me, *not least* because he's adopted a North-Eastern accent *not unlike* Gordon's. 'I can be a giver or taker, but I'm *never* a faker! My passion will never cease and I *always* seek to please, *so call me!'* He then quotes Gordon's mobile phone number. Strauss is so amused with this he *still* fails to observe my presence. When he does *eventually* go into the pub I follow tentatively in an attempt to make sense of *all this*. I don't process much of what is said over the next hour. I've been persuaded to join this peculiar duo in drinking a couple of lagers, but my incomprehension is less to do with my low tolerance for alcohol than to bewilderment due to Kevin's *increasingly* bizarre behaviour. After ordering a round

I excuse myself to leave, and am predictably implored to stay. I stick to my resolve *however* since I sense this situation *needs* to be addressed sometime soon, and *only* with a sober approach.

I *once more* join Kevin and Gordon at work at yet another location the following day. I feel I'm about to make a breakthrough, the specifics continue to elude me but I'm certain *something* dramatic is soon to occur.

'*Whose* phone is ringing?' Gordon calls out. It's mine for a change, having left it on by accident. The caller I.D. reveals that Stan -my occasional sound recordist- is trying to contact me. I have *little* use for this freelancer now since my video camera (*which I also operate myself*) has ample audio ability. And so I turn my mobile phone mode to silent.

'*Offloading someone useless?*' Kevin is addressing me. 'I can see *myself* doing the same thing any day now.' I'm curious to know precisely *how* he's conscious of my wish to dispense with Stan's services since I *don't* recall sharing such a confidence with him.

'I've sanded everything down now,' Gordon says as he appears from around the door getting painted. Perhaps Strauss is distracted because his brush then comes into contact with his Colleague's face, transforming it into a sloppy shade of white. '*What the fuck?!*' Gordon grabs Kevin's decorating utensil then reciprocates by slapping it fully into his face.

'Leave it out, Geordie- it was an *accident!*'

'*Bollocks!*' the Northerner bellows back. 'You told me there's *no such thing as an accident*. And *stop* fucking calling us "Geordie"! ' His voice is steadily rising, a protruding vein throbs at his forehead. 'My name is *Gordon* and I'm *not* from fucking Newcastle, I'm from *Sunderland* so *why* the fuck does yous' call us "Geordie"?!'

'*You know…*' Kevin attempts a smile in the hope of disarming his usually passive partner, who has now *clearly* lost his temper.

'Nooo, I *don't* fucking know! *Why don't you try to explain it to me, Kevin?!*'

'Well, you know, "Geordie" sounds kind of…' he seems less sure of himself now, 'like catchy, *like*…like a cartoon character.'

'*I'm* a cartoon character?!' Gordon's pitch has lowered but I sense threat emanating from him like *never* before. 'Now, I'm asking you to put your words together *very* fucking carefully when I ask you the next question -*am I a fucking cartoon character?!*' I have to tear my attention away from the vein throbbing at his temple to instead study Kevin's reaction. His lips quiver in what I sense is a compulsion to make a clever or witty reply but he falters. I sense he's *finally* aware that saying the wrong thing now might have *dire* physical consequences for him.

'No Gordon,' he replies at last, swallowing hard, 'you're *not* a cartoon character at all. You are *Gordon*…Gordon from Sunderland.' For the *first* time I see Strauss sober, serious, subdued. The man from the North-East exhales loudly, turns on his heel and struts out of the room.

'I'll be in the van,' he calls out as we hear him thundering down the stairs. Kevin turns to me and slowly the mischievous grin creeps back across his face. He picks up a tin of paint, walks to the open window and proceeds to place it on the frame, thus tipping then upending it to spill its *entire* contents out down below. Subsequently a violent bout of coughing can be heard. Gordon is heard attempting to shout again but sounds as though he's choking. Strauss then looks alarmed at something occurring at ground level below. He winces and moves away from the window. Suddenly *an object* impacts against the pane, causing it to shatter and cascade flecks of glass down upon Kevin and myself like potentially *lethal* confetti!

The journey to the pub is long, tense and silent.

Strauss visits the toilet, and so I enter the premises alone whilst Gordon parks the van. My attention is drawn towards a group of a half a dozen or so men of *varying* ages. They are laughing and joking among themselves.

'He's *only* gone and put his number out on gay chat lines,' a florid-faced man of around sixty guffaws.

'Who?' asks a younger man whose resemblance to him suggests this might be his son.

'Kevin,' the older man continues, 'he goes on them, telling all and sundry his name is *"gobbling Gordon"* and the like, giving it, *'come on, big boys, come and do some filling in!'* Gordon hasn't *even* got a Scooby when these benders call him back!' Laughter erupts around the table but the face of the teller of this tale *suddenly* falls, and others present follow suit when they *also* observe Gordon entering the pub. Initially the tall man from the North looks sullen, cadaverous even. Then his expression becomes a snarl to quell any *remaining* amusement present. It registers *clearly* now that *Gordon had heard all that had been said.* Just then Kevin enters. Clearly *oblivious* to this situation he proceeds to warmly greet those present, *all* of whom appear

to be of long and close acquaintance. Their reception *in turn* is somewhat muted: some look away whilst others *leave* the table on the pretense of another appointment or activity *away from here*. Several of them discreetly relocate elsewhere to observe from other vantage points around the pub.

'What do you want to drink, Geordie?' Strauss asks whilst approaching the bar. He remains ignorant to both his Workmate's glowering demeanour, and to the fact that space has cleared around them in anticipation of what *might* be about to occur.

'How many times have I had to tell you?!' Gordon suddenly explodes. 'It's *not* fucking Geordie!' The angered man then lurches forward. Alarm is *only now* registered upon Kevin's face. He turns and runs for the exit, with Gordon in close pursuit. Strauss manages to push the door shut behind him but this serves only as a *temporary* obstacle for his nemesis, who is soon also outside to resume this chase in the pub garden. The drinkers flock to witness this through the windows. I'm forced to eke out a space for myself to film this *inevitable* debacle. Bets are called concerning the outcome: some of the pub's patrons speculate that Gordon- the taller man with the longer legs- will quickly catch his prey; others are certain the stouter fellow can apply his *slippery approach to Life in general*, and so dodge his potential *attacker*.

Several garden features are damaged and up-ended in this fracas. Kevin manages to escape this immediate location but *only* to the shambolic children's play area nearby, where he attempts to use a swing to fend off Gordon's prolonged charge. Then there's a scramble around a see-saw. Strauss eventually breaks free to make a *clear* route towards his van.

One of the men to my side is giving a detailed narration of *all* these developments in a faux-clipped tone as though commentating on an *especially* dramatic horse race. Gordon manages to clip Kevin's heel, causing him to fall. Subsequently he sets upon him but, as they begin to wrestle, the man from the North-East also stumbles and loses balance. This allows Strauss to spring up and make a *fresh* dash to sanctuary within his vehicle. Once inside he activates the central locking, provoking a ranting Gordon to clutch at *whatever* he can inflict damage upon. The first casualty is the radio aerial, which is soon broken off. Then comes an attack upon a windscreen wiper but Kevin manages to fire up his van and therefore affect his escape. Gordon narrowly evades being hit by the vehicle though *continues* charging after it. Soon however Strauss accelerates off to be safely in the clear. His van escapes from view. The wagers amongst those observing inside the pub are then duly honoured.

'*Who's that?*' a familiar voice hisses.

'It's only me.' I'm hovering on the front garden pathway.

'I got a *"dear John".*' My Subject emerges from the nearby hedge. 'Or in my case a *"dear Kevin"!*'

'What do you mean?'

'*She's only gone and changed the locks on me!*'

'Who?'

'*My wife, of course.*' Strauss looks drained of all his *former* confidence. '*I can't believe* Glenda could do *this* to me. She *must have* had someone make this decision for her, and I've a *good* idea who that might have been. *So Fabio- what did you say to her?*'

Kevin is settling down for the night in his van. It has taken me quite some time to calm him and dissuade him from the *delusion* that *I* had somehow convinced his wife to evict him. Eventually he's come to the conclusion that it was *Gordon* who'd poisoned Glenda's mind.

'It's a temperate evening', I tell him, 'you'll be fine.'

'*Why, isn't there enough in your filming budget to afford me a hotel?*' Strauss huffs amidst an envelopment of blankets.

'That would be *manipulation* of the Subject,' I inform him, 'besides which, we're *still* waiting for *full* commission.'

'*All this was all on spec?!*' There is exasperation to his tone. 'Can't you *at least* put me up at your place?'

'I have family over. I'll meet you here at six a.m. tomorrow morning. I'll bring coffee.'

'*Tea,*' he grunts back, '*six sugars!*'

Once more we're stuck in traffic. Fulfilling our *prior* arrangement I'd been surprised by the presence of a large man of East European origin, whom Kevin had introduced as "Andrew Gollata," and who'd subsequently corrected this *several* times before *eventually* giving up on the task as fruitless. This giant now sits with us, the three of us crammed within Strauss's van.

'You *weren't* kidding, Andy,' Kevin concedes as he indicates to join the Great West Road, 'you *really* are a high standard, high quality Tradesman. I'd be more than proud of the work you done today, *even* if I'd done it *myself.*'

'*Yeah, yeah,*' the huge Pole replies, 'I'm the best painter-decorator in *all* of Krakow.'

'I can see us doing *lots* of work together.'

'I tell you earlier,' Andrew booms back, 'I don't fuck you and you don't fuck me. I did the work *so now you pay!*'

'We've *just* got to go to the client's house first,' Strauss replies. 'He'll pay us *right away* so no need to fret.' Ten minutes later the traffic has become less congested but Kevin is pulling over.

'What's happening now?' I ask.

'We're losing revs.' We've come to a stand-still. 'You'll *both* have to give me a push to restart the engine.'

Andrew and I climb out of the van. The East European's eyes narrow as he looks at my camera equipment then waves me off as though I'd *only* get in his way before proceeding to push the van *alone.* He must have the magic touch because the vehicle immediately fires up. But Andrew begins snarling because Kevin, *instead* of waiting for him, *accelerates off!* Then the Polish man-mountain is in hot pursuit, yelling unfamiliar curses such as "*I will eat your children*", "Swine herder" and what sounds like *"I spit on your Mother's moustache"!* Eventually Golotta gives up on this vain exertion as the van disappears altogether from sight. The huge Pole turns back and catches sight of me. His eyes blaze *anew* as he now begins to run towards *yours truly!* Luckily I've already hailed a black taxi and climb inside to safety. As we pull away the driver proceeds to make speculative criticisms about *anti-social* foreigners. And so Andrew becomes a fading image, disappearing as resolutely as a flawless camera dissolve.

Kevin gets in touch with me mid morning the next day. He summons me to *yet another* job, this time at a block of flats not far from my production office.

'You're *still* finding clients? …*All* from your advertisements?'

'Something *like* that,' he grunts from a ladder overhead. Upon my arrival he'd evaded any type of explanation for his *especially* erratic behavior yesterday. 'Have you received your budget *yet?*'

'Kevin, have you given *any* thought concerning my presence these last few weeks?'

'*Yes,*' he replies whilst tinkering with tins of paint and less identifiable objects on a ledge above me, '*you're a jinx, Fabio!*'

'I *meant* concerning your brother, Roland, and his *most specific* needs.' I now notice the utensils he's handling are not work tools as I'd *initially* thought. I move away from the wall to get a better view of *precisely* what he's doing. He opens what looks like a bottle of white spirit before taking a large gulp from it! Could *this* be a suicide attempt? 'Kevin, *what* are you doing now?'

'*I'm trying to work!*' He takes *another* gulp from the bottle before extracting his mobile phone to make a call. The speaker is on. Subsequently an urgent ringtone echoes about our surroundings. Eventually there comes a voice but this is merely an answerphone message, which according to my *transcript* is thus:

'This is *Glenda's* phone,' a voice from the North-East cheerfully states, which I immediately recognize as *Gordon's*, 'Kevin's ex-missus and now the *very* welcome new partner of someone who has *long* held a torch for her.' A girlish giggle is heard in the background. '*We* won't be around for some time because we're out on the razzle *big-time*, a lovely cruise courtesy of Glenda and Kevin's *joint* bank account. Don't wait up, *kidda*, we might be away *quite* some time!'

First to impact upon the ground is Kevin's phone. Luckily I'd moved aside to be clear of this. The next object to fall is *Kevin himself*. It later transpires his ladder had become dislodged from the wall, *probably* as a result of shock from this painful revelation, and so giving cause for his *considerable* injuries. I'd had, *of course*, the presence of mind to film *all* this. I am an unwavering eye. *I am a camera*.

I next encounter Kevin on a visit to the hospital he's been admitted to.

'Happy now?!' he asks as we enter the room. I have my occasional sound recordist, Stan, with me today.

'You've been given a lovely private room here.'

'I should fucking hope so,' he spits back. *'It's my fucking charm what swung it!'*

'Charm *indeed,'* I reply.

'Yeah, fucking charm!' Strauss growls whilst rummaging through the gift bag he'd snatched from me upon my arrival. 'I've got an abundance of fucking charm, fucking shit loads of it! *I've got so fucking much charm that I got it oozing out my arse!'*

'Have you had *any* visitors, Kevin?'

'You *really* know how to kick a man when he's down!' he replies whilst devouring the bunch of grapes I'd gifted him. 'No wife, no workmate, I've *even* been boycotted by the *entire* Polish Community for an *alleged* slur upon their fine craftsmanship.'

'Yes, I've heard they are *very* proud people.' Kevin has a black eye which I'm sure *hadn't* been sustained in his fall from the ladder: had Polish Andrew tracked him down to *here* at the hospital?

'And sweetest irony of all is that I should end up here at the *same* infirmary they are treating my brother. There's gratitude, eh? *He's not even come to see me!* I'm sick of making *all* the efforts with that lazy sod!'

'We've been told that he's *completely* incapacitated.' Stan and I had attempted to visit Roland earlier but the medical staff had told us he was spending *all* his time either under dialysis or resting.

'He'd use *any* excuse to gall me,' Kevin huffs before casting aside the now empty gift bag. 'And just to think I was about to sabotage *my* own health further by donating him one of *my* kidneys-well, *he can whistle for that now!*' There's a knock at the door. A young man in a long white coat enters. He has all the appearance of a doctor, and eyes our camera equipment with suspicion. 'It's alright, Doc, *just* visitors.'

'I've *some* news for you, Mr. Strauss,' this person says sternly whilst staring me straight in the eye. Or rather, into the eye of my *all-seeing* camera.

'It's perfectly alright, Doctor, I give you my permission for you to talk medically in front of these *agents of destruction.*'

'Well, the *good* news is you have *not* suffered any fractures from your fall,' the Physician relays, 'but tests show that your liver has had quite some *considerable* damage.'

'That *can't* be true!' Kevin gasps. '*But how?!*'

'I'm inclined to think it's connected to your lifestyle, Mr. Strauss. You'll *have to* drastically change if you're hoping for *any* type of recovery.'

'I knew the *paint* would get me in the end!' Kevin's bottom lip is trembling. 'Have you got *anything* to steady my nerves?' he asks once the man of medicine has left.

'Drink is *not* the answer,' I tell him, 'it's very likely *the cause* of your current condition.'

'*Doctor, are you now?*' he scornfully replies. 'Damn that brother of mine-*the curse of Roland strikes again!*'

We didn't see Kevin again for several weeks. By this time we'd given up hope on him altogether, and had therefore approached one of his brothers, *Dougie,* who appears to be taking us a lot more seriously, and so seems to be *more genuine* in becoming the donor to offer a kidney to aid Roland.

Our re-acquaintance with Kevin is quite by chance. Stan and I are passing the public convenience filmed in the preceding month when we catch sight of a familiar looking beaten-up old white van.

'*Hello Kevin,*' I call out as we film him emerging from the toilet. He looks startled then attempts to compose a demeanor we're more familiar with.

'You got my message then?'

'*What* message?' There had been *no* further effort from him to contact us.

'It got all a bit heated after my accident,' he elaborates, 'I said many a thing in *jest.* Of course I was willing to donate a kidney.'

'*You were?*' My tone is understandably doubtful since we have footage *very much* to the contrary.

'Of course! But then you were there when they gave me the bad news about my *own* kidneys.'

'*Your liver, surely?*' He seems to be trying to convince us of some *Alternative Reality?*

'Yes, my *multiple* organ failure,' Kevin retorts bitterly. 'I'll just have to try putting a brave face on it… I'm going back to the hospital any minute now for my *own* daily dialysis.'

'What have you been doing *here?*'

'Working, of course,' he replies at last, 'more painting work…*Doing it properly this time*'.

'*Where* are your work tools?' My question registers alarm upon his face. He subsequently returns to the toilets in haste. We remain stationary for several minutes but Kevin fails to re-emerge. Eventually I call out to him, albeit fruitlessly. I then try his mobile phone, and even hear the ringtone echo amidst the public convenience. *He neglects to answer.* 'We're *not* going away *anytime* soon, Kevin,' I yell out to him. *Finally* he comes out from the toilets. His hands are empty. His expression is unfathomable: shame? *Rising anger?* I expect him to barge past us to escape to his van but he now appears resigned and rooted to the spot. I *now* feel relieved that several weeks *previously* -amidst much drunken bonhomie- I'd gotten him to sign our consent form, therefore giving me *complete and unconditional permission to use this footage in any way I choose*. Strauss's bottom lip is wobbling. The weeping begins. I suspect this will serve as a *suitable* end sequence: credits rolling down his wet face to accompany those *much anticipated* tears.

Episode Three:

Dougie, Entertainer

'Sometimes I've a good mind to deny this cruel,
ungrateful world the great gifts I have to offer.'
Douglas Bader Strauss.

I'm having a repeated viewing of a video emailed to me of an Entertainer -introduced by a caption as "Dazzling Dougie Strauss"- performing to a crowd at a public venue. He's deeply attentive to his audience, which compromises mostly of mature females. Their reaction to him comes across as positive, enthusiastic even. I cannot be *absolutely* sure of the quality of the performance *itself* because this was sent to me *sans* sound, whether willfully or through some technical fault I cannot yet be certain. As the footage continues I observe that the intimate connection between Performer and Audience has a chemistry converging almost upon sacred devotion. They look as though they adore Dougie, and he *seemingly* reciprocates. It comes as a great relief I've *at last* found a Strauss sibling devoid of the toxic misogyny of Robby, and free of the senseless, belligerent nihilism of another brother of his, Kevin, with whom I've *also* recently dispensed with. The fact that Dougie has immediately expressed interest in being a kidney donor to Roland, apparently with *none* of the mercenary motives of his predecessors, genuinely makes me feel I've *finally* found both a worthy Subject for documentation and the selfless saviour of an ailing hospital patient whose condition will only worsen if not *soon* installed with a fresh new organ.

'Blue eyes!' Dougie is wearing a garish, near-identical dressing gown to the one worn by Robby: perhaps these had been purchased wholesale? His wife dutifully trots off then quickly returns with a pair of cowboy boots. 'No, the Elton John version.' With this she again exits the room before reappearing with another form of footwear, fluffy slippers, which she tenderly places upon his feet. 'Good girl, but you're forgetting.'

'Ah yes,' replies Doug's wife, 'baritone means with a cup of tea'.

'These are code words?' I ask after she's gone to the kitchen. He remains silent until she re-arrives with a cup and saucer.

'Blue Moon,' Strauss issues, still enthroned within his armchair. He takes a sip from the cup. 'No, this is *no* good-this is *"Blue Hawaii"!'*

'You're *off* sugar?!' his wife whimpers. 'I didn't think you liked that brand of artificial sweetener I got last time?'

'I'll settle for Blue Hawaii then,' he replies sharply. 'The *live* concert would have been preferable to this studio-bound version.'

'I'm trying to keep up here, what do you mean?'

'*Where's* the teabag?'

'You won't drink it if it's stewed!'

'Blue Velvet!' With Doug's new command she again leaves the room, clutching a biscuit tin on her return. 'I didn't mean the A Cappella version. I want full orchestra accompaniment!'

'Why couldn't you *just* say you wanted your snacks on a plate?' she bleats back.

'Begin the Beguine,' he instructs whilst munching away at the biscuits once they have been presented in a way satisfactory to him. 'Not next week!…Beguine the Begin!...Make it a medley.' This is code, *I later learn*, for clearing away the cups and saucers. 'Can't get by without you.' His Spouse shuffles behind his chair to massage his shoulders. 'The more *livelier* version!' She obediently moves in front of him then sinks to her knees. His robe slips open as she massages his chest. 'Stairway to Heaven…Skip the acoustic– go *straight* to the anthemic overture!'

'This could be *my* highway to hell!' I mumble to myself as her face disappears into his lap.

'Oh *yes!* The *extended* version!' I hear him cry out as I retire to the kitchen. 'Crescendo!...Encore!...Reprise…Three steps to heaven!'

'Lazy Sunday afternoon?' I hear her mutter as I'm considering slipping out of Doug's home altogether.

'Did Elvis Presley have a similar technique?' I ask gingerly after returning to the front room, *thankfully* having missed most of that particular private performance.

'He wasn't the *only* king,' Strauss replies, still wedged within his recliner. I'm beginning to suspect that his thick, black mane of hair is a wig. 'L. Ron Hubbard had a similar approach.'

'The Father of Scientology?!' I gasp. 'Surely he wasn't *also* a singer?'

'He shared a few of his secret techniques with me.'

'You knew him?' This could become an *altogether different* project to the one I'd originally planned.

'There are *certain* things I've been sworn not to reveal,' Doug replies as his wife grooms *"his"* hair. 'Let's just say that I didn't *have to* be transformed into a *"clear"- I* was *born* clear.'

'That seems all very clear,' I reply, even though there's nothing *even remotely* clear about *any* of this.

Perhaps I've gotten ahead of myself. This hadn't been the *first* time I'd met Douglas Bader Strauss in person. Our initial encounter in the flesh had happened several days previously. 'Good morning!' He's greeting me at the front door of his home, which is situated within a council tenement block.

'That was a quick answer,' I tell him. Perhaps he'd observed my approach along the balcony?

'I *sensed* you on the Astral plane- I know when I'm about to get a visitation.'

'Yes, hence our ten a.m. appointment?' I'm curious why Strauss hasn't yet invited me into his home until I realize his attention has been drawn elsewhere. I look behind me to see a figure seemingly gliding along the walkway on the balcony at the far side of the building. I notice something familiar about their attire. It takes me a several seconds to process the fact that this person has a near identical outfit to Doug, complete with the same hairstyle. But this man is taller, slimmer, younger looking. These garments suit him better, and are in sharp contrast to those worn by – or rather *containing*- the man standing before me. 'Who's that?'

'Nobody!' Doug replies at last, once this apparition has disappeared from view.

'Oh, you've adapted.' My comment is in response to a sign on the front door stating "beware of the dog" , which has had the letter "u" inserted after the "o" to appropriate it as "doug", hence *"Beware of the doug".*

'Adapted?!' His demeanour lightens upon noticing what I'm referring to. 'In a way, though his Spirit is *still* with us.' I consider asking him to elaborate upon this but he's motioning me to follow him. 'And so to the Vortex.' Just then Strauss barges into a large plastic bin left in the hallway, thus spilling its contents of waste products and empty packaging out across the carpet. I decline to follow this *exact* example.

'Hi,' I say to the plump, middle-aged woman I encounter in the front room. 'I'm Fabio,' I add in an attempt to defuse this long, awkward silence, 'and you are?'

'Wife,' Doug answers for her.

'Yes, I surmise this lady *is* your good wife- I was enquiring after a name?'

'It's Wife,' she replies blankly.

'We felt it far *less* complicated that way,' Doug explains, as though this were the most natural thing in the world.

'You changed your name by deed poll?!...How precisely did you two meet?' I enquire after my initial question is met by nothing more expansive than a prolonged vacant expression.

'In the park,' she quavers after looking to him for approval.

'The eponymous wife, eh!' Strauss's tone is sharp. 'You *always* make it about *you*, don't you! Make yourself useful, blue eyes'. This is a peculiar comment, *not least* because her eyes appear to be brown. 'Where can I start?'

'Try starting at the beginning, Dougie?'

'I'm more than happy to give *something* of myself, hence your presence here.' I attempt to ask him directly if he's serious about donating a kidney to his ailing brother, Roland, but he presses on. 'You're more than welcome to call me Dougie, *granted there*, fella. Right, the beginning, you say? I distinguished myself from *all the rest* of my brothers because musically I was the child prodigy of the family.'

'What instrument did you play?' I ask. 'Piano, brass or strings?'

'I was drawn to the drums,' he replies without a beat.

'By whom? …You must have been very young?'

'The clue is that I was a *child* prodigy. Keith was a very good teacher, I learned from his personal tuition.'

'A friend of the family?…Who was this Keith?'

'Keith Moon from the Who. He instructed me on the spirit plane.'

'*The spirit plane?!*' *What* am I to make of this?

'My abilities were superior to Moonie's though.'

'*They were?!*'

'Of course,' Strauss carries on regardless to my incredulous tone, 'because I had the advantage of playing the drums like a *live* guy.' There seems to be *some* form of logic present *somewhere* within this. 'I had advice from *all* types of people who had passed on.'

'Such as whom?'

'We'll come to that in good time. We don't want to go down the whole History of Rock just at this *precise* moment, do we?'

'I suppose not,' I reply, somewhat dazed. 'Perhaps you can *elaborate* on your formative years as a musician?'

'I started hanging out with, jamming and gigging, with older musicians, ones that were *not* dead in this case. Far *more* practical that way, of course. I got recruited by a Prog Rock group of some note but unfortunately at that point they were in recess, so had reverted back to being a Country and Western act.'

'I seem to recall just after that you had a hit single with a New Romantics group you joined in the mid 1980s?' I'm referring to the copious notes I've brought with me today: unlike his brothers, Dougie had at least *some* residue of fame beyond being merely one of Sextuplets.

'Less New Romantics, more *new,* new romantics meets pre-nu metal with a Goth sensibility applied against a hard rock crossover attitude that *resisted* selling out.'

'Hence your *one and only* hit.' My comment elicits a dark look from my Subject. '*Quite* a niche act then?'

'It was rave culture that killed the cult of the rock star, but don't tell Bono or Michael Hutchence that.'

'Bono?'

'Just kidding, I know he's *long* dead already,' Doug shrugs, 'but you get my drift?'

'I think so.' *I don't, of course.*

'I mean, the Musician was *no longer* the Star. With some weird little bleep noises, not dissimilar to that catchy tune

Roland has got going on with his hospital gadget, and with the aid of a little pill, Rolly's territory *once again*, the Ravers themselves became the so-called Star rather than the *genuine* talent such as myself.'

'Was that *so* bad? A truly egalitarian youth culture?'

'Anarchy!' Strauss proclaims. 'And *not even* in an exciting rock 'n'roll type of anarchic way. And so I was forced to go *against* the grain.'

'Indeed,' I respond, referring to my notes, 'your concept album?'

'I see you've done your homework.' His face lights up. 'Perhaps you were one of the very few who *got* it? Or rather, to *understand* it,' he adds to rectify this unfortunate terminology.

'Yes', is all I can manage, and eventually, 'and *what* a marvelous title for an album!'

'Journey to the centre of my ego!' Doug exclaims, his chest puffed up with pride before a coughing fit gets the better of him. 'Well, the public weren't *quite* ready for it yet.'

'You mean concerning the disappointing sales?'

'With the advance of Evolution it might *still* take quite some time *yet* for them to catch up with my ideas. Roll on the monoliths!' I must have looked confused because he's then attempting to explain himself more clearly. '2001…the film… *rather* than the year of my unsuccessful court action.' Nothing amongst my notes gives any *further* clue to this last reference so I avert his gaze to feign consulting my paperwork till happy distraction comes from *"wife"* entering the room with cups of tea.

'Blue Hawaii and Blue Velvet,' she sing-songs.

'Thank you very much,' Strauss says in a complete change of demeanor. 'Wife, *now* you can tell Fabio how we met.'

'How we met,' she responds as though making a well-rehearsed performance, 'me and Dougie met in the local park. His inspiration came from taking a walk in the said park, whilst my *own* inspiration came from walking my dog, Oscar, in that self *same* park. Hence, *this* is *how* we met.'

'I noticed her pet dog,' he adds. 'And later noticed her, *of course.*'

'He did!' "Wife" states emphatically.

'This is when I picked up on vibes from her pet dog.'

'Vibes?' I reverberate. 'What *sort* of vibes?'

'A psychic link,' he replies, his tone suddenly very serious. 'Myself and this canine had an instant psychic link: a meeting of minds, *as it were.'*

'This is *how* Dougie picked up on the fact that I was in an abusive relationship,' "Wife" explains.

'Through your dog?'

'Yes, amazing really,' she continues, 'the power of second-sight, being psychic and *all that* stuff. It truly was a life-changing experience for me.'

'How so?'

'Previously I'd been blocked. I had been married, and *seemed* happy at the time but the fact is I wasn't *even aware* that it was an abusive relationship I'd been in with my now *ex-*husband.'

'You learned *all* that from your dog?' I enquire.

'Dougie did,' she tells me.

'Is your dog *still* psychic?' Suddenly her face drops. Behind her Dougie is doing a mime of sorts: is he trying to tell me something? First he gesticulates an index finger run along his throat. Then -possibly as a result of my quizzical reaction- he pretends to wrap an invisible cord or rope around his neck then proceeds to lift it, hoisting both arm and upper body up as though by a noose. By the time he has played out a further charade where he's giving himself what appears to be a fatal injection and, with tongue protruding from the corner of his mouth and slumping back within his armchair, I surmise the fact that *the said dog is now dead.*

'We're not sure,' she replies gloomily.

'Oh, how so?'

'We used to get postcards from him but have not received one in a while now.'

'Postcards from your *dog?'*

'Yes, you see, he went to live on a farm.' She turns back to Doug, who is then forced to adapt his *"her dog is dead"* mime into the more innocuous action of brushing the garments he's wearing.

'You really *should* have pressed this outfit more carefully, my love,' he tells her. 'I'm expecting a visitation from an *especially* important guest shortly.'

'We are expecting company?' I enquire.

'Indeed,' Doug responds with a smile, 'perhaps even from Mr. Mozart *himself!'*

'Oh, a spirit visitation like the one from Keith Moon you mentioned?' Strauss responds with a self-satisfied nod. I consider putting to him that Wolfgang Amadeus might *not* be quite so receptive to being greeted by a chubby middle-aged cockney in a creased, Vegas-years, too-tight Elvis jumpsuit but choose to remain silent since I am a *mere* observer. And a camera. A camera that *observes.*

'The spirits *however* might *not* trust you just yet.' Is it possible that on some psychic level Dougie has been able to pick up on my skepticism? As an open-minded Journalist and Broadcaster I *should re*serve my judgment till some later time. 'You shall have to impress upon them that you are *not* their foe.' These words cause a chill to my spine.

'Will Mr. Mozart be ok with artificial sweetener?' Doug's wife asks, which elicits a pained expression from him.

'Any sign yet?' Several hours have passed.

'It's not a tap that can be *just* turned off and on,' Strauss replies bluntly. He's now wearing a white, powdered wig (presumably to make Maestro Mozart feel at home) and a stick-on bushy black beard whose purpose seems less clear. 'I'll have to go into a *deeper t*rance.'

'Does the bushy beard have any significance, Doug?'

'Silence!' he booms. 'I bring you news from my astral travels, for *I* am the Oracle.'

'As in the one from Delphi?'

'Well, I'm *not* talking about the long defunct television listings guide, am I?!' comes his caustic response. *'I* am the vehicle that is the bridge between our world and the next… *world.'*

'Is the beard an aide?' I persist. 'A useful prop to help you?'

'Is *not* the Sorcerer's crystal ball *merely* a prop to untangle and tame the sea of dreams?'

'I'm not sure.' On reflection I suspect this might have been a rhetorical question?

'Besides, the ends of this hair work as tiny transmitters, *antennae*, if you will.'

'Which? That wig or your *own*…hair?'

'This hairpiece, rather than my own natural *full* head of hair.' Doug glares at me for emphasis as though to dispel my suspicion that he *is almost certainly* bald. 'This was woven from the locks of a saint, none other than Saint Desmond of Tutu.'

'He was made a Saint?!'

'I return to give you tomorrow's news today.' Strauss closes his eyes and roars with the intensity of an Old Testament Prophet, 'Hark, leaders of Nations go insane, those governed by them…really become *quite* anxious actually…A stranger comes to town to paint everything…lime green!..He makes an awful mess, not least of his blouse.'

'What of predicting something *useful*, Dougie?' I enquire. 'Something to help Humanity avert some natural, *or unnatural,* disaster?'

'The 4.10 at Haydock,' he splutters before slumping back in his armchair as though fully spent. The sporting pages of yesterday's newspaper are open on a nearby table.

'That particular race meeting would appear to have *already* been and gone?'

'Some data is often *post dated*,' Strauss replies after regaining consciousness. 'The spirit plane isn't *always* the information super highway we want it to be.'

'Are there any *further* revelations you can relay from the Other World, Dougie?'

'Reliable accounts coming from my Spiritual Guides can categorically both confirm and deny certain conundrums which have been confusing Mankind, such as the fate of evil dictator Adolf Hitler.'

'What of him?!'

'I can categorically *confirm*, despite speculation that his brain was saved by mad scientists, that evil dictator *Adolf Hitler is now one hundred percent dead!'*

'A great comfort *indeed!'*

'Furthermore,' he continues, 'I have been given vital information concerning the circumstances of Lady Diana, the former Princess of Wales.'

'I'm *fairly* sure she's also dead,' I counter, 'unless you are privy to some conspiracy where she faked her death to live in some remote location under a new identity?'

'Let's keep it *real,* Fabio,' Doug sighs, 'she's as dead as last night's lamb chops! I'm referring to the conspiracy concerning her *untimely* demise.'

'Of course you are,' I concur. *'Which specific conspiracy?'*

'The specific conspiracy to prevent her from wearing a seat belt! And now an *especially* special Revelation for my psychic friends…' Strauss's stare into the camera becomes exceptionally intense at this point. Eventually I recall that he has a background in Hypnotism so I avert my *own* gaze in case he's attempting to use it upon me! I leave my camera running however, with a mind to study this footage in a *safer* situation at some later time. 'Thank you my friends,' he says at last. It is *only later* I'm aware he'd sent out a lengthy message I'd been unable to initially pick up upon. He then moves over to the corner of the living room and places himself behind an electric keyboard before attempting to play a few notes. Only a series of atonal noises emanates however. 'This subversion of my *vital* organ could *well* be a sign!'

'What type of sign?'

'*Agents of destruction* are at work. The Shitegeist in the machine, as it were.'

'Doug,' I say, trying to bring more relevance to the filming, 'have you given *any more* thought concerning your brother Roland and his search for a new kidney?'

'Fabio,' he replies, turning to fix me once more with his piercing gaze, 'I'm not sure I'm *quite* ready to perform for you *just* yet.' Has he misunderstood my plain and simple question? Perhaps he'd been distracted by some other enquiry, possibly coming from the Spirit World?

'I don't follow.'

'Indeed, I can tell that you are *very much* your own man. You're an educated, informed person, Fabio, and I'm sure you're aware that sometimes even the most accomplished of Spanish Flamenco guitarists has occasion to face away from his audience so they can't steal the secrets of his most skillful licks.'

'Something has come to my attention, Dougie.' I'm no longer able to remain silent concerning something that has increasingly been giving me cause for concern. 'I'm beginning to become aware of *something you've been attempting to do* during the course of this documentary.'

'Oh really, Fabio?' He again fixes me with that look which seems designed to probe deeply into my most cavernous core. *'And what would that be?'*

'I'd like to talk to you about the stage hypnotism act that you attempted to take on tour in the early '90s?' I produce the specific research notes saved for this *very* moment.

'I'm not trying to hypnotize you, Fabio,' he counters with a dismissive chuckle though I detect he's disturbed by the appearance of these documents, which include newspaper articles.

'Did you anticipate that I would present you with this? Did you pick up on *this* on a psychic level?'

'Of course, that is *why* I told you from the onset on our correspondence that I'm *more* than happy to speak about it.'

'*You did?*' I shall have to re-consult the various e-mails that went to-and-thro between us to check if this *were indeed the case.* I'm *not* sure what happens next but I suddenly find myself out in the hallway of the flat, with Mr. Strauss bidding me a safe trip home. 'I seem to recall…*something?*' I hear myself say as I'm guided on my departure.

'*Indeed, you do.*' Before I know it I've descended the staircase of the tenement block and am on my way home.

I must have been tired. This is the *only* possible explanation. After waking from a mid- afternoon nap (something I'm *most* unaccustomed with) I look for the files presented to Strauss earlier in the day. I'm unable to find them so try my best to recall their contents from memory.

'Dougie, there's a few points I'd like to go over again if possible?' I ask him over the 'phone later that evening.

'Of course, but I'm about to begin a gig.'

'On a *tuesday?*'

'Supply and demand. I'm free during the day tomorrow so why not pop round again mid- morning?'

I have a curious dream that night. In this visitation I'm again presenting the research files to Dougie, who in *this* instance is far more receptive.

'You can't believe *everything* you read in newspapers, Fabio,' he attempts to convince me, 'it's *just* a make-believe story.'

'Can you confirm or deny this, Mr. Strauss?' In this current avatar I'm a crusading Lawyer intending to incriminate a *guilty* Party in the dock. 'Can you confirm or deny that during the course of your act, the only person to get hypnotized was you *yourself?*'

'Do you believe *everything* you read in the gutter press?' I notice that Doug's bottom lip has begun to wobble. His hairpiece is becoming lop-sided.

'That was *not* my question!' I persist. 'What is your response to the account that your dissatisfied audience turned the tables on you and began to chant *"dance-puppet-dance,"* to which, in your suggestive state, you *complied to?*'

'It didn't happen like that, *at all,*' he bleats back, suddenly tearful. 'It was all a plot against me, I swear!'

'A plot?' I soften my approach: I'm *not* a sadist; 'A plot hatched by *whom?*' Strauss responds but unfortunately at this point I'm unable to hear him, in what becomes a strange reprise of the mute performance he'd sent me by e-mail.

I'd woken shortly after that.

After documenting this dream in my journal I go in search of my video camera to view the footage. For some inexplicable reason the interview appears to have been cut short. Filming stops *just* at the point I'm removing the incriminating files from my bag. Upon inspecting this same bag, in the *present tense*, I discover I'm *no longer* in possession of these documents: had I absent-mindedly left them with Doug? I shall have to devise a *suitable* approach of enquiry about this when I meet him again later today. I'm drawn back to the silent concert. Something unfathomable has been troubling me about this from the very outset. I subsequently make a forensic examination of *every* detail of the video yet again unfurling across my computer screen. I focus on the loving attention of the females watching Strauss perform. I also notice, *for the first time,* a number of details concerning this *excessively* indulgent audience: a protruding Adam's apple here; a forearm that would be the pride of a brick-layer there; fifty shades of grey would be an *apt* way to describe the gradations of five o'clock shadows upon the otherwise heavily-cosmetisized visages of those present. It only *now* becomes apparent that my Subject had been performing to a group of crossdressers, transsexuals and myriad of other *self-definers!* This is no problem to *me,* of course, since I'm the *least* homophobic of people but it does lead to some *very* pertinent questions, such as *why* would Mr. Strauss send me a video of a performance which *remains* silent?

To confirm my suspicions -just before the footage comes to an end- I catch sight of one of the *pseudo*-females sitting (rather *un*lady-like) at a table in a position that could be defined as "*man spreading.*" I freeze the frame to witness that the strapping device this person installed has failed, and so escaping from their thong -despite having been conscientiously shaved- is clearly identifiable as a roving, *exposed* testicle!

'Come in,' I hear Doug's voice call out from some distant place within his flat. I hadn't yet knocked at the door, which presents me with several possibilities I shall explore more in depth at some *later p*oint. I proceed through the front room to find Strauss immersed within his courtly armchair once more. His wife stands behind him massaging his scalp. I still can't decide whether this black mop is his *own* hair or from some other, *less organic* origin. It might appear churlish to ask at this particular point in time.

'*How* did you know I was here, Doug?'

'My precious...' I imagine he's addressing me until I'm furnished further, 'you really are my rock. She helps me in my war with the Mediocres.'

'Who are "*the Mediocres*"?' I enquire

'Did you enjoy your nice little holiday?' Strauss asks, turning to his wife. She nods and smiles. Was the brief act of giving him a scalp massage seen as a *holiday* for her?! 'Blue Eyes.' She dutifully leaves the room, skipping along in an act that belies her heavy frame. 'Blue Hawaii for our guest.'

'Thanks,' I call out after her.

'She's a fine woman but I *can't* help being tormented by her mother's presence.'

'Is her mother here?'

'No Fabio,' replies Doug, 'I meant her mother's presence here on Planet Earth.'

'Is that not a little cold? Surely you can't resent her *just* for being alive?'

'You *haven't* met her,' he retorts, as though if I *were* to come face to face with her then I'd agree with him. 'There's *only one* thing worse than that.'

'What is this one thing worse than her being alive?'

'*Hard to believe*, I know,' he sighs, 'but the one worse thing is that the wife is *always* going on about her.' As yet I've not heard her make a single mention of her mother though remain silent so that he can explain himself. 'It's "mum" this and "mum" that, it's "mother knows best" one day and the next day exactly the same. It's always "mum wouldn't like this", then it's "mum said you'd do something *exactly like that.*" Then she'd say, mum's…gone to Iceland- *if only!* There would be polar bears up there with their ears chewed off!'

Just then his wife returns with a tray containing a pot of tea, cups, saucers and a biscuit barrel. My attention is drawn towards a wholly *more* disturbing sight however. She's now wearing a French's maid's outfit, or what was possibly *once* such attire but which is now torturously stretched at every seam by her swollen shape. Stocking tops are frayed, the apron straining at her waist is stained and the little maid's hat she wears would look more at home on a prized pooch's head rather than upon the obese woman wobbling before us. To make matters worse she turns and bends over to retrieve something, which prompts both Doug and I to grimace and avert our gaze. I eventually notice she's now brandishing a vacuum cleaner, which is switched on then pushed and pulled noisily up and down the room. Again my senses are assailed as Mrs. Strauss gruesomely wiggles, inclines and squats to reclaims items stuck within the increasingly tormented machine.

'What did you mean earlier, Doug', I enquire, more as a way to dismiss this disturbing imagery, 'when you mentioned your *"war with the mediocres"?'*

'*It's obvious,*' he replies, raising his voice to be heard above the din of the vacuuming, 'mediocre entities will *always* band together to attack those who are *truly e*xceptional.' It seems this newest point comes as a welcome distraction for Doug also. He then waves his wife away in a theatrical gesture as though, *I imagine*, to banish her from his sight *altogether.*

'Tall poppy syndrome, eh?'

'Was Lucifer not the most beautiful, brightest angel?' I suspect this is another rhetorical question. 'He was struck down by those who were jealous of him.'

'*Surely* it was for the sin of pride?' I counter.

'Can't you do *that* later?' Doug bellows at his wife. 'Maestro Mozart would think a vacuum cleaner to be some instrument of the Devil, so I expect if you haven't already scared him away with that terrifying outfit then I'm sure that infernal thing *certainly will!*'

'I thought only dogs fear vacuum cleaners?' I'm attempting to defuse this awkward exchange. 'Unless you mean Beethoven, whom I *seem* to recall from a movie, is also a dog?'

'*A dog?!*' Dougie roars above the cacophony of the carpet cleaning device. 'Turn that shit off!'

'But *you* bought me this outfit,' Mrs. Strauss bleats back once the din has subsided, 'you said it suited me.'

'It did *thirty pounds ago!*' he yells as though still at war with the machine which is now being packed away. 'Go get your feather duster!'

'But that just moves dust from one place to another,' she replies tearfully.

'Where was I?' Doug says, turning back to me. 'Look, that bloody noise is *still* ringing inside my head so let's go out for a drink?'

'Most people are stuck on a defective frequency full of static,' Strauss pontificates at the bar.

'What's yours?' I enquire.

'Same again thanks,' he shoots back, *'a pint and a shot.'*

'I meant what exactly is your own frequency, Dougie?' I reiterate once having bought another round. I abstain from alcohol myself after having learned a valuable lesson from Kevin Strauss: I *do* hope this won't also be a problem for the brother I'm currently conversing with?

'My own currency is pure, unadulterated light,' he replies after quaffing a mouthful of lager, 'I'm lucky enough to be tuned into a Celestial radio station that gives off *only* pure light and the music of the Spheres.'

'That's *quite* a playlist,' I'm intending this to be a compliment of sorts.

'Just because it's light *doesn't* mean you should make light of it!' Suddenly Doug has become *very* serious.

'You mean you feel things that other people are *not* aware of?' I'm hoping he'll pick up on the fact I've now finished my tomato juice, and that he *should* reciprocate by purchasing me another, not least since I've bought him three lagers and as many shots in the last hour!

'Please don't subvert my message,' he replies before draining the spirit I'd purchased only a minute previously.

'*How* am I being subversive?' I've never been accused of being subversive before so this charge is not completely without appeal to me.

'Do *not* incur the wrath of *the Great Clown!*' Strauss is then looking around him to make sure nobody else has heard what he's just revealed.

'A great clown?... Can you reveal more about this please?'

'Perhaps I've said *too much* already,' he replies sourly.

'I won't be able to get the picture of a clown out of my head now.' I'm trying to lighten the tone, and to coax more from him. 'There, I know a little now so you may as well reveal *more?*'

'Very well, Fabio, but upon *your* head be it.'

'I can keep a secret.' I gesticulate for the barman to replenish our drinks since my Companion clearly has no intention of doing so.

'He's at the centre of *all* existence, mocking *all* our efforts.'

'*Who?* This clown you mentioned?'

'Eight pounds forty please,' the barman says whilst placing our drinks down upon the bar.

'He has to be kept at bay!' Strauss declares once the member of staff has receded. '*I alone* see this.'

'You alone?'

'It was part of the Faustian pact I made.'

'*A deal with the devil?!*' I splutter back, after having choked on my tomato juice.

'Like Prometheus I had to pay the piper for my share of the fire I stole and gifted to my public,' my Subject reveals in a stage whisper.

'That's *quite* a metaphor salad you tossed together there!'

'Of course,' he replies, 'for I am the Master of the sign, I *alone* know the secret life of street signs.'

'If you were a road sign, Dougie, what would you say?' I'm attempting to get him to make himself clearer.

'Do *not* read this sign!' he proclaims with histrionic aplomb. He seems very pleased with what he's just disclosed but only a moment later his face falls. I look along his line of vision to see the reason for this sudden dismay. Again I see the tall, slender man I'd observed the previous day on the far side of the balcony at the block of flats where Strauss lives. 'Shit! We've got to go!'

'Why?'

'A bad smell has arrived,' replies Doug before draining his drink and motioning for us to leave.

'Thank you everybody,' Strauss calls out to his audience after his opening number. I've finally heard the current Subject of my documentary sing and, whilst *not* expecting a Tom Jones, I'm truly flabbergasted by the yawning chasm between Dougie's *own* estimation of his vocal talents and his *actual* abilities. My previous suspicion that he'd hypnotized me is now shattered by my latter certainly that I'm not in the *least* impressed by his *extremely* limited capabilities as a singer, nor am I convinced he's even entitled to define himself as an "Entertainer". The possibility then occurs to me that I might possess the mental strength to resist *all* forms of Mesmerism. This likelihood will moreover ably prepare me to be as *objective* a film-maker as possible, and which should be kept in mind next time I'm applying *for official* funding. More of this later.

In the present tense I observe my Subject beginning his second song. Unlike the cover version which served as his introduction it seems this is an original composition written by he himself. It's a pastiche of sorts, and I detect allusions to various geographical places. Soon I divine references to the seven wonders of the Globe. All becomes clearer in time *however* when these following locations are mentioned:

"The hanging baskets at the Babylon petrol garage and convenience store."

"The Colossus of Rhodes Kebab shop."

"The Grand Pyramid scheme which you bought me for my birthday."

'Thank you *very* much,' Strauss issues with the close of this number. There's only a muted response, with what sounds like just a solitary pair of hands clapping. I pan my camera away from him, past the sprawling *"happy birthday"* banner, across the end of a slightly raised area that serves as the stage, and onward finally to the Audience. I'd surmised this venue to be a Retirement Home but it's only now that my digital eye focuses upon the Residents themselves. Doug will later try to convince me that all present were suffering varying stages of arthritis, which prevented them from applauding, and unable to voice their verbal appreciation for a *myriad* of other reasons.

'Thanks everybody,' the man at the microphone reiterates, as though he'd not been heard. Later he will insist that the sound system was *"misperforming"*, and that *all* present were profoundly deaf. 'That was an original song written by yours truly, that's none other than *I*, myself, Dazzling Dougie Diamond, here for *your* pleasure, here at the Spring Grove

Rest-Home, *here* this very afternoon. Thanks so much for the great turn-out everybody, and thanks to you all for making it here.'

'Will he be calling out the bingo numbers?' an emaciated, bewildered looking Octogenarian of indeterminate gender asks.

'Cool your heels, old timer,' Strauss retorts. Later he will define this as *"heckling"*. 'Now, where were we? You know, *guys and gals*, it really warms my heart to be here on this most special of *special* occasions, and I mean that *most* sincerely. It gives me the greatest of pleasure to bring a bit of sunshine into your dull, *lonesome* little lives.'

'Is that your son?' an ancient man asks a woman of similar age sitting across from him. I detect sarcasm in his voice. 'He's always here to see you … *not!*'

'Leave her alone!' another elderly man tells the first, before also getting derided for the lack of visits he receives from relatives.

'Calm it down, folks,' an earnest appeal comes from Bill Jones, a middle-aged man who'd earlier introduced himself as the Manager of the premises.

Dougie now launches into his third number, a strange song I'm unable to identify either as a cover version or one conceived by he himself. Squabbling continues amongst the Residents.

'Thank you, very much,' my Subject proclaims at the close of that tune. The response is more tepid yet but this seems not to deter him. 'It really is such a *very* moving experience being here today, folks. It's so great to feel so very close, so *quickly* here tonight, *sorry*, this afternoon, kind of like we've been a big happy family for years already. *Without* all the resentments that goes with that, *of course.'*

'Surely he *is* your son?!' the offensive elderly man then caws. A busty young redhead, I suspect to be a Caring Assistant, descends upon him in an attempt at appeasement.

'When is Countdown on?' the ancient woman -who'd been harassed a minute previously- asks.

'Now, I'm picking up on *something,*' Strauss says in an attempt to re-engage his audience: I begin to have the awful foreboding that he's about to regale them with his *alleged* psychic abilities. 'I'm getting a message…Is it somebody's birthday?' He seems to be having an unobservant episode because behind him is a banner that declares this very fact clearly and precisely in letters *as tall as himself.*

'It's Jeff's birthday,' the manager, Bill Jones, interjects in what seems a genuine attempt to be helpful.

'Jeff hasn't been here,' a previously silent Resident claims.

'He was,' the young red-headed Nurse cheerfully counters, 'but all his raging and sobbing about the past tired him out so he's having a little lay down.'

'What's *that*, birthday boy?'Dougie calls out to Bill.

'I was referring to *Jeff.'*

'Get up here, Jeff,' Strauss insists. Bill then unwisely approaches to explain but is denied the chance. 'So Jeff, did you get any nice presents today?'

'I'm not Jeff,' he perseveres, 'I'm Bill Jones, manager of this establishment.'

'He's a card, isn't he?' my Subject says to his audience before turning back to Bill, whom he addresses in an infantilizing tone. 'So, you little scamp, how many years young are you today?'

'I'm fifty six,' he limply replies: his entire demeanor has changed; it seems it *no longer* matters that he's been misunderstood; could this have created a camera-worthy crisis for him?

'Isn't he a sprightly gentleman,' Doug appeals to his ever diminishing audience, 'how *marvellous!* Give him a round of applause, everybody?'

'Look at his little face light up!' the elderly trouble-maker from earlier shouts out. But Bill isn't smiling. He looks as though he's about to burst into tears. The young Nurse has joined the heckler in clapping but soon stops abruptly, possibly *only now* aware his intention is to ridicule.

'Dazzling, do you do requests?' she asks, possibly to defuse this increasingly awkward situation.

'Such as *"piss off"*?!' the toxic Pensioner yells out before again erupting with laughter.

'Yes…requests,' Jones whimpers from the stage. Perhaps he's coming to his senses at last?

'Oh my,' Strauss responds, 'he *is* an impetuous one, isn't he!'

'We often have a sing-song,' the flame-haired young Nursing Assistant calls out.

'Yes,' Bill meekly responds, 'a sing-song.' He still seems dazed.

'Not on my stage, *pal*,' Strauss firmly insists before taking the Manager by the elbow and gesticulating to the young Nurse to remove him from the proximity. She obediently complies.

'Move along carefully now, Jeff - we don't want you breaking a hip.'

'*Don't we?!*' the elderly Hoodlum exclaims.

'And now for my next number,' "Dazzling" declares as he moves towards his electronic keyboard. He plays a few notes but *as before* it's out of tune. He then throws me an anxious look, which transports us back to his incident a few days previously where he'd claimed some malevolent force had taken charge of his organ.

'Ghosts in the machine,' somebody says. I look to see who's uttered these words but *nobody present* is the obvious and immediate culprit.

'That's not on my playlist,' my Subject retorts, 'just a few glitches…Now, *she'll* be ready for some hot action again soon in a minute. Yes Madam, I'm referring to *you!*' A tiny bird-like woman at the periphery gives off a bashful smirk in response to this much-appreciated attention. She reciprocates by flashing her bra at him.

It's another few days before I see Strauss again. In this interim I'd had a few contentions of my own to attend to. I'd had to re-establish contact with *two* separate Commissioning Editors from *competing* television channels. I shall elaborate upon this at some later point.

'You're just jealous,' I hear Dougie's distinctive voice call out to somebody. I've just reached the storey where he lives, and delay my arrival to attempt to get a clearer sense of this unexpected situation. And so I prepare my camera to film whatever dramatic developments might be about to occur. 'Well jel!'

'*Jealous?!*' comes a doubtful, less familiar voice.

'Well, so called "*Johnny Nemesis*", that's all you need to know about my gig!' I catch sight of my Subject but am yet to observe who he's addressing. 'You'd be having multiple orgasms over something half as good.'

'Whatever, Douglas Strauss!' I stand out in the exposed part of the communal balcony to signify both my presence to Dougie, and to see with whom he's arguing. 'All the best to you, and all that but I need to go off now and prepare for a *proper* performance tonight.' It's only now I view this opposing person. It's the tall slender male I'd first observed across the tenement walkway a week or so previously, and then again a few days later in the pub which had prompted us to leave.

'And don't think I *don't* know what you been spreading around town!' At this point Strauss notices my presence. Initially he smiles then his expression changes, perhaps now feeling self conscious and regretful that I'm filming this heated exchange.

'*What* are you talking about now?' the taller, slimmer, better-looking version of Dougie replies.

'That incident about the balcony. You've been boasting about that fictional incident which simply didn't happen, and which is all merely a fig tree of your twisted little invention.'

'Balcony incident?' This opponent's expression is one of bafflement but eventually a dawning recognition spreads out across his finely-constructed, symmetrical features. 'Oh, yeah, I recall now. Come on, Douglas, all old water under the bridge, *or balcony*, if you prefer?'

133

'Try it *now?!*' This has not appeased my Subject at all, quite the opposite in fact, his tone becomes louder and *more* shrill yet. 'I'd like to see you try to dangle me off the balcony now, go on, *try it now-if you dare!*'

'Look, let's cool it?' This Rival's tone becomes more passive, tender even. 'All I can do is apologize for some regrettable thing we can't even be sure really happened at all.'

'*Can't be sure*?!' Strauss reverberates in tremulous rage.

'It was so long ago. *Who* can really be sure? *If* indeed it did happen then we were both still at school together and, as you can see, we're *far* different people now.'

'What's *that* supposed to mean?!' Dougie bellows back- he seems *completely* committed to continue this confrontation.

'Well, it wouldn't be so practical *now!*' This put-upon person is clearly losing patience with this prolonged verbal attack.

'What, you mean, with my weight gain?!' My Subject is yelling again. 'Go on, say it-*I dare you!*' Then the recipient of this wrath gives a pained smile to the camera, shrugs and silently slips away. '*Where* do you think you're going?' Strauss hollers after him. 'That's it, you coward, get back to your dump!' There's no further response from this person, who merely strolls back the few yards across the walkway to his own home, lets himself in and gently closes the front door after him.

'You're back,' Mrs. Strauss beams.

'No, it's a hologram resembling me!' he retorts caustically as I follow him into the front room. 'Where's my fucking dinner?!'

'Oh Dougie,' she replies regretfully, 'I'm not used to your new routine. I'm so sorry. I'll make a start now.'

'I *don't* believe it?!' he exclaims as she dashes off to the kitchen. 'We as a species didn't go through millions of years of Evolution *just* so you can sit on your lazy, fat arse watching the afternoon soaps!'

'I'm trying my best,' she calls out from the next room, 'and you seem to be forgetting that I'm the only one around here that does a full-time job, *as well as* waiting on you hand and foot.'

'What job does your wife do, Dougie?'

'I didn't come home for this!' he yells out. 'Come on now- less talk, more...*housewifery!*' A humming sound comes from the next room. Strauss recedes into a pregnant silence. This is eventually shattered by a dinging noise. 'If that's a microwave meal then it had *better* be for you! If it's for me then you'll see *fists-a-flying!*' I've noticed my current Subject has given me -much to my disappointment- examples of the family trait of chauvinism, *misogyny even*, now moreover I'm growing concerned he might *also* be prone to inflicting *physical* attacks. 'Relax,' he says, seemingly reading my mind once more, '*tis* but banter.'

'There you go,' the wife triumphantly declares when she eventually places a large dinnerplate with all the trimmings down before her husband.

'Oh, Mr. Ambassador,' he sarcastically responds, 'you really know how to spoil us!'

'There's enough for Fabio if you want to join us?' I politely refuse her kind offer.

'*What* precisely is it?' he demands.

'Why, it's your favorite, of course,' she chimes in a tone one might use to placate a very fussy child, 'Elvis bangers with Presley mash. I'll just get you the Colonel Tom Parker gravy.'

'I'll just eat a *little* bit so not to upset her.' He proceeds to wolf down this food. 'Wasn't a *real* Colonel, you know?' he says when she returns with a gravy boat fashioned in the image of his favorite musician.

'Who, Elvis?' she guilelessly replies, which elicits a familiar grimace from him.

'Sorry *pard'ner,'* the South Asian shop Keeper explains in response to Strauss's enquiry, 'we're all out of 'Elvis-the King, monthly' magazine, I'm afraid.' This man is dressed as a cowboy. His whole way of communicating, *I soon discover*, is in a style more suited to that of an 18th century frontier man from America's Wild West. 'I'm sure it's coming in on the next stage coach delivery.'

'But I don't understand,' Doug replies, 'it's been advertised on the telly.'

'Small flicker box speak with fork tongue.' I cast a glance to see that these words have come from a tiny, elderly white woman dressed as a Red Indian, complete with frayed feathered head-dress, or as I *should* say, attire of Native American origin.

'Back to your duties, *you!*' the South Asian Cowboy tells her. 'And stay off the fire water!'

A familiar-looking figure approaches as we're leaving the shop.

'This town ain't big enough for the both of us!'

'I come bearing an olive branch,' this tall, rangy man replies.

'Olive branch?' My Subject's eyes narrow with suspicion. He stands side-wards on as though making a smaller target of himself.

'I'm not trying to throw you a bum-steer here,' the man -named as Johnny Nemesis on our previous encounter- issues, 'this here is two *free* entry tickets for my performance at the Naval club this Friday night.'

'Whoa!' Doug retorts with an extended hand to ward off the offer. 'There's a new Sherriff in town.'

'There is?' Johnny's brow is knitted with incomprehension. 'Who's that then?'

'*Me, of course!*' Strauss virtually shrieks back. 'And he's performing that *very same* night at the British Legion.'

'Hold your horses, kid- due to last week's Senior's hoe-down, or *"showdown"*, as the local newspaper put it, the electricity is still down. Did they *not* tell you?'

'Well, cowpoke, that's just where *you're wrong*- the powers that be let us re-saddle at the Ex-Serviceman's club in Barrow Street!'

'I guess you were lost somewhere on the range when that place closed for a refurbish.'

'*What?!*' Then my Subject regains his composure, along with the Wild-West themed barbed banter. 'High noon, desperado! I'm raising ya'- the *true* venue is the Black Swan Inn.'

'Why lie then?' Johnny replies, coming out of character.

'I know you, Nemesis, you'd be trying to head me off at the pass. Well, tenderfoot, I'll be performing at Joe Sad's café the following Friday evening. Come along to see how it *really* should be done?!'

'Thanks, I would do,' he responds, 'but I'll be competing in the Elvis Tribute Acts Final in Blackpool next weekend.'

'Give me proof, old timer!' My Subject has become irate again- 'Let me see that wanted poster!'

'Howdy!' The Cowboy Shopkeeper emerges from his business premises to hand Johnny a magazine. 'It's all true, Deputy Douglas, Marshall Johnny here is starring in this month's "Elvis-The King monthly," surely the finest publication in the whole wild West!'

'Much obliged, pard'ner.' Nemesis takes possession of this periodical.

'But you said you had sold out of that?!' Strauss fumes.

'I said *no* such thing, mister', the Indian-looking Cowboy responds, 'the Marshall reserved this one but if another blows into town I give you my word on the Cowboy Code that I will deliver it to you myself, by Pony Express *if need be!*'

'Forget it, Tonto,' Doug retorts rather rudely, 'you can poke that right where the Prospectors don't mine!'

'By the power invested in me,' the Shopkeeper judiciously declares whilst puffing himself up and placing his thumbs within the breasts of his tan suede waistcoat, 'I will see that you are *no longer* welcome at Khalid's Stand-Off license and Ok Newsagents Corral!'

'The smoke signals don't bode too well for you, hombre,' Johnny snorts with derision.

'The Cavalry won't always arrive to save you, Johnny Nemesis!' Strauss has a vein pulsating at his temple.

'Save it for your lame mules, tumbleweed - blow yourself out of town!'

'You'll die a lonely death, you... *clown cunt!*' Doug turns to me and, judging by his expression, *only now* seems aware I've filmed the *whole* confrontation. *'Are you with them or me?!'* I follow as he marches off, cursing all and sundry.

'He'll die with his boots on,' I hear the diminutive, elderly Native American lady croak in the wake of our departure.

I accompany my Subject until he halts in his tracks after having caught sight of something which causes him to grimace. He then tells me he'll return home alone, and will call when he's ready to be filmed again.

Once he's gone I scrutinize what had arrested his attention. It's a poster for his cancelled gig. Someone has written *"wanted"* over the image of his smiling face and blacked out several of his teeth. It hadn't been this, I suspect, which had been so much the cause of offence, more the words *"reward, dead or alive: 1p"* scrawled underneath.

'What's going on?' I ask Mrs. Strauss, who's preoccupied with a celebrity gossip magazine.

'Danni Monogue is making a comeback.'

'No, I *meant* what's up with Dougie?' He's rolling around on the grassy area of the communal gardens as though wrestling with some invisible adversary.

'Oh, that?' she listlessly replies. Her eyes never leave her reading matter, her broad behind remains wedged within the confines of a besieged camping chair. 'It's Shaman Sunday.'

'Shaman Sunday?!' I'm thrilled by this most unexpected development, and furthermore gratified to *already* be filming. *'What's that?'*

'On a Sunday afternoon, after the EastEnders Omnibus, he goes into shamanistic communion with his spirit guide.' She makes this sound the most humdrum of incidents but I'm fascinated to learn *more.*

'Who is his Spirit Guide?' I avariciously enquire. 'Possibly a long deceased Native American Witch Doctor? Or perhaps an ethereal Guardian from the South American rain forests?'

'Nah,' she replies as though bored, 'nobody or nothing like that.'

'*Who* then?' His wrestling bout has become more manic yet. 'Most natural cultures, mistakenly categorized as *Primitive,* adhere to the concept of the holy man or woman that is the *Shaman*, from cultures as supposedly disparate as those from the Philippines, all the way to Siberia. What form does your husband's Spirit Guide take?'

'A bear,' she mumbles before yawning.

'I'd heard these Guides could take the form of a beast. Forgive me for saying this but your husband's animal Spirit doesn't seem very much in harmony with Nature. Is this bear-guide righting some *great* wrong within the Ecosphere?'

'I doubt it,' she sighs, 'the bear in question is rather anti-social and doesn't get on very well with the other bears.'

'That would *seem* to be the case.' Strauss appears to be writhing in agony. The other Entity looks to be getting the better of him but eventually my Subject finds the strength to throw off this Opponent and *bear* down upon - *if* one can excuse the pun?- this other beast to score a *hard-fought* victory.

'*Oh look!*' Mrs. Strauss exclaims with sudden enthusiasm. I look back to her spouse but she still fails to observe him, choosing instead to quote from her magazine. 'Her from Celebrity Big Brother is making a comeback.'

'I dare say,' I reply whilst bearing witness to her husband eventually finishing off his mortal enemy.

'Once more I triumph!' Doug exclaims, having returned to the sanctuary of his armchair.

'Who *is* that person?'

'Was it not obvious, Fabio? My Spirit Guide is a grizzly bear who resides in Alaska.'

'No, I meant that man who lives across the way from you- that same person you had a confrontation with at the newsagent's shop?'

'I was saving the right moment to explain all about that,' he retorts whilst fixing me with his trademark stare. I suspect he's again attempting to hypnotize me but I'm *increasingly* confident that I now have immunity to this! 'That was Nemesis.'

'The person that you *perceive* to be your Nemesis?'

'If only! His name *literally is* Nemesis- he was christened John Douglas Nemesis! I've *even seen* his birth certificate to prove it.'

'What's in a name?' I attempt a quote from Shakespeare but am cut short.

'You *have to* understand something, this person was born in the same hospital as me, brought up in the same town- even attended the very *same* school as me.'

'Who was born first?'

'He even had to beat me to that!'

'I'm not convinced,' I appeal, 'traditionally a nemesis follows *that* which it sets out to thwart.'

'That's just it,' Doug bleats, his former composure now seemingly fully eroded, 'I was the Star *'til he decided to usurp me.'*

'You were Salieri to his Mozart?'

'*Look,*' Strauss raises his voice, 'it's *your* fault that Wolfgang didn't pay us a visit.'

'How so?'

'The likes of the Maestro won't come out for such a modest shoestring of a production as *yours!'*

'You're *not* making sense, Douglas.' I have to be careful not to rise to his baiting. 'Try to explain *precisely* how this person is attempting to usurp you?'

'He learned the power of persuasion to convince people he has talent,' my Subject explains, now having calmed down a little, 'and so I was then *forced to learn* Mesmerism myself to counter-balance this curse.'

'So in a way it's *you* who serve *as his* Nemesis also?'

'Are you *even* listening?' It seems he's at risk of losing his temper again. '*He's persecuting me!'*

'How so?'

'He's often used the disabled as offensive weapons against me!' I'd be interested in a demonstration just how this could even be achieved but the litany of perceived slights continues. 'He's conjured up a group of Elvises, an *Elvi*, as it were, in order to disrupt my singing act.'

'Is there *any actual* proof?' I'm sensing paranoia. 'Perhaps they were *just another* disgruntled audience who happened to be dressed in a similar way?'

'It gets worse- he's the main suspect in putting my name and photograph on a website to expose criminals!'

'He did?' It now occurs to me that I should check if Doug has a criminal record as well as investigate *all* his brothers also.

'It's even been said,' he continues, increasingly wide-eyed, 'that Nemesis has fashioned a graven image of me, a diabolical facsimile, a counterfeit version of my *own* form for *nefarious* purposes, intended then to remotely visit some spiteful act upon it in order to smite me!'

'A devil doll?!' I gasp.

'And all *without* merchandising rights!' he breathlessly ejaculates before pausing to regain some composure. 'Do you know a good patent copyright lawyer?'

I made the effort that same evening to search the history of all the brothers Strauss for evidence of convicted criminality. This was with the help of both Google and an Acquaintance of mine in the Police Force, whom I'm unwilling to divulge more information about. Having completed this investigation my only certainly now is that my current Subject, Douglas Bader Strauss, is the *sole* sibling amongst this brood *not* to have a criminal record. Some of those who've heard his music committed to vinyl *however,* might beg to differ! Three of the brothers (Kevin, Billy and Peter) have convictions for both theft, and for receiving stolen goods. Peter had- sourced from National Newspapers- been on *more serious* charges (more on this later) but had been acquitted. Surprisingly, Robby has not had *as many* convictions as I might have imagined.

My research on Mathew Strauss was altogether *less* enlightening. *Even* with the help of my aforementioned Contact within the Constabulary my efforts were frustrated by the fact that a 'D' Notice -effectively a gagging order- have been placed upon whatever charges he may have been on. I will be forced to attempt some *further* approach towards this *most curious* member of the Strauss Clan at some later point.

'Artists are all too often a misunderstand breed,' Doug laments. He's sat at the keyboard in his front room, playing the occasional note. 'Take for example a hero of mine, the late, great Oscar Wilde- playwright, poet, all round clever dick. Not *so* clever where he actually put his dick, of course.'

'That's not entirely the right way to define such matters, Dougie,' I admonish him, 'we've moved on *a lot* from there.'

'You're right, it's more likely *he was a taker rather than a giver.* Do you think he'll reveal *all* if ever he pays a visit?'

'He hasn't come across you on the spirit plane yet so I suspect this should remain a moot subject.'

'*What*, and allow homophobia to continue to thrive?!' Strauss seems to have missed my point *entirely*. 'We need to get this subject out there. We need to ask Society just how could it have *done something so terrible to someone so talented?*'

'I'm fairly sure the Gay Lobby has already done all that, Dougie?'

'And just for doing something that happens in every pub in Soho, every day of the week,' Strauss continues regardless. 'Even the House of Commons has *more than its fair share* of bumming going on!'

'I'm not *quite* sure that's the case.'

'I hope you're not homophobic, Fabio?' This comment leaves me genuinely speechless, which *in turn* gives my Subject *further* credence to continue. 'I've got the deepest of reverence, well, respect...let's call it *tolerance*, to irons. I won't have anything bad said about the gay-*ers*. I *even* have a couple of brothers who are benders.' I'm desperate to probe this claim but remain dumb-struck by his miscalculated tirade and *deep* misunderstanding of the *whole* matter. 'It is with this great reverence that I've adapted Maestro Wilde's life and works into a stage musical destined for the West End and Broadway.'

'How far have you gotten in composing it?' I ask once I've regained the power of speech.

'I'm at the tail end,' he smirks. 'Would you like to hear an excerpt?'

'I suppose so,' I confirm since it's unlikely I have a choice.

'Rent boys! Rent boys!' Strauss sings what I presume to be the opening number- 'Roll up and get your rent boys!' Then he halts playing his keyboard to address me in speech once more. 'That was in his earlier, care-free days, of course. Well, what do you think?'

'I'm...speechless!' I manage at last.

'That good, eh? You ain't heard *nothing* yet, to quote Kenny Lynch. Here, I'll play you one I've scored dealing with a later, less jolly part of Wilde's life. This bit is when Oskey, as mates called him, was consigned to Reading Gaol, or *jail*, as *now* known to the likes of me and you...'He then sings along again to his own accompaniment- 'Oh, for a hole in gaol, they say every hole is a goal, *especially here in gaol!*'

'*Really*?!' I stutter, once he's thankfully finished singing.

'Yep, Fabio, I don't arse about when it comes to banging out a tune. Did you know as well as all his other achievements Oscar Wilde also invented the glory hole?'

'*He did?!*'

'Oh yeah,' Doug elaborates, 'I've written a number about that too, it rolls right of the tongue. Do you want to hear it? It's quite a mouthful actually.'

'Perhaps some other time?'

'I know what you're thinking, Fabio.'

'You *do?*'

'I've got some darkness to counter the light moments,' Strauss explains, suddenly adopting a more sober demeanour, 'some gravitas to bookend the catchy ditties. I've prepared my fair share of Requiems for this.'

'Requiems in the plural?'

'Indeed yes,' he solemnly confirms, 'never will there have been a more moving light musical about the pain associated with sodomy. Trust me, there won't be a dry eye in the house.'

'Hasn't there already been a musical written about the life of Oscar Wilde?' I ask, having eventually recovered from a state I can only describe as petrifaction.

'There has, Fabio. Written by Mike Read. The funny one rather than the dead one.'

'It *wasn't very* successful from what I remember?' I'm hoping this will deter him.

'It's hard labour here, breaking rocks, 'Doug once more breaks into song, 'just because I was into rock hard c-'

'Dougie!'

'See- show stopping numbers like that!'

'Show stoppers, *indeed!* Do you not think this approach you're taking may appear to be at best, insensitive, and at worst, positively homophobic?'

'*Homophobic?!*' Strauss wails back. Then he's laughing. Finally he regains his composure. 'Fabio, dear *misguided* Fabio, I have a *unique* claim that will dismiss all such bum raps.'

'*You do?*'

'Indeed I do, dear Fabio,' he states with great confidence, 'you see, the truth is I have *at least* two gay brothers.'

'You *do?!*' Being in the company of someone as exasperating as this seems to have *decreased* my vocabulary.

'I read your mind, Fabio.'

'*You did?!*'

'Yes, I know you think that it's Roland who is the gay one but luckily getting given a gay name didn't have that effect on him.'

'*It didn't?*'

'No. And I know you think it might be Billy but the fact is just because he can't pull a bird, despite all his motivational coaching, does not mean he's a shirt-lifter or pillow-biter.'

'I thought Billy is a mechanic?' I enquire, after having found my voice at last. 'I would have thought, what with all that *over-compensation*, that the brother of yours who might *actually* be gay would be Robby?'

'Don't be a prize plum! Here's a story for you. I remember it was that difficult age as an adolescent. I summoned up all the courage I could to sit my parents down and tell them a truth that had *long* been troubling me. I said "*mum, dad, there's something I really need to tell you*".'

'You did?!' I'm suddenly spellbound by this unexpected candour.

'Indeed, I did. I said to them that this secret I'm about to reveal is the fact that *your son is gay.*'

'You revealed to them that *you* are gay?' I'm on the edge of my seat: it isn't so very improbable; even though Doug is in a marriage *this isn't so uncommon* amongst homosexuals.

'*Of course not me, you numpty!*' he erupts. 'I'm as straight as they come! I was talking about *Peter!*'

'Oh, Peter?' My research on this brother is only sketchy, and I can't seem to find out any more about him other than he had a middling boxing career, failed marriage and that he's *currently* employed as a security guard. 'What was your parents' response?'

'They didn't take it well,' my Subject replies ruefully, 'especially Dad. He punched the wall *then* slammed his first hard down upon the table.'

'Did he say anything?' I'm hoping to get more of an insight into this Pater familias, who seems to have *so much* to answer for.

'He did indeed, he shouted, "I've told you a dozen times, Douglas, your brother Peter is *not* gay!" See, *totally* in denial!'

'Denial?'

'Not half,' Strauss scoffs, 'he wouldn't even believe Kevin is a poof *too!*'

'*Kevin?!*' I'll need to re-examine my video footage for evidence of this fanciful claim.

I've been forced to re-examine *much* over the last few days, not least concerning the *outlet* my documentary shall take. There is *still no confirmed commission* for my project but the most likely exhibitor -let's call them "Broadcaster A"- has expressed considerable interest. There's also *much* curiosity coming from a rival of theirs. "Broadcaster B" does *however* have ideas concerning context and format which I'm not altogether comfortable with. I will be resisting compromise and maintaining my integrity as best I can, and shall expand upon this at some point *hence.*

In addition to these discussions I've also received several curious emails from a mystery Sender who appears to have an insider's perception into my Project. I suspect these betrayals have come from a former production assistant, or perhaps someone who'd been taken into an intimidate confidence. I shall devise some tactful, discreet way to consult Stan, my occasional sound recordist, perhaps with the offer of more work by way of an incentive to induce him to reveal something he may *or may not* be aware of. I'm intending to reveal more about the precise content of these e-mails at some later stage, together with any subsequent correspondence received in the meantime.

Concerning my *more immediate* plans however, those of Douglas Strauss offering one of his *supposedly* healthy kidneys to his brother Roland, well, *this seems less certain still,* not least since I'm having my own intuition of some impending situation which shall force me to make *alternative* plans.

'I shouldn't be getting so anxious before a gig,' my Subject reveals. I've visited him again several days after our previous encounter.

'I'm surprised with this dip in your confidence, Dougie.' He appears to be limbering up, albeit from the confines of his armchair.

'I'm *not quite* the full-time all singing, all-dancing confidence machine you might have imagined me to be. The truth is I've had some poor counsel.'

'You have?' I survey a nearby table where a number of bottles of medication reside. 'From *whom?*'

'Whom indeed,' he grunts, 'I knew it was a mistake consulting more than one Physician.'

'There's no harm seeking a second opinion. Is your G.P. local?'

'Vienna,' Strauss replies, and for a second I imagine I've misheard him before he adds, 'Austria.'

'That's *quite some distance* to go for a medical consultation.'

'And time too,' he expands. 'It's quite a stretch, not least since they'd qualified just before the twentieth century.'

'Dougie, does *all* that medication belong to you?' I sense this could be a window into his very troubled soul.

'Most of it belongs to the wife. I've attempted to use the science of persuasion to snap her out of her *ridiculous* claims of being depressed. I mean, *what* on Earth could she possibly be depressed about?!'

'*What indeed?!*' This conversation appears to be robbing me of all rational thought. 'Doug, can you explain your *own* condition please?'

'Ah yes, I digress. Initially I was offered medical help by a physician claiming to be none other than Doctor Sigmund Freud himself.'

'Much esteemed help *indeed!*' I exclaim, whilst wondering where all *this* could be leading.

'One would have thought so,' Strauss sighs, 'but Freud's decisions began to become increasingly erratic. His advice was becoming as ill-judged as my own brother Billy's, if indeed *such a thing were possible?*'

'Ah yes, Billy?' I interject, hoping to shed more light on this curious sibling but I'm not allowed the chance.

'To be honest I was beginning to think Herr Doktor Sigi had relapsed on the cocaine. Then an *even more* curious occurrence happened.'

'Could it be possible you were getting your wires crossed, and that it might have been a *living* Entity contacting you?'

'No, Billy is too limited for that.' Strauss is seemingly once more reading my mind. 'There was a new arrival on the Astral scene, undermining the great Sigmund.'

'How so?'

'This new guide was offering fresh advice, claiming Freud, or *"Fraud"* as he called him, had stolen most of his theories.' Doug explains all this with an ease as though it were merely a common, *everyday* occurrence. 'Well, what could possibly go wrong there?'

'Well, *what* did go wrong?'

'You've heard the saying *"Two Jews, three opinions"*?' I nod even though I'm *not even remotely* familiar with this: I cannot let *further* digression steer me away from what I suspect he's attempting to reveal, albeit in coded form. 'Well, in the After-Life that applies two-fold.' Then he frowns. 'Or is that *four-fold?*' I've not got the *vaguest* idea what he's trying to tell me! 'The long and short of it is, *don't* trust *long dead* Jewish doctors.' I shall have to take his word for this. 'Not least because they are now currently speaking about you and I.'

'*They are?* What are they saying?'

'Fuck knows - how's your Yiddish?'

'Do *they* advise you in taking medication?' I ask in a sudden flash of inspiration: I myself am no stranger to Psychoanalysis; more about this sometime hence.

'I will need your help, Fabio,' Strauss replies, suddenly sombre: perhaps I've achieved my very *own* breakthrough concerning my Subject? 'Do the tuning fork exercise I taught you how to do earlier?'

'Happy to help!' I pick up the fork, which he'd referred to as 'mystical''and "lucky" then dutifully hit it off against another metallic object -an old tin pot- to effect what he'd told me is a *key* sound to tap into the Spiritual Realms beyond our World.

'Kindly spirits, give me guidance,' Doug drones. He closes his eyes for what I assume is greater concentration in achieving communion with powers beyond our limited comprehension. 'And I don't mean you couple of jobsites from Vienna…And again please, Fabio?' I oblige once more with another impact of the fork, an object (using my *own* intuition) he'd likely stolen from the local pub on our last visit there. 'Yes, that's helping… I think I'm beginning to go *fully* under now. Help me now, kindly Spirits, in this my *own* time of need. Previously I've done so much good for others but I call on you to help *me* now…Give me guidance?…Yes…*Yes*…I see someone.' Doug's demeanour has become one of calmness, even serenity, the level of which I've not witnessed within him before: perhaps he now *truly is* consulting with the Spirit World *at long last?!* 'I see you…Yes, you seem familiar?…Oh yes, you *are* familiar…Oh *no!-* What the hell do *you* want?!' Suddenly Strauss's face has altered, his expression transforms into a grimace, and he seems as troubled as I've *ever* seen him. His aura has gone from one of bliss to frustration, despair, even anger and *full-blown rage!*

'*What's* happening Dougie?' I'm then aware my enquiry might be counter-productive, and *possibly even dangerous!* Fortunately my camera is rolling to document *any* eventuality which might occur. 'Who, *or what*, do you see?'

'*What, indeed!*' he replies, then appears to be in a bizarre three-way conversation where we've been joined, or rather interloped, by some *malevolent* spirit. 'It's *her!*'

'Who?' I entreat in order to indentify this potentially hazardous foe my Subject has unwittingly summoned.

'*The wife's bloody mother!*' Then he's addressing this other Entity once more. 'Get out of here, Elsbeth!… You're *not* wanted here, you *never* were!… *Don't you* wag that finger at me!… I don't care- *get out of here, you toxic witch!*'

'But Dougie, I don't understand- I heard your wife talk to her mother *only earlier today* on the 'phone.'

'Leave me alone!' he roars in outright fury. Soon I'm relieved to surmise Strauss is *not* talking to me but rather to his Mother-in-law. 'I do good work with worthy spirits in the After-Life, must you hamper me *even here?!*'

'Dougie,' I reason, '*surely* there's some rational explanation for all of this!?'

'Shut up Elsbeth! *Go haunt somebody else!*' Just then the living room door opens, causing me almost to jump out of my skin by imagining this phantasm to have taken a *physical* form! The face confronting me, however, is not one of the living dead but *still* one that unsettles me *all the same*. It's Doug's wife. She's blubbering uncontrollably.

'It's Mother...' she snivels, 'she's...*she's*...' Mrs. Strauss does not need to finish her sentence on account of this terrible Revelation *imposing itself* upon me. She begins to sob and wail.

'Well,' Doug shrugs philosophically, 'her Mother's gone off to live on a farm.'

'Is that not a little bit insensitive?'

'Talented as I am, Fabio, bringing her back is not something *even I'm able to do*. I mean, it's not as if *I* put her over the other side *myself*.' Suddenly he fixes me with a worried glare. 'Come on, you were with me at the time-you *wouldn't* deny me my alibi, *would you?!*'

'No Dougie,' I reassure him, though not without distaste, 'I wouldn't deny you an alibi. I just think you could give a tactful amount of time to let things sink in?'

'Come on, my Missus *already* had an hour to sort herself out. As Bill says-'

'Your brother Billy? Did you consult *his* advice?'

'Of course not, you donut,' Strauss scoffs, 'I meant Bill Shakespeare.'

'The Bard?'

'No, *Shakespeare!* Try to keep up?! Well anyway, in the words of Shakey- "The show *must* go on".'

'You're *still* going to do your gig tonight?' I rasp in exasperation. '*Surely not?!*'

'Wife!' Doug calls out. 'Have you pressed my stage costume yet?' He then turns back to me. 'Let's hope she hasn't stained it with tears.'

'*Really?!*' My response is tremulous, and appears to accompany the music playing on the stereo: something about someone crying in a chapel; I suspect the singer is Elvis Presley?

'Wife!' She appears red-eyed in the doorway. Mucous is running from her nose.

'I know ironing my stage costume is the probably *the last thing* on your mind right now,' he tells her, 'but trust me, it *will* be *therapeutic* for you.' She blubbers back a reply that is incoherent to me but which he appears to understand and respond to, 'More importantly, I've got a big gig to get to'. Again Doug's wife sobs out some unintelligible response which continues to elude me but gets another harsh reply from him, 'Look, she sabotaged me in this World so please *don't* allow her to do so from the After-Life also!' The wailing returns, as do words which remain beyond me. 'That's *exactly* what she wants!' Strauss has raised his voice to meet the heightened pitch of his now hysterical Spouse. 'How many times *precisely* do you want me to say how very sorry I am she's brown bread?!' The wife is now inconsolable. 'How the hell am *I* responsible?!' he barks back, 'I only predict-don't shoot the messenger!' Her response is now one of undisguised rage, and yet these are still words *only* my Subject seems to understand. 'Look! You've a big woman but you're out of shape. With me it's a full time profession-*now behave yourself!*' Suddenly she fails silent, and disappears from the scrutiny of my camera into the adjacent kitchen. I see only Doug's reaction then as he winces and ducks down into a crouch for some reason. The explanation for this becomes apparent in the next split second as a large object -similar in size to Strauss's head- is hurled towards him, missing him by *mere* inches. He turns to see where this projectile has impacted, somewhere in the bathroom.Then he also disappears from view, apparently to retrieve this object, which *I suspect* to be an iron to press clothing, and likely the *same* one I'd seen her use to remove creases from his wide selection of stage outfits. This object makes its appearance again (confirming that it had *indeed* been an iron) when it flies back to the location from where it had originated, therefore prompting me to determine it's now been thrown back at his wife by Doug. The sound of this most recent impact is heard but quite unlike the previous clatter in the bathroom. This time it's the dull thud of hitting something softer, *broader,* and which is accompanied by a yelp followed by a rising wail. Soon I hear *something heavy* crash down to the ground. Then silence. I now feel confident in concluding that the said iron has *almost certainly* hit Mrs. Strauss, and that she'd dropped down to the floor after having sustained an injury from this *considerably* heavy object. Doug emerges from the bathroom. Alarm registers upon his face, which intensifies with his wife's prolonged silence.

'Look what you've done *now!*' he tells me, looking up horrified into the lens of my camera.

'I *would have* taken her to Casualty but there wasn't time.' We're sitting in my vehicle outside the venue where Strauss is about to perform.

'I could go back and take her there?' I suggest.

'She'll be alright,' he replies stoically, 'she's been through worse. *Besides,* I need you for moral support.'

'Do you have any advice for young aspiring musicians?' I ask, for want of anything else to say.

'Yes, I do,' he replies, his confidence suddenly returning. 'If you are lacking in musical abilities you can mask that by dating a Supermodel.'

'*Come again*?' This is Left-field even by Dougie's standards!

'It worked with the lad Doherty. He was doing shifts at my local mini-market 'til I took him under my wing.'

'Pete Doherty?' I enquire. '*You* were the one who suggested he should date Kate Moss?'

'Well, it beats stacking shelves,' he replies with nonchalance.

'I can sense *he's* here.' Doug is pacing up and down inside the toilets of the venue. He's *very far from* nonchalant now.

'Pete Doherty?'

'No, you numpty,' he growls back, 'Johnny Fucking Nemesis, *of course!*'

'I haven't seen him.' I've only just now come into the gentlemen's convenience after my Subject's prolonged absence. 'I've been positioned at the bar all the while waiting for you, and had a clear view of the entrance so I can confirm categorically that he's *not* here.'

'That's the impression he *likes* to give!' Strauss fixes me with an intense glare: it's likely he's suffering from acute paranoia.

'I can go out to check *again* if you want?'

'I'm getting an impending sense of doom about all this.'

Doug is pulling at his hair, a recently developed nervous tic which has become especially pronounced this evening. Suddenly his hairpiece comes loose altogether, making it appear as though his scalp is sliding off.

'Relax, I'm sure it will all go well.' I'm now getting vexed *myself* on account of not filming this. I resolve to visually document the *remainder* of this occasion. 'I'll get you a drink?'

'An Elvis cola,' Strauss meekly bleats back.

'Diet?'

'Kick me while I'm down, why don't you?!' he replies bitterly.

'*No* charge for the King,' the barman says as he places a drink down before me. He's also dressed as Elvis, complete with Vegas-period shaggy wig and full-rhinestone bejeweled jumpsuit. 'I'm *quite* the fan myself.'

'As I can see,' I tell him.

'So you're making a documentary about our Performer tonight?'

'That's *if* he ever comes out from the toilet?'

'Nerves, I guess,' the barman replies. Suddenly he's looking very concerned. 'Somebody told me the *real* Elvis died sitting on the toilet. *You* don't suppose it's true, *do you?*'

'Dougie,' I call out upon my return to the toilets, 'I've gotten you a drink.'

'You've brought it *here*?' he replies irritably from a cubicle. 'What d'ye want to do that for?!'

'It's at the bar. The Landlord is saying he'd like you to perform soon, like, right *now*!'

'Just one minute.' This reply comes with an accompanying

splash: I suspect Strauss is having a bowel movement; a foul odour *confirms* this. 'I'm having a consultation.'

'*Indeed!*' I'm choking as I go to leave this unhygienic place.

'With the Spirits,' he elaborates, 'wait!'

'*What?!*' Smelling Dougie's shit is *not* my precise idea of a good night out!

'Can you hear that?!' he enquires with much anxiety, and so I listen to him wrestle with his clothing.

'I'm *not* privy to your psychic visitations.'

'Not *that!*' I hear the flush mechanism. He emerges at last from the cubicle, struggling to get back into his all-in-one jumpsuit. '*Somebody is subverting me!*'

'It's *just* a soundtrack.' I'm only now aware of the music playing in the bar. 'I expect it's merely to get your audience warmed-up?'

'You *don't* understand,' Doug yelps as he barges past me to run out to the performance area, 'it's a plot against me!'

I follow him to see that attendance here has swollen, with more people present than any previous audience I've yet witnessed him perform in front of. A sea of people part as Strauss labours towards the stage. I *now* comprehend that there had *not* been a pre-recorded soundtrack playing but in fact a *live* Performer. I see a taller, slimmer, *better looking version* of Dougie singing for the crowd. It takes me only a second to process that this is Johnny Nemesis!

'*Get off that fucking stage!*' I hear someone rant. It's hardly surprising to realize this comes from my Subject. 'This is *my* gig!' This fails to break the concentration of both Singer and Audience, who are already mutually engaged. Strauss is now attempting to mount the stage. I zoom into these angry antics as he slips and falls back against a few patrons, some of whom voice their displeasure. He ignores this to eventually climb successfully up upon the raised area but this is no deterrent to Nemesis, who continues to sing *even* whilst Doug is attempting to wrench the microphone from him. Johnny merely raises his arm and, *still* projecting his voice into the amplified device, continues to evade Strauss's restricted reach. Nemesis is now adapting the words he's singing to personally address my increasingly tortured Subject. I sense this is the culmination to the conflicted relationship they've both harboured since early childhood.

'*You've* let down your public, and *you lose again!*' Nemesis goads all this and more in the form of song, 'Only *you* could have been so wrong- so very wrong!' Eventually the shorter, squatter man wrestles the slimmer Performer down, twisting his arm and eventually regaining control of the mic. Then Doug attempts to push his tormentor off the stage altogether but the nimbler man deftly sidesteps this, and so forces Strauss to stumble and again fall. With this, two things happen: firstly the audience cheer and applaud Nemesis; then an *even more troubling* blow for my Subject; the sound system comes to an abrupt halt, rendering the pub silent in *so* sudden a way it seems pre-planned. Doug scrambles to his feet and attempts to interlope the same song a Capella-style but all that comes across is his raw, unvarnished voice now devoid of the technological enhancement which had made it *only barely* tolerable. The air soon becomes filled with dissatisfied voices. Booing becomes increasingly louder, coming from *every* angle within the venue.

'Just a few teething problems,' Strauss attempts, having now given up all pretense of singing. He goes to a corner of the stage where his keyboard had been shifted during his prolonged absence. But the amplification fails him. No further sound comes from this instrument.

'He's *not* Elvis,' an elderly woman croaks from the bustling bar, 'he's rubbish!'

'Guidance…Guidance!' Doug is calling out as through to summon help from some Spiritual, even *Celestial* Source. He begins to bash his fists down upon the keyboard, again and again but still with no success. 'Play keyboard, *play!*' Alas all this is to no avail; the gods of music appear to have abandoned him *completely.*

'Get off!' a voice calls out. Then this unequivocal request is echoed by others until it grows to become a combined, continuous chant which is eventually shortened to '*off!off!off!off!*' ad nauseam, ad infinitum. This is accompanied by no shortage of booing, wolf –whistling (in response to my now profusely-sweating Subject having popped a couple of buttons from his jumpsuit after so much exertion against his inert organ) and a plethora of imaginative, inventive heckling from the audience to express their consolidated contempt.

Suddenly Doug jolts as though stricken with some form of inspiration. He goes to his props trunk, which had also been marginalized during his sojourn in the toilets, and rummages through it in search of a solution to his *many* woes. Eventually he pulls out a few items then shakes them out vigorously as though in prelude to a sacred ceremony. Unfortunately this is *not* in the *least* way placating the Audience, who've now taken to booing *yet louder*. I zoom into these objects, recognizing the wig and beard he'd used in a bizarre ritual at his home. Strauss begins to groom the wig tenderly. He soon becomes less assured in this task however, choosing *instead* to mop his streaming brow with this hairpiece before discarding it altogether. He then places the woven beard over his glistening jawline. Still with no musical accompaniment other than the baying audience, my Subject resumes with intoning further appeal for guidance. He then goes into a peculiar series of motions similar to old documentary footage I've seen of Native American ghost dancing.

'Are you picking up anything, Dougie?' I call out but maybe my request has been drowned out by the discontented crowd, *or he's gone into a trance*, because the dance becomes more frenetic yet. A rhythm establishes itself within his motions. The Audience, either to pour further scorn upon him, *or perhaps even as encouragement*, begin a slow clap of hands which increases in pace, with Strauss's movements becoming increasingly faster. I'm now certain this situation is similar to the stint he'd had as a stage hypnotist, which had backfired and rendered he *himself* suggestible to the cruel whims of a pitiless audience. Faster and faster, more spastic still are his actions in accordance to the callous crowd. I then recall where I'd observed a similar spectacle: it was amidst the tenement block communal gardens on the previous Sunday where Doug had consulted with his Spirit Guide, an *especially* confrontational grizzly bear. His contortions and convulsions become greater still, his teeth become bared. Saliva drools from his mouth. Armed with a new confidence, *or fevered compulsion*, Strauss now heads back to his keyboard and proceeds to bang his fists down upon it repeatedly, time and again, with increasing ferocity. Suddenly a loud bang comes from the vicinity of this fevered activity. A flash of sparks and puff of smoke issues from the instrument, along with a ghoulish sound that might be a death cry for both it and the crazed man assaulting it! Doug looks alarmed, standing bolt upright from his previous Navajo crouch before crashing down to the ground, tumbling, then rolling off the stage. By the time he hits the grimy pub carpet I notice that his fake beard has caught light! A burgeoning blaze soon spreads to his *equally* artificial hairpiece. *Luckily* several of the patrons to the fore of this sensational spectacle have the presence of mind to hurl their drinks over him, thus quelling the fire from becoming *completely* out of control.

Upon watching this footage it seems most probable that Douglas Bader Strauss had electrocuted himself in his ill-judged attack upon his own instrument. It had subsequently burst into flames, and so caused *further* injuries to the man I'd been tirelessly documenting.

'Did you hear what he said?' the elderly woman (who'd earlier heckled Strauss) had asked as the ambulance arrived to take him to Casualty.

'I think *everybody* heard what he said,' I'd replied to her.

'*Look again*,' she'd said with a wry smile as Johnny Nemesis was returning to the stage.

Once home I play back the footage to see what the old woman (whom I now recognized as *"red Indian lady"* at the Off License) had been referring to: I see Doug bang his fist repeatedly down upon the amplified piano; I witness what I *now* know to be a potentially fatal electric shock; '*Et-tu, keyboard-clown-cunt!*' I hear Strauss issue just before a spark hits his fake beard and hairpiece to turn him into a most *ungracious*, great ball of fire.

'Dougie will be missed,' his wife says directly to my camera, two weeks after the event which has so drastically changed her life.

'I'm sure there is someone out there who will miss him?' I'm encouraging her to open up.

'I'll certainly miss the great personality I knew,' she continues, 'and I'll never stop trying to get through to him. They know what they're doing at the After-Life place. I'm sure he's got plenty of new fans there now.'

'Did you say the " *After-Life*" place?'

'Sorry, I *meant* to say "*After-care*" place,' she replies with a nervous giggle whilst readjusting the medical dressing upon her head which serves as a reminder of the iron attack. It seems I'm *finally* getting to know this person. 'They fit him in on Tuesdays and every other Thursday.'

'As part of his rehabilitation?' I enquire. 'What are the chances of a full recovery?'

'Traumas aside,' Strauss's wife confides as she spoon feeds her husband, 'the doctors call it a *complete* breakdown.'

'Has he been fully comatose *all* this time?' Doug is wearing a surgical turban matching hers, in his case utilized to aid recovery from the multitude of wounds sustained on that fateful night at his local social club.

'He's been pretty much as you see him now, although he *did* have a moment of lucidity at some point.'

'How so?'

'It's silly really,' she replies with a chuckle, 'but one night he sat bolt upright in his cot and said the most strangest thing…I *shouldn't even* mention it really.'

'Please do?' I detect a twitch within her otherwise incapacitated husband.

'He sat up and, just like the old Dougie we know and love, made reference to my mother.'

'Lord rest her soul,' I say by way of encouragement. '*What did he say?*'

'He said that it was *she* who had caused all this- silly, really.'

'Please elaborate?' I persevere.

'Well, he said that she had been *urging him to join her* on that fateful night of his injuries, and that right at that very moment of trauma she'd been seeking to drag him over to the Other Side to torment him for *all* Eternity…Well, *can* you imagine?' She chortles. 'Back to his old laughing and joking ways.'

'And then what?'

'Then he fell back into this stupefied state you now see him in. But I think there's a more *rational* explanation for this.'

'There is?'

'I'm sure he's *chosen* this as a respite from his creativity,' she explains, looking off wistfully into some middle distance I myself am unaccustomed with. 'Like his hero, the King himself. He also flew too near the Heavens, only to be struck down.'

'Like Icarus?'

'No,' she responds abruptly, 'Elvis Presley!' Then her demeanor softens as she attempts to feed her husband what appears to be baby food. 'The King who shall *never* die.' Strauss is responding at last, albeit to sup feebly at the spoon as a mere infant would. Her tone becomes softer still, as though addressing an *actual* new-born. 'His glory marches on…*doesn't it!*'

'I suppose so,' I reply whilst observing the slop ooze back out of Doug's limp mouth.

Episode Four:

Billy-motor mechanic

Parts for people, people for parts; I'm working on it.
William N. F. Strauss.

Our search has now led us to another member of the Strauss family, Billy, a self-employed motor mechanic who, after only the briefest of correspondence, immediately appears to have grasped the objective of our documentary.

'Hello, I'm Billy,' he says, emerging from his work premises, a car maintenance workshop. 'I'm *certainly* interested in your production and *all* that entails. Please come in.' Billy shares the same short, squat stature of all the Strauss siblings I've as yet encountered. There's also a facial semblance though he differs from his brothers in having a mustache and, *I suspect*, that he grows his sandy-hued hair longer on one side of his head to comb it over to conceal his baldness.

'We're certainly relieved that you're interested in making a contribution,' I tell him whilst he makes me tea.

'"*We*"?' he enquires.

'I was referring to my film production company.'

'But you've come *alone* today?'

'I employ staff *as* need be.'

'I can relate to that,' Billy enthuses, 'I'm mostly a one-man-band myself, and sub out work when I get inundated. This also seems to work for Broomhead.'

'Broomhead?'

'Mick Broomhead, *of course-* your *fellow* documentarian.' I think he *means* Nick Broomfield? 'He very clearly does his own sound recording judging by that boom he always holds. Surely somebody *else* is filming him though?'

'Evidently,' I confirm, 'I use similar Spartan technical approaches myself.'

'No harm keeping production costs down too.'

'That's *not entirely* the reason,' I retort.

'But what about that character Louisa Thorax?!'

'I'm certainly not *that* type of film maker,' I reassure him.

'That's a relief! Why does he *always* have to end up making the documentary about *himself* every time?'

'Well, I certainly *won't* be appearing in front of the camera as they both do.' I've written a manifesto I'll share at some point, concerning this very *specific* matter. 'So Billy, perhaps we can get back on track-would you care to share some information about yourself?'

'Gladly,' he chirps, 'I'm a great joiner-in of things; social clubs, volunteer charities, organizations in need… Jury service! I get voted in for virtually everything I take part in. Then it's only a matter of time before they make me their Chairman.'

'Why's that?'

'I suppose they sense my leadership qualities, and all that,' he embellishes in a monotone that differs from the verbal deliveries of his brothers. 'But then, *what* is leadership without humility and insight?'

'What *indeed*.'

'How do you take your tea?'

'Do you have artificial sweetener?'

'The radiator of your production vehicle was loose so I've fixed it for you,' Billy tells me as I emerge from his Portaloo: you might recall the opening statement of my *first* transcript on judging a person by their bathroom; this particular toilet looks as though it's been used for a *succession* of music festivals, *never once* having been cleaned or, judging by the stench, *emptied!*

'You did *all* that while I was having a pee?'

'I'm something of a one man production line,' he quickly counters, 'I'll tell you more of that later.'

'I'm sure you will,' I respond with bemusement: I'm sensing a family trait; if he's anything at all like his brothers then I'm sure he'll be giving me *much* mileage.

'No charge. For my work, that is, *rather* than me furnishing you with information you *might* need. That will be free also, *of course*.'

'Thanks!' It's refreshing to meet a genuine Strauss at *long* last. 'Billy, do you have many clients?'

'Parts for people, people for parts,' he confidently replies, 'I'm *working* on it.'

'That's your *work* ethos, is it?'

'I'm glad that comes across.' He smiles for the first time: his teeth could *certainly* do with some extensive dental *work*.

'Yes, you've used similar mantra-like terms in *all* our phone calls. And you've got those *exact* words on your web pages.'

'Glad you've done your homework.' Strauss's smile is slipping: perhaps I haven't gained his *entire* trust just yet? 'You see, I'm not *just* an automobile technician, I'm also a sporting coach, and I approach everything in Life that same way.'

'Football?'

'Of course! Then outside of the season it's cricket, *depending* on the time. But when the transfer windows for the football comes upon us I often have to turn off my 'phone.'

'Why?'

'That's when I get pestered by the big teams, where they are asking me *who* they should buy, and for *how* much.'

'By *"the big teams"* you mean those in the Premiership?'

'I've been asked *not* to *name* names, 'Billy replies, 'but yes, I act on behalf of the big boys.'

'So, you're a Consultant?'

'Yes indeed, though I can only give them so much advice before I'm forced to ignore them. They drive me mad but I am *so* terribly flattered by their attentions. Anyhow, I digress- concerning this project, I'm *more than happy* to be involved.'

'That's a great relief because we did have *some* problems with your brothers who, forgive me for saying, were *not* true to their word.'

'There will be *no* chance of that in my case!' Billy gives me a craggy smile. 'I'm happy to be generous with myself. I shall to the best of my efforts apply myself like a fluid science.'

'That's an interesting analogy, is it part of your philosophy?'

'A philosophy indeed,' he confirms, 'but so much *more* than that. You see, I myself *am* a *Method,* a *different* angle, sort of like a finely-tuned engine. When I was playing for Wimbledon F.C.-'

'You played for Wimbledon football club?!' I'm a little disconcerted because *at no point* in my research had I discovered that Billy had played professional soccer.

'Well, they've airbrushed me out of History, on which I shall elaborate more upon later.'

'As you wish?'

'Sparks!'

'*Pardon me?*'

'"*Sparks"* was my nickname at the Dons, on account of me firing up everyone else. Not *literally* burning them, *of course*, more a case of me serving as a combustion engine to ignite *all* those around me.'

'I can imagine.' I'm shuffling through the scant information I have on the man sitting opposite me.

'That, *in turn,* caused the trouble there,' Strauss states between sips of tea, 'even though, and probably very likely *because of*, the team hurtling their way up the divisions, things got very messy.'

'How so?'

'The *Powers-that-be* got fed up of getting upstaged by me so I was *bound* to fall foul of them'.

'Do you *still* maintain good relationships with your former colleagues, the other players?'

'Of course,' he replies without a beat, 'I often get asked advice from Vinnie, usually acting tips. It seems it's working out well for him over in Hollywood. Oh, and I'm always hearing from "*Fash the bash*", him pestering to help him with his latest crazy scheme. And *"Wisey"*, of course, I gave him the best advice he's ever had.'

'Concerning his post-sporting career?'

'Not as such, more of a case of advising him to avoid taxis! Anyhow, my dealings with the club became *less* cordial. There's gratitude, eh! Still, no need for me to be bitter because look at them now-living in Milton Keynes, of all places! Yep, I've certainly had the last laugh there, *thank you very much!'*

I politely decline joining Billy for lunch to instead answer my e-mail correspondence on my smart phone. So far there's been a lack of potential participants for my intended documentary about cuckoldry: I'd made contact with several mutual acquaintances of Robby Strauss's, whilst approaching others online; *no* replies *as yet* alas.

I have *however* had more success in receiving information from my contact within the Police Force: this person -whom I've resolved *never* to reveal their true identity- has provided previously elusive information concerning Mathew Strauss; it seems he was recently found *not* guilty on a drug trafficking charge after the Jury were convinced the "*evidence*" was *nothing more substantial than* a series of tapped phone calls proposing a *fictional* feature film *rather than* (as the C.P.S. claimed) a multi-million pound narcotic deal.

Less enlightening is a peculiar e-mail that comes to me from an unknown Source by the name of *"John Cade."* But more about this later.

'Now Fred, it's very important for you to listen to me now...*Fred?*' Billy is having a conversation with someone on his landline, a phone that is mounted upon the wall of his workshop. 'I speak to you now *not just* as a therapist but as someone who is *almost* a friend...You're talking *again*, Fred, so *how* are you going to hear *what you need to know?*...Yes, that's better. Now Frank, are you ready for help?... I called you *Frank?*... Oh, well maybe that's more appropriate *now* that we're being frank with each other?...Well, let's just suck it and see...Ok Frank, you've *got* to face your demons...I *know* your wife is dead and the funeral is tomorrow but do you hear *her* crying tears for *you?!* You've got to listen to common sense now, Frank...Well, *of course* you do but if you're feeling all alone now then you just wait for Christmas!... Yes, that's exactly what I meant, pal, so best to head it straight on...Tea and sympathy are demons too, Fred. See what I did there?...Look pal, this *isn't* 'Kramer vs. Kramer'-stop that blubbing!...Yes, those tears *won't* get her back...That's *exactly* what I meant, Frank...Now you take *these* words with you, Fred- *I have spoken!*'

'Forgive me for saying, Billy,' I remark, once he's placed the phone down, 'but that didn't *precisely* sound like a conversation between a motor mechanic and a client with a problematic car.'

'I might not have mentioned this but I have a very rewarding sideline,' he proudly states, 'I've learned to use my sports-coaching skills I have to serve a *broader* benefit.'

'You mean advising people in *other* facets of their lives?'

'In a nutshell,' Billy beams back, 'you've hit the proverbial thingy both straight and squarely upon the head.'

'Perhaps you can tell me more when we both have more time?' I'm trying to think of some valid excuse to attend to other concerns currently on my agenda.

'Capital idea!' he responds with enthusiasm. 'Maybe we can discuss over a pint sometime? Not that I patronize drinking establishments *too* frequently, I wouldn't be considered one of Britain's *leading* sporting Gurus if that were the case. I'd be happy to offer advice to you, Fabio.'

'*How so?*' Perhaps my tone is severe but I hadn't thought Billy would presume to be qualified to advise me, of *all* people, in *any shape, form or capacity*.

'We can *all* do with some fine tuning occasionally.' He's possibly sensing my alarm. 'We are *all of us* not so very different from motorized vehicles.' I might have found this comparison more comforting but for the fact the car currently in his workshop is *no more than* a shell! 'We can go through the whole A-Z of your life just in case you've missed something.'

'*I'm not* the subject of this documentary, Billy.'

'Indeed. And I *won't* shirk in what's expected of me as a Subject. The advice I can offer you *specifically* is local knowledge.'

'Such as?'

'You're not from around here, are you?'

'No Billy,' I agree, 'I'm *not* from around here. In fact I've never had the opportunity to visit Stevenage before.'

'I'd be more than happy to show you around town sometime, add some local colour to your production. By the way, *is* there an allowance for that in your budget?'

'I *really* must be getting back to London now. I won't be able to visit you again until next week.'

'That's fine by me,' Strauss replies with an affable smile, 'we can make a social thing of it too. Now, as much as I *love* indulging you I've got stuff to attend to *myself.'*

I study my e-mail correspondence more in focus once I've returned home. I pore over the limited details of Mathew Strauss's criminal trial: my secret Acquaintance tells me this transcript was *not* available to the Press, in what was effectively a gagging order known as a 'D' notice. More information will hopefully be forthcoming.

I'm not sure what to make of this individual *"John Cade."* He, *or possibly* she, is accusing me of wrong-doing; "exploiting people who *shouldn't* be exploited"-what could *possibly* give this person grounds for imagining *that*?!

'Game, set and match to Billy Boy, methinks!' Strauss declares as I pull up outside his motor mechanic garage in our second meeting in as many weeks.

'What's that?' I enquire while climbing out of my vehicle.

'Ah, Q.E.D., my friend!' He's gesticulating towards a parked car it seems he's claiming to have just fixed, 'I rest my case.'

'Your case?'

'I'll look at that creaky door of yours now if you want?'

'But *is* my door creaky?'

'Not to the *unqualified* ear, at least,' he explains. 'You sound a little run down yourself. I've kept my magic sponge from my professional coaching days so I'll give you a rub-down later, *depending on time.'*

175

'Both myself and my vehicle have recently had a *full* M.O.T., thank you!'

'Concerning Roland's illness, ' Strauss says whilst surveying my car, 'it's likely his medical people can take a *mere* sliver from one of my kidneys, which in turn would most probably revive my ailing brother to *full* recovery.'

'*You think so?*' I ask with skepticism. 'Have you actually investigated the medical process for such a situation?'

'I've *intuited* as much,' he replies, momentarily looking up from the wheel arches of my vehicle, 'you see, my *own* organs have *such* vitality that even the *smallest* portion from me would have the desired effect.'

'Do you have *actual* grounds for this claim?'

'Oh '*ye of little faith,*' Billy admonishes me before beginning to inspect other parts of my automobile. 'My nickname is *"Champ"* on account of being a sporting *all-rounder*. Not just football but cricket, rugby, and *even* women's sports such as tennis. I also had a very promising career as a boxer but I got out of the sport whilst I still had my good looks intact.'

Strauss insists I should remain in town to join him in a visit to his local boxing gym.

'Billy is a good lad,' his trainer Harry says for the benefit of my video camera, 'and a very dedicated fighter.' Both men currently stand within the ropes of a boxing ring. Harry is a couple of decades older than his protégée, and has an interesting history etched upon his face. 'Nine very tough boxing matches, all resulting in knock-outs. Then in his tenth fight he *eventually* won one.'

'Brilliant!' Billy whoops with laughter, 'This, *dear viewer*, is what's known as *boxing banter*.'

'This is what's known as **objective fact!'** Harry reproaches, suddenly becoming very serious-looking. 'Punchy, sorry, I *meant* Billy here, had to pack it in though on account that one of his Opponents didn't make it.'

'One of his opponents died in the ring?' I ask. 'Knocked out fatally by Billy?'

'Knocked down in the car park after the fight,' Harry replies solemnly. 'Luckily the Coroner was satisfied.'

'That must have been the greatest of regrets?' I make a mental note to investigate this further.

'Not quite,' Harry retorts, 'we missed out big-time with commercial exposure.'

'You mean with furthering Billy's boxing career?'

'I meant advertising,' the stony-faced boxing trainer elaborates, 'it should have been on the bottom of Billy's boots *the amount of times* he ended up on the canvas.' Billy is now evading the gaze of my camera: it seems this interview has not *quite* gone the way he'd have wanted. 'His brother Peter was a better boxer.'

'Can you tell me a little bit about Peter?' Suddenly Billy looks petrified.

'*Nothing* on Earth will compel me to talk about Peter,' Harry replies curtly, 'I'm closing the gym now so you'd both *best* leave!'

Note to myself: investigate Peter's boxing career when time permits.

'I'm not sure *what* I was watching out there,' Billy delivers by way of coaching advice, 'but two words spring to mind- one of them is "shit"! And can anyone here guess the other word? That's right- *"very* shit"! And what a big steaming pile of it that was too! Don't waste your time and mine if that's *all* you've got to show. I want to see 150% extra effort out there for the second half. But if you can't do that then you might as well fuck off back home *right now!'* I pan my camera across the faces of the team: these nine-year old boys look shocked, terror-stricken even; several weep and one is sobbing uncontrollably!

'May I point out something?' I enquire, once the second half of the football match has started.

'I know what you will say, Fab,' Strauss -rather annoyingly abbreviating my name- responds, 'you're going to favor the carrot *rather* than the stick, but name me *one* lasting architectural design that solely consists of carrots?'

'That *wasn't specifically* my point, Billy. I'd just like to refer to something you said in your coaching speech where you mentioned the figure of 150% - technically there can be *no* higher percentage than one hundred percent.'

'Funny you should mention *that*.' A sardonic smirk spreads out across his features. 'Young Malcolm Albright, who usually plays Left-back insisted that very *same* point last week but take a wild guess *who* got dropped?'

'Left back, *indeed*,' I muse as Strauss's attention is drawn back to the activity on the pitch.

'What the fuck do you call *that?!*' he screams out to his youthful team. 'I told you that I want *nothing less* than one hundred and fifty fucking percent!' At this point the Referee blows his whistle and sprints towards a couple of boys from opposing teams embroiled in a dispute but then runs straight past them to confront Billy, to whom he presents a red card for his unacceptable behavior.

'Certain undesirable elements have crept into football,' Strauss pontificates from the bar of the clubhouse after the game, 'elements that can *hardly* be good examples to young aspiring players.' With this he downs his pint of lager and chases it with a shot of spirit.

'You're referring to the Premiership?' I enquire.

'Of course,' he wheezes whilst gesticulating to the barman to duplicate our order. 'Tales of away match shenanigans, champagne cocktails, the *disunity* of the shower cubicle. It was a team bath in my day and *no* mistake! Then you have your betting syndicates with nefarious forfeits-'

'*Forfeits?*'

'Post-play penalties, substances referred to as *"sports* gels," and *all* the applications that entails, not to mention vibrating mobile phones utilized for *immoral and unsanitary* acts in hotel rooms for away matches.'

'I'm sure this only applies to a *tiny minority* of professional footballers?' I reason.

'Perhaps,' Strauss shrugs, 'but I'd resist buying a second-hand mobile phone from one *just* to be sure! I put *all* of this down to a sinister infiltration within the F.A.!'

'Infiltration by *whom* exactly?'

'By those whom you *wouldn't* welcome to join you in the team bath, *of course.*'

'Interesting coaching technique…' I'm attempting to change the subject since we've broached on something that makes me feel awkward in a way I cannot *precisely* explain.

'They've defined sticking a mobile phone up someone's bum as a "*coaching technique*"?!' Billy gasps with exasperation.

'No, you misunderstand,' I quickly counter, 'I was referring to your own very unique coaching style which I was filming earlier- it reminded me of "Kes".'

"Ah, yes, the new Sheffield Wednesday signing?'

'Oh,' I then realize, 'a player is called-'

'You'll have to try harder than that,' he shoots back with a sly grin, 'I'm *all too* aware you're referring to a bleak old film made by Britain's leading gritty Northern Miserabilist and Pallywood Perpetrator, Len Roach. More importantly, it's *your* round.'

'I have *neither* the facilities *nor* the inclination to wash the team kit!' I respond to Billy's bizarre request. Over the last two hours he's become progressively, or rather, *reductively* drunk whilst I remain teetotal and sober.

'Look at it as a bonding experience?' he perseveres.

'No Billy, I *won't* be doing that.'

'Look, Fab,' he pleads, 'why not hang around a bit?'

'*Why* would I want to do that?'

'It's Saturday night,' he replies as though this should have some relevance, 'we can go on from here to a few places, grab a curry if you like? There's not a bad little nightclub not so far away too.'

'A *nightclub?!* I've got an early start tomorrow, Billy.'

'Me too, but that never stops me being *up with the cock!* Anyhow, I say nightclub but it's *more* an exclusive bar with licensing reserved for the likes of us.'

'The likes of *us?*' I'm not sure how he's qualified to quantify *me* personally?

'Truth be told it's a heaving nest of crumpet, bring your shit-coated stick to beat them back! I've *never* failed to pull there so come along and I'll show you the ropes?'

'That's a very kind offer, but I have very *specific* plans early in the morning.'

'I can put you up for the night,' he persists. 'Here, let's get down Magnum's. It's happy hour there. Who am I kidding?! It's happy hour *whenever I'm out!*'

'I thought I'd visit your brother Roland in hospital in the morning.'

'Be sure to give him my regards', Billy replies before necking his drink. 'Can you drop me down Magnum's before you head back to the Smoke?'

'Yes sir,' Strauss tells a customer over the phone, which is secured to the wall inside his garage, 'your car is now restored *almost completely* to its former glory.' It's now Monday morning: *still* a solitary vehicle -no more than a shell- sits central within the workshop; *surely* this *can't* be the car he's boasting about having "*almost completely*" restored?! 'Best to give it two more weeks, sir…' I sense opposition from the Caller but Billy perseveres, 'because I have commissioned France's *finest* polisher to handle the upholstery, and since he's still completing his obligations to Lord Beaull…lo-jo and the Getty Museum…

As I said, *sir,* he's the finest in his field…But any sooner would be premature, sir…I'd like to assure you that your vehicle is in the *very finest* hands.'

'I was hoping to have seen you at the hospital yesterday, Billy,' I mention once he's completed the call to his Customer.

'A rush job, as you can see. So Fab, how's Rolly?'

'He's *not* terribly well, Billy'.

'Any of my other brothers visiting the hospital whilst you were there?'

'It seems Douglas has been discharged,' I relay, 'to a convalescence home of sorts, *according* to his wife it's situated on a farm.'

'I've left him enough coaching tips on his answer phone so when he comes round he'll have a useful lifeline.'

'Have you offered *much* advice to your other brothers?'

'I've given Robby a series of mantras.' He's looking very pleased with himself.

'Have you heard from him recently?' I venture. 'And what of Kevin?'

'You've just reminded me about my eleven a.m. client!' Suddenly he's dashing across the workshop. I imagine he's about to start work on the bare chassis but instead returns to the wall-mounted telephone. 'Norman, it's me, Billy,' he announces when eventually his call is answered, 'don't worry about that, Norman, your treatment is *really* coming along now, Norman. Now tell me, Normal Norman, what is your name?… That's right, you've got it…That's how people will know you *in future*…Normal Norman!...That's right, and remember what today is?...That's right- it's normal Monday!..Then tomorrow you can ease off the gas for semi-normal Tuesday. Then if you *really* feel you've made progress by then you can kick your heels back for casual Wednesday, before you have formal Thursday and thoughtful Friday to contend with…Now you take that away with you, Norman- *I have spoken!*'

'Part of your Life coaching?' I ask, once he's completed his call.

'I'm going to have to cite client confidentiality there, Fab, I'm afraid,' he replies whilst *finally* inspecting the hollow shell of the car. 'But *one* thing I can share with you is that one has to be very, *very* patient with the sick and twisted. And luckily for them I am *fairly* patient.'

'Does your life coaching and sports advice ever overlap?'

'Obviously with the kid's football team it does,' he affirms, 'I'm attempting prevention rather than cure for the young'uns so they'll grow up to be *"Normals"* rather than *"Normans"*.'

'Is not your approach a *little bit* stigmatizing? Is it possible the Normans in this World-'

'Discipline *has* to be maintained!' Billy cuts me short. 'Not *precisely* the type of discipline handed out like a brutally exacting Father because that's *technically* illegal now but discipline *all that same*. Parts for people, and people for parts-*I'm working on it!*' There seems something manic in his conclusion but *more* curious still is the reference to a Father-figure, leading me to suspect he's making an allusion to *his own* Father.

'How much do you draw upon from *actual* existential experience?'

'I'm glad you've come to the subject of me drawing from a bunch of stuff I *really* know *all* about, Fab, I've noticed how *un*economical that production vehicle of yours *must* be.'

'I wasn't referring to anything *remotely* like that *at all*, Billy!'

'Why don't you consider a lovely little run-about? A pristine little car I've set aside for you, more immaculate than Mary and I'm *not* talking about Magdalene! I can give you the bargain you've *always* been looking for. Perhaps we can discuss it over a curry sometime?'

'I'm really *not* interested in that, Billy,' I state emphatically.

'No worries,' he concedes, 'Mexican or Thai food it is then!'

'*That's not going to happen!*'

'Ok, I understand.' Suddenly he looks crestfallen, which *almost* makes me feel sorry for him. 'You're absolutely right, of course. Besides, I'm just finishing up some business with a Client who needs a little discretion. How's about you grab yourself some lunch and we meet up after to tie up all our loose ends?'

It's at this point I *should* mention certain incidents I've as yet omitted concerning the previous Saturday. Rather than head back to London immediately after delivering Billy to his requested nightspot I'd instead remained in town to meet up with a local Acquaintance, my Police Source, who'd acquired some useful information. Once having made contact, and received news which had *indeed* proved helpful -more about this later- I sensed it appropriate to remain in the locality to get a better angle on my most recent Subject.

Two hours after dropping Strauss off, I'd returned to that same premises. He was no longer there but *was* inside the second bar I ventured into. A sudden inspiration took hold of me: rather than approach him directly I would first observe him at length until the *inevitability* of recognition. He was *not* to notice me however, neither at the furthest span across the establishment (from where my recce was to commence) nor in the middle distance, behind a useful pillar where I continued my candid study. Billy *even* failed to see me upon later visiting the bar *closest* to me, which would have put me in *direct* eye-line with him! The thought eventually crossed my mind that, as a former pugilist, he might have chosen to force me into approaching *him* first. The actuality eventually dawned upon me *however* that he was simply unable to countenance my presence there this night! And what was Billy doing whilst I was observing him? Drinking, *naturally*, speaking to a few fellow male patrons he already seemed to know then later, after *several more* drinks, approaching a succession of women, *none* of whom appeared to have much time for him.

I'd left after an hour or so, still invisible to Strauss's scrutiny. Conversely I *had* gained some useful technical advantage: I'd filmed some of his fruitless labors with my smart phone, which confirmed *this* medium would suffice to capture such telling imagery; and even *when* approached by the establishment's security team (enquiring about my motives for filming) I was met with bemusement, even astonishment as to *why* I should express interest in a *"fantasist non-entity"* such as Billy! Despite their incredulity they agreed to retain my confidence, and even promised to keep me posted should anything dramatic befall *"that pointless, baldy-fraud, ginger-Minge 'tache-twat"*.

'Sorry about that earlier,' Strauss says when I return to his workshop, 'I was having a clear out.'

'As I can see.' His work tools have been placed out across the floor. 'I sense *some* kind of order.'

'Order is *everything*,' Fabio.' Thankfully he's refraining from abusing my name at long last. 'My tools are my children, however *not* the disorderly, ungrateful children who refuse to return valued, nay, *priceless* sporting memorabilia.'

'Did you ever have children yourself, Billy?' I'm suddenly compelled to ask, even though I'd found *no* evidence of offspring during the courses of my research.

'Forgive me but I *must* continue with my work,' he replies abruptly whilst feigning to continue sorting his works tools in an order most probably *only* making sense to himself: have I touched upon some raw nerve? 'Pride in the job!' he re-issues about ten minutes later, attempting to impress upon me that he's completed the task in hand. *'That's* my byword, Fabio. Tea?'

'Thank you,' I say after he hands me a hot beverage.

'Not everyone is *so* lucky, Fabio.' I sense he's about to open up to me, possibly concerning *something* I'd broached upon earlier. He nods consent to be filmed when I point to my camera. 'I had to let one young fella go from my employ. You see, he'd become a danger both to himself and others- he'd taken to drink.'

'What is your *own* relationship with alcohol, Billy?' I'm zooming in to capture him in close-up: it's likely he's attempting to reveal something about *himself,* albeit in coded form.

'Not alcohol,' he sharply retorts, 'this young man had taken to drinking car engine oil.'

'Surely that would be harmful to his health?'

'Not half! He would start to make bizarre noises.'

'Choking?'

'Peculiar noises not unlike an old, pre-German takeover Skoda,' Strauss elaborates. 'It was pathetic really, here in my employ was a tender youth who'd become convinced he was an elderly East European automobile.'

'Have you stayed in contact with this person?' I ask in as sensitive a tone as I can muster.

'If you're watching this, son,' Billy responds, looking directly into the lens of my camera, 'whether you're in hospital or hostel, hotel or hovel…get well soon, *champ*. I'm *sure* you'll get through your next M.O.T.' He then displays a sad smile before removing his overalls. 'Forgive me, Fabio, I've just remembered something I must attend to.'

As I'm driving out of town (fortunately *early enough* to avoid the afternoon rush hour traffic back to London) I again catch sight of Strauss. He's once more approaching the same watering hole I'd dropped him at the preceding Saturday evening.

There is still *no* response for my intended documentary about cuckolds. It has *not* escaped me that people who indulge in this *extreme form of intimacy* might be inhibited about a broader audience -possibly even family members- discovering this about them. And so for this reason I'd issued assurances concerning their anonymity, with their voices and facial features obscured *should* they insist. I shall have to throw my net out *yet further* to find suitable contributors once time allows.

I receive another e-mail from "John Cade": It seems ever more likely this person has *inside* information on me; I've been accused of exploiting an unnamed man suffering from alcoholism, whom alleges I'd induced him to destroy both career and marriage; it's *possible* this comes from Kevin Strauss, specifying his *own* decline. But then I recall that he is both illiterate *and* unlikely to find an accomplice willing to help him with such fanciful correspondence.

And so I block incoming messages from this *"John Cade"*. Within the hour an additional peculiar e-mail comes from another unknown Source going by the handle *"Agent Provost"*. This is quite possibly *also* from *"John Cade."* I resist blocking this person however on account of something I shall *later* disclose.

There is *no* further information about Mathew Strauss from my contact within the Police Force.

'Sorry I've kept you waiting,' Strauss says, emerging from his vehicle outside his workshop, 'I've just come from visiting my two brothers in hospital.'

'That's ok, Billy, I understand.' I do *indeed* now *fully* understand: I'd not long myself left the hospital so it's *hardly likely* he'd been there! *'How are they?'*

'I've brushed up the performance of their Life Support machines,' he smugly replies whilst climbing into his work overalls.

'I would have thought those machines are *extremely* sensitive?'

'I imagine *merely the aura* of my healthy kidneys will do them the world of good,' he boasts whilst putting the kettle on.

'You are very likely to hear there'll be a very great improvement with *all* of my family very soon.'

'You had time to visit Dougie at the hospice too?'

'I have the healing hands, you see.' My subject carries on as though he'd not heard my last question. 'I'd be glad to give you a rub-down with the magic sponge sometime soon, *indeed* these hands, these tools, *do indeed work wonders.*'

'I can imagine,' I sigh.

'These are *not* toys!' Strauss is suddenly holding his fists up, possibly angered by my doubtful tone. Eventually he feigns calmness to deliver a familiar mantra, 'Parts for cars, parts for people-*I'm working on it!*'

'Billy,' I venture as we both sip tea, 'have you been *completely* honest with me?'

'Ok, you've forced my hand. The truth is I'm being stalked.'
'*Stalked?!*'

'Yes Fabio. I've had a stalker, or rather a *series* of stalkers for *quite* some time now.'

'A spurned former lover?'

'Oh, that's just par for the course,' he replies with a chuckle, 'they come by the legion. No, these stalkers I specifically refer to are a *certain* racing team that I shouldn't really name.'

'A racing team?'

'Yes, you know- the type who race on the professional car racing circuit such as Formula One.'

'*Why* would they be stalking *you*, Billy?'

'Oh dear,' he responds with a series of tutting noises, 'somebody *clearly* hasn't been doing their homework. Well Fabio, if you *had* looked more into my former life you would have discovered I used to work as part of a successful team that would be defined as *a racing team.'*

'Why did your work discontinue with them?'

'Much the same as my sporting career, Fab- it only had a certain shelf life.'

'Burn out?' I venture.

'Only a few minor prangs,' he replies. 'The same old story, really-jealousy, envy, stress.'

'You were suffering stress?'

'Of course not,' Billy chortles, 'I created stress amongst jealous competitors who failed to keep up with me. So I got out to come work in this modest little garage, having *chosen* a life of being anonymous here.'

'*This* is a Life choice?' I survey the shambolic state of his workshop.

'Of course! A bit like the way T.E. Lawrence, after his military miracles in the Middle East, neglected to be blinded by shallow fame and empty glory to instead chose a life *away* from all that. I mean, *what* can you possibly do after conquering a continent?'

'So you prefer to project your energies into *other* fields now?'

'I do, indeed, such as my charity work, which I choose *not* to talk about.'

'Very wise,' I agree.

'I insist *not* to talk about my *considerable* work for charity but for one unavoidable factor…'

'And *what* would that be?' I ask against my better judgment.

'My secrecy clause was compromised. I'd ticked the optional box to remain anonymous but *agents of destruction* swooped in to exploit my former fame.'

'They did?' I've heard this term "*agents of destruction*" before but *precisely* where currently eludes me.

'Of course they did! But I'm *hardly* going to sue a string of various charitable organizations for breach of confidence.'

'But I thought the whole point of using Celebrity Status was to the *benefit* of collecting money for charities?' I put to him.

'*If only!* I didn't come out from amidst the dizzy heights of fame and the gilded corridors of power without learning *some* very valuable lessons.'

'And *what* lessons would they be?'

'Whether it's Big Brother, or The Man, or indeed the Fat Cats, *the Great Terrible Clown* or even the Chubby Controller, they are all euphemisms for the *same* thing.'

'Which is?'

'To conquer, control and domesticate the likes of me and you. And it might be fine for you but *not* for me, my friend, no thank you very much-*you don't get me!*' Suddenly there's a loud and furious banging at the garage door. Then a rattling noise as though someone is wrestling with the outside handle. Entry is denied to whoever is doing this because Billy had earlier locked us inside. I go to speak but he motions for me to remain silent. Eventually this disturbance subsides.

'Who was that?' I whisper at last.

'That was *precisely* the point I'd been making,' he murmurs before going to the garage door to peek out through the gaps in its structure.

'Did you never think to start your *own* racing team, Billy?' I ask once I hear a vehicle outside drive off. Suddenly he picks up a carjack type object which I've heard referred to as a *"spider"*. I initially panic, suspecting that he's wielding it as a weapon to go after the person or persons who'd been at his door, *or worse still*, to attack *me* for some perceived offence he's imagined I've committed. But eventually he holds the object in both hands as though it were a crucifix to ward off vampires.

'Away with thee, Satan!' he booms, 'I *cannot* be tamed!'

'Yes, I *think* I get your point.'

'I should take this with me tonight.' A calmer Billy is referring to the cast iron cross.

'For protection against *physical* attack?'

'Possibly, but I've also been asked to officiate over a religious ceremony so...Bless you! Let's wind down here because I'm expected at that place and already running a bit late.'

I've had my hand forced. Due to certain developments I've been compelled to get back in contact with my inept, former sound recordist Stan, in order to make sense of some *most* perplexing recent events.

Several days after having last seen Billy I receive an online video. It's been sent most helpfully by the staff of Magnum's nightclub. There's no footage of Billy inside the bar area but he's shown emerging from the venue. A man a decade or so younger than him approaches. There's no sound but I surmise a heated exchange. Then this man physically attacks Strauss before the Security Team intervene to prise the two apart. A brief paragraph within the email gives the context of this incident. This is in keeping with my general and overall impression of Strauss.

Just minutes after watching this *however* I'm sent another video of Billy, this time from a different Source. As I take in the events unfurling onscreen I realize this puts a whole *new* perspective on the man who's my current Subject.

'Billy,' I call out at the door of his workshop, 'it's us, your film crew.'

'*Us?*' he replies from inside. 'Is that really you, Fabio? Who is this "*us*"?'

'Myself and my sound recordist, Stan.' I'd been unable to contact Troy these last few days so unfortunately had been forced to call upon the services of my existing production assistant.

'*Stan?*' Strauss echoes. Then I hear a series of locks and security bolts getting de-fastened and un-shot. The garage door opens ajar. I observe a frowning Billy. Upon seeing me his brow unfurrows, and I'm given a broad gappy smile before allowed entrance. Once inside I notice he's got a black eye.

'You missed an amazing night at Magnum's club last night,' he claims whilst making make us tea, 'it was absolutely chock-full of crumpet.' The time-coded video footage sent to me just hours previously showed very *few* females present, and certainly *none* that were responsive towards him.

'Did you pull?' Stan asks. I'm *already* regretting having brought him here.

'*Did I pull?!*' Billy reverberates with incredulity. '*Where* did you find this one, Fabio? He clearly *doesn't* know me from Adam!'

'Well, *did* you?' Stan reiterates whilst setting up his sound equipment.

'*Yes, I did!*' Strauss emphatically states, before reverting to his usual unconvincing bonhomie, 'I copped off with a *few* birds actually, a selection of snogs before selecting my suitably desirable victim. Well, I use the term *"victim"* in a *non* serial killer sense, but you get the picture?'

'Sounds a fun place,' Stan replies: I'm *really* hoping Troy rematerializes soon so I can dispense with this idiot *altogether.*

'I gave her a proper one-man football team roasting, gave her *all* the trimmings. She even had a mate whom I found it in my heart to let join us for a threesome.'

'*Both* of them?!' Stan gasps.

'Indeed,' Billy boasts, 'and some post-match play, I mean, a *full* extended proper replay! I can see me getting into the Champions league yet- *even* my brother Robby would have been proud!'

'Have you seen or heard from Robby recently?' Stan has a useful question *at long last!* 'We were wondering what's happened to him?'

'He's found a publisher for his autobiography. And it seems he's doing a documentary for *somebody else* now.'

'*Really?!* I interject. 'Can you enlighten us about these new plans?'

'He's doing a new feature called *"Sexploited Migrants,"* a companion piece to his *"Rape-ugee"* series.'

'Is there *nothing* too low, exploitative, iniquitous and plain *wrong* for your brother Robby?!' I castigate.

'Nothing to do with my brother,' Billy replies cheerfully, '*those* are the titles of the Bafta-nominated films made by this famous guy who's now doing the documentary *about* Robby.

He's had the good sense to follow my life coaching tips *at long last.*'

'Billy,' I say, tiring of all this, *'how* did you get that black eye?'

'*This?*' he responds, suddenly less sure of himself. 'It's nothing really.'

'Sound recording levels all fine,' Stan confirms. I remain silently waiting for Strauss to explain himself.

'It was a bit of a misunderstanding really,' he mumbles, groping for an excuse which continues to elude him.

'It *was?*' I *must* play the Inquisitor in this instance.

'Well, you know how generous I am with myself,' Billy continues, his confidence slowly returning. 'Reality *itself* dictates the fact that I couldn't physically get involved with *every* single available woman at that venue last night, so what you see upon my face now is just a little love wound that came as a result of unrequited lust.'

'So what you are trying to tell us,' Stan ventures, 'is that a woman gave you a black eye because you rejected her?' I find this ironic interjection not *quite* as intrusive as his other comments: I'm not wholly convinced *however* that *either* man *fully* comprehends the *actual* Concept of Irony.

'The poor creature just *couldn't* handle the dread of forming an orderly queue.'

'Very strange.'

'You think so?' Strauss quibbles. '*How so?*'

'Yes, very strange,' I expand, 'since a barman at Magnum's claims that your black eye was given to you by one of the fathers of the children's football team you manage, for yelling at his son.' Evidence of this had come by way of CCTV Footage within the email I'd received.

'I can see what's happened here,' Billy replies, suddenly subdued, 'Hell hath no bitterness than Pedro the barman scorned.'

'So the barman *confected* this story *because you rejected him?*' I ask with incredulity.

'I'm not quite *that* charitable, Fabio.'

'The type of charity that *modesty* prevents you from speaking about, Billy?'

'This is *not* in *any* way, shape or form related to my *very* worthy charity work in Africa, Fabio,' he counters in an indignant tone.

'Oh, you do charity work in Africa?' Stan lights up. 'How *very* admirable of you.' I now regret *not* giving him a lengthier, *more detailed* brief concerning our current Subject.

'Not only do I achieve *so very much* for those poor unfortunates out there in famine-ravaged Africa, I also spend whole weeks of my life collecting money here in England. I was even persuaded to deliver the funds *directly* to them to avoid it falling into the hands of local despots.'

'How did you manage that?' I'm hoping he'll incriminate himself *further*.

'By parachuting onto the African Veldt,' he replies without a beat.

'Savannah?' Stan queries.

'Nah,' replies Billy dismissively, '*none* of those Showbiz types had the guts to join me out there.'

'That *can't* have been easy?' I respond, with undisguised sarcasm.

'I'll say,' he unheedingly proceeds, 'not least for brandishing an eight foot by four solid cardboard cheque.'

'Surely those are *merely* props purely for publicity purposes?'

'I beg to differ,' Strauss disputes, 'it certainly worked as an effective tool for me to ward off marauding lions.' Just then a wrenching noise is heard at the entrance of the garage. I turn to the door to see it being forcefully yanked open. It then occurs to me that Billy had earlier failed to complete his usual ritual of shooting all the bolts shut.

'Would you care to explain something to me?' a giant of a man asks in a gentle tone that belies the violent nature of his entrance. He proceeds to join us.

'Good afternoon, sir,' Billy whimpers. He's attempting to smile but his expression is more a terrified rictus. 'We were about to have some tea so would you care to join us?'

'No-tea-ta,' this visitor replies calmly though I sense great menace within him, which is partly confirmed in his next words, 'I expect you've got a story for me so you'd *better* make it good.'

'I'm assuming you're referring to the repairs to your car, sir?' I now infer the empty shell, this mere ghost of a vehicle which I've *yet* to see the Mechanic do even the *slightest* amount of work upon, belongs to the terrifying man present. 'This process has taken *quite* some time on account of *several* good reasons.'

'*One* good reason would be a start,' the glowering, thickset Customer states.

'In…*fest*…ation,' Strauss manages at last.

'*Infestation?*' the man repeats as though it were a provocative challenge towards him. 'On *my* car?'

'Yes sir,' Billy blurts back, having appeared to step up a gear in his attempt at a credible excuse, 'it leaks like you *couldn't* possibly imagine, sir! And while, *granted*, that the repairs to your automobile have taken *a little longer than* anticipated due to absent staff, *staff* I *should* have insisted work upon your car *even* when some of them were *genuinely* injured, one even mortally wounded on at least one occasion, during the mending of your car *specifically*, I can at this point *guarantee* a new and *concerted* effort to *fully* restore your motor car.'

'You can guarantee?' Everything about this Customer seems cold, frozen even, all with the exception of his eyes which burn with a terrible ferocity of threat.

'A guarantee that will be honoured at haste in accordance to the technological developments being achieved *as we speak!*'

'What *type* of technological developments?' I turn to see that it's my soundman, Stan, who's asked this question. I look back to the menacing man, expecting him to explode but instead he's merely smirking.

'Go on, Billy,' he says, 'answer the gentleman's question. Answer *my* question!'

'Indeed sir,' he continues, though his delivery becomes increasingly halting, 'some parts needed to mend your car are still *yet* to be manufactured in accordance to your *understandably* high standards as a customer, and so *as soon as* technology has caught up with your needs then I shall be *more than happy* to install them and *fully* complete this service.'

'I don't care for any more excuses,' the man eventually replies. I can see that he's straining desperately hard not to lose what little patience he has remaining. 'Just repair my car by the end of the week or there will be no more business, no more garage and certainly no more *you*! Is this quite understood?' Strauss nods obediently. The man then gestures farewell to each of us in turn before making his departure. Once he's gone Billy shoots every bolt on the door to ensure *no* further visitors.

'They will have to try *harder* than that!'

'*What?!*' I exclaim. 'Who are "*they*" and *what* are you even talking about?!'

'The race team sending amateurs like *that* posing as punters,' my Subject snorts with derision. 'Another two seconds of his nonsense and I would have been kicking his arse all around this garage!' Suddenly there's a loud crashing sound upon the garage door, followed by several more blows.

'Have you got something to say *now*, maggot?!' a ferocious voice yells out, followed by another series of heavy impacts against the entrance, which seems about to be breached. 'Give me a *single* reason why I shouldn't break your neck?!'…Well, maggot, what's it to be?!' Strauss stares with alarm directly into the lens of my *all-seeing* camera: I see a wholly different Billy now; one that is terrified, vulnerable and no more than a pitiful, immature imposter stripped bare; this new Billy is bereft now of *even* self-deception, which had been his *only* barely adequate, blunted tool against the all-too sharp realities of existence.

'I *only* keep the doors locked in accordance with the petty bureaucracies of health and safety,' this inept Mechanic tells us over a cup of tea. It's around an hour since the angered Customer has been persuaded, even *begged and pleaded with* (in a surprisingly impressive feat of negotiation by my Soundman) not to break in to commit physical retribution against Billy,the garage and quite possibly myself and Stan *also*. 'That guy will thank me for that later.'

'How so?' Stan questions. 'By him deciding *not* to break your neck?'

'As if!' I sense the old Billy returning. This is *not* confidence *however*, this- I'm increasingly certain- is a pathological self-preservation against *certain* unacceptable truths which might possibly destroy him if he were to *actually* face facts. 'Has it *not* become obvious *yet*?'

'Hasn't *what* become obvious, Billy?' I marvel.

'That guy, the one who was posing as a customer- he's a patient of mine.'

'A *patient?*' Stan gasps.

'Of course! I'm helping him out with his anger issues. This was *just* some roleplay to help with his rehabilitation.'

'Billy, may I ask you a question?'

'Which is, in fact, *already* a question,' he retorts with an unconvincing smirk.

'I've noticed you have accrued quite a few personal effects here in the garage recently.' There has been a recent accumulation of food stuffs, toiletries and even a sleeping bag. 'Are you now living *here* at your garage?... Is this *where* you sleep at night?'

'Please excuse me,' he counters, suddenly grim-faced, 'I have to make a most urgent call to a Client of mine.' He returns to the landline mounted against the wall to once more dial a number. 'Hello Patricia,' he says after a duration of ten seconds or so, 'yes, it's me, Billy…Now down to specifics, Patricia, *before* you have children you should ask yourself, are you emotionally and *mentally* qualified to have children?... What's your sister got to do with all *this*?...This isn't a *"two for one"* offer, she'll have to seek her *own* form of therapy…Just tell Mary *that*… Yes, but she's a point in case of someone who *should* have been prevented from having children…Patricia?…Are you there?... Well put your sister on the phone and I'll tell her *myself*…' And so this conversation continues *even* after Stan and I tell Strauss we're leaving. His reaction is a mere wave and gesture that he'll call us sometime.

This phone call from Billy was never to come. Further, *more* revealing developments *were* to be occur *however*. My Contact within the police force, *true to his word*, was to furnish me with additional information: there had recently been an attempt to arrest Mathew Strauss. My confidential Contact emphasizes "*attempt*" since after the arrest it transpired the man taken into custody was *not* Mathew Strauss but *in fact* the much respected film critic Mark Kermode! This misunderstanding was later explained due to the uncanny resemblance between the two men. By the time of Mr. Kermode's release, Strauss's Solicitor had provided adequate counter-evidence, a series of alibis and *other* Intel which would appear to implicate the Diplomatic Corps! And so this makes both the criminal charge null and void and renders the *whole* incident *subject* to a Media black-out. Subsequently the Official Secrets Act, and very likely the Data Protection Act too, forbid me discussing this episode further. But this is hardly an issue now since my *own* comparative form of omission continues concerning correspondence with my most recent Subject- the possibility has *not* escaped me concerning the likelihood that Billy has been implicated in his brother Mathew's plans!

There is still no reply from Troy (my hoped-for new production assistant) or from *any* potential Subjects for my "*cuckold*" project.

The following day was to bestow me with *additional* points of interest concerning Billy Strauss, this time in the form of a video emailed to me by the person calling themselves "*Agent Provost*," whom I suspect to be my previous troll going by the name of *"John Cade"*. In this file I see an image of Strauss in his garage, filmed at an elevated angle to suggest it is CCTV Footage, even though I'd at no point seen or heard him refer to having utilized this medium.

'Hello Norman?...'On this video the Mechanic is on the familiar landline suspended from the wall, a place I'd myself seen him positioned at on *many* occasions. 'No, Norman, it's not a trick.' There's something uncannily familiar about this footage. 'It's a courtesy call to see how you're getting on… That's ok, *all* part of the service…Well, yes, the treatment, the *very* special treatment.' I myself had previously witnessed Billy address a "*Norman*" on this phone, and so I'm now given enough clues to confirm this to be the *same* individual. 'Yes Norman, that's correct…Now, Norman, some people might call that progress, those who are unenlightened, of course… I hear you, Norman, but it sounds like you are living *too much* in the mind, what with "*I think this*" and "*I think that*" but once you realize there's *no real* thinking mind behind your actions then *that's* when you can make some *real* progress…Well, it might feel like you're content at the moment, Norman, but that too shall pass, so *then* what?...Listen Norman, further progress you can make is by you taking interest in a very reliable,*great* value, *lovely* little motor car I just happen to have for sale at the moment...Yes, I *know* you never learned to drive but that's part of the brain-block controlling you...Don't let the medication make those decisions for you...Ok Norman, I want you to stay in touch for a focus group that I'm forming...Yes, I *shall* be in touch to give you the dates...' As this video comes to a close my earlier suspicions seems confirmed that someone had secretly filmed this exchange *without* Billy's knowledge or consent.

I subsequently call my occasional Soundman but he's unable to deliver any further specific information.

'I've been able to find out something else though,' Stan says towards the end of our phone call. 'That documentary film-maker about to have your brother Robby as the Subject...'

'*Yes?*' I reply in anticipation after an unnaturally long pause. '*Well?*'

'Well, he's got his current documentary pipped to win *every* award from the Palm d'Or to the Golden Bear and Silver Lion.'

'That's *very* nice for him.' I'm wondering where on Earth this facile conversation is leading?

'It's a documentary about cuckoldry- were you not *yourself* planning a project on that *same* subject?' Stan has, *of course*, been the prime suspect in being the leak within my organization: I shall have to conceive of some cunning plan, a suitably *ingenious* mousetrap, to coax out the conscience of this rather dim-witted rodent.

Yet *more* news arrives the following day, giving me the uncanny feeling that some great, unfathomable Force has been drip-feeding me further pieces of the puzzle. First comes more CCTV footage of Billy patronizing the Magnum's bar. Initially I'd assumed this to be more footage -thoughtfully though fruitlessly- sent by the staff to show the *full* extent of Billy's lack of success with the opposite sex. But to my surprise the current evidence shows him speaking to a woman at the bar, and *even* kissing her passionately, with her *seeming* to fully reciprocate this embrace! Once this video ends I check the identity of the Sender once more to see that it was *not* (as I'd presumed) sent by the bar staff but *instead* from the same obscure person, or persons "*Agent Provost,*" who'd sent me the preceding Life-coaching phone call.

To make matters even *more* baffling I receive *another* video only an hour or so later, this time from Billy *himself!*

'Hi Fabio,' he directly addresses the camera, 'funny how things have panned out. Well, it seems like the disgruntled racing team *finally* got to me. They used the old honey-trap on me, and like a fool I fell for it. My weakness, *you see,* even *I* have one of those. And it came in the form of a busty blonde.' The CCTV footage I'd received earlier had shown Strauss with a plump woman, likely to be this suspect. 'So, I did the foolish thing and went back to her place, well, down an alleyway, *anyhow*. And that's when it happened!'

'When *what* happened?!' I hear myself ask my computer screen.

'A female Spy's 21st Century version of the clap!' Strauss continues, a sad smile upon his face. 'You see, she infected me *not* with a sexually transmitted disease but instead with something far *more* ingenious, in this case a time bomb within my system that *even* the magic sponge wouldn't be able to cure.'

'What the fuck are you talking about, Billy?!'

'I suppose I *should* explain more clearly, Fabio,' he says as though replying to me in the present tense, 'it was a patent I *myself* developed whilst working at the racing team. Now, this substance can be to the benefit of your own racing car, given in *very* small doses but it can also sabotage your rivals if smuggled into one of their automobiles in *larger* dosages... Well, that deceitful woman certainly gave me a *massive* dose! And now I wait for the *full* onslaught of this destructive element so very ironically invented by me *myself*.'

'So what will happen to you, Billy?' I quiz the image onscreen.

'Spontaneous combustion!' he explains, as though sitting right here before me, 'I will spontaneously combust, that means blow up, explode, within mere hours so it's likely I'm *already* dead when you get to watch this. Well Fabio, all I can say is I'm very sorry things didn't work out between the two of us, and *all* I can do is wish you the very best luck in what you're *trying* to do. Take care now.'

The video cuts out at this point. The time-code has yesterday's date.

'Stan,' I say over the phone line in our second conversation in as many hours, 'are you available tomorrow?'

'I'll just check,' he replies, causing me to gnash my teeth: *surely* he would know whether he's working *or not* the following day?! 'I *think* I'll be able to fit you in,' he responds after a prolonged delay.

'Billy,' I call out as I knock upon his garage door, 'are you there?'

'I can try calling him again?' Stan offers.

'I'm sure there's no need,' I reply but my occasional Assistant is already doing this. To my surprise a ringtone sounds off within the workshop.

'Perhaps a car had fallen on top of him again?' the sound recordist says whilst attempting to peer inside the premises through gaps in the structure.

'*Again?*' I respond with incredulity. 'When did he tell you that?'

'I don't know,' Stan replies, 'maybe when you were busy with something else?' I demand additional data about this but he's now busy wrenching open the garage door. 'I guess Billy has ditched his security regime,' my Assistant quips as we enter to investigate inside. The shell of the car remains, as do Strauss's personal effects, only now they seem to have been ineffectually set fire to. Smoke still lingers amongst these blackened rags and only partially burnt papers.

'He was inept *even* in destroying his legacy,' I muse.

'Do you think so?' Stan retorts. 'You don't think it possible that we're actually looking at Billy?'

'I suppose if you mean this is *all* his life has amounted to then that's a fair point.'

'No Fabio, perhaps he really *has* been the victim of spontaneous combustion!?'

'What do *you* know of spontaneous combustion?!'

'You were *not* the only one to receive his last video message,' Stan replies. 'Did you not notice the *other* recipients in the e-mail?'

'I think I've got more leads on our mystery,' Stan tells me over the phone a week or so later.

'You *do*?' I query. 'I thought you were pretty much sold on the idea Billy had spontaneously combusted?'

'I'm not sure it was so spontaneous, *after all.*'

'What do you mean?'

'I returned to Stevenage to investigate further,' he earnestly continues, 'and perhaps there *is* more to this. The landlord of the garage wasn't very co-operative but the local shopkeeper had, *according to him*, been told by Billy that he was off to join a religious Order, promising to pay his store account once he was fully inaugurated within that Organization. It's possible Billy is off to Africa again.'

'All the while *still* appealing for donations, *no doubt?*'

'I'm glad you see my logic. But I have yet *another* theory concerning the disappearance of William N. F. Strauss.'

'*Enlighten me?*' I reply in a bemused tone he seems entirely blind to interpreting.

'A football Club in Mexico has just employed a manager for their team who they call *"the masked coach"!'*

'And this would be *Billy?'* I continue in the same sarcastic tone.

'I *knew* you'd be receptive to my investigation,' Stan replies guilelessly.

I have my *own* theories about Billy. Having found *no* convincing trace of him on my return to his garage, I'd picked up mail addressed to him which had survived the fire: it was only then that I'd become aware that his full name was, and likely *still is*, William Norman Frederick Strauss; this *certainly* throws up tantalizing possibilities concerning both the "*Norman*", and "*Fred*", with whom he'd been in frequent phone exchanges with. If this sounds a stretch of the imagination then I should *also* point out the bizarre coincidence concerning the two sisters "*Mary* and *Patricia*," *also* recipients of his Life coaching skills. These siblings happen to have the *same* Christian names of Billy's Mother and her only Sister, *both* of whom are still alive! If you're *still* failing to see a pattern emerging here then I should explain *another* factor that puts all this into a very sharp and specific context: amongst Strauss's surviving mail, which I'd *appropriated* on my departure, had been a telephone bill; this was to inform Billy that -as a result of prolonged *non*payment- the communications provider was cutting off his phone-line with *immediate* effect; this letter had been dated a whole month before our filming had begun!

'I don't think "*The Masked Coach*" was Billy, *after all*,' Stan tells me, two weeks after informing me of his initial theory.

'Really?' I say with what limited interest I can muster. 'Why are you not so convinced now?'

'There was a group brawl on the pitch,' he explains from the other end of the phone, 'and the Masked Coach ran on to break it up.'

'That's *all* very fascinating but *what* are you *actually* trying to tell me?'

'Well, in the fracas the Coach got *de*masked- someone pulled the disguise right off!'

'And it wasn't Billy?' I sigh.

'It wasn't *even* a man!' Stan explains excitedly. 'It was a woman!'

'Wonders *never* cease,' I groan in response.

'She did have a mustache *however*,' he adds cheerfully as though this should explain some *great* elusive mystery, 'not a ginger one like Billy's though!'

Episode Five:

Mathew: businessman.

'I am not Mathew Strauss...I don't know what this Mathew Strauss does, or have any idea who he even is- please leave me alone?!'
Mark Kermode.

'But how, and in what way precisely, would it profit a rich man to travel through the eye of a needle?'
Mathew Strauss.

A black leather-gloved hand is groping the bare bricks of a wall. This mitt then explores a selection of household furnishings before coming to rest upon an old-looking stereo system. A button is pressed which prompts the soundtrack of a crude stag-show Comedian, complete with receptive, raucous response. The location shifts to a boxing gym, and so a montage unfurls: a skipping rope; a punch bag; boxing gloves; these props are then utilized for their practical purposes. Additional images are inserted within this increasingly quick-cut sequence-manacles and work tools such as hammers, pliers and nails, *all* of which have what appears to be blood upon them. The audio becomes more bestial still, less a rowdy night out and *more* a gladiatorial celebration of torture-porn! A bruised, bloodied human arm spills from a rip in the punch bag, prompting the Viewer to speculate upon the sadistic scenario behind this. Then the equally battered, abraded head of a man also rolls out from this torn parcel. This is followed by a zoom-in upon the blackened eye which subsequently slips shut, rendering the frame in silent darkness. Out of this blackness a caption materializes: "A Mathew Strauss production."

'State your business please?' a metallic voice blasts from the exterior speaker of the apartment block.

'It's Fabio from the film production company,' I tell this disembodied Entity. There's a pause so prolonged I'm about to speak again but get intercepted by a klaxon-like din granting me entry to this new-looking structure. Once upstairs I'm about to knock upon the door specified in my most recent email correspondence when I notice it's ajar. I'm unable to peer inside yet sense that I *myself* am being appraised.

'I'm Fabio Bordino,' I reiterate, 'from the documentary film production company. I'm here to see Mr. Mathew Strauss.' Eventually the door opens wider. I'm presented with the sight of a smartly dressed, *very* tall black man wearing sunglasses.

'You've been expected,' he says at last, 'this way please.'

'Mr. Strauss?' I call out to a seemingly steel-quiffed man wearing a white bathrobe. He appears to be eating breakfast. There's a quizzical tone to my voice because whilst he *does* resemble the rest of his siblings, the person he *most* reminds me of is the respected Film Critic Mark Kermode! I *now* see the reason behind the case of mistaken identity and *subsequent* arrest.

'You're a little early for our lunch appointment,' he replies presumably by way of confirmation, 'but may I offer you brunch?'

'Lunch appointment?' I'm genuinely perplexed. 'But I was *led* to believe we were to have a short, informal-'

'You're the film guy, *right*?'

'Yes, the documentary film-maker.'

'*Documentary*?' Now it's Strauss's turn to look confused. 'Who *precisely* sent you?'

'I'm Fabio Bordino, an independent documentary film-maker with whom you have been exchanging correspondence concerning your brother, Roland?'

'Is that right?' Something about the tightening of his jaw, and chill within his tone and expression discomforts me. '*Who* precisely are you, and *what* are your credentials?'

'Did I *not* explain *all* that in the emails I sent you?'

'Refresh my memory?' Strauss transfixes me with his cobra-like stare. I sense a presence behind me, likely the tall black man who'd let me in. This, together with the fact I've not been invited to sit, increases the unease I'm feeling.

'My training, you mean?' There's no reply so I nervously continue, 'I graduated from Bournemouth University, followed by some post-graduate stuff. And my previous projects have been on diverse subjects...'

'Such as?' a low rumble from behind me comes.

'A Sports Personality,' I stammer, as a result of feeling hot breathe at the back of my neck, 'various enterprising individuals of interest and an Entertainer.'

'Spielberg must be shitting himself!' Strauss snorts back. I then notice a change in his demeanor: he lightens?

'It would *seem* there's been a misunderstanding? We've been discussing...your sibling Roland and the search for a healthy replacement kidney for him.'

'That *is* possible,' he replies. 'I was thinking about another project.'

'Is there *another* project *more* pressing than the life of your *own* brother, Mr. Strauss?' I assert boldly.

'You *actually* propose a documentary film project about my brother Roland?!' A look of incredulity spreads out across Strauss's broad features.

'Did you really get *none* of my emails at all?' I enquire, expressing my own lack of comprehension. 'But *someone* replied to them!'

'They did?' He looks concerned. 'I'm going to have to investigate this myself then get back to you, not by email for *obvious* reasons, you understand?'

'Naturally,' I reply, even though there's nothing *remotely* natural about this situation.

'My colleague Mr... Black will take your digits on your way out.'

'Thank you, Mr. Black,' I say after the tall gentleman has punched my phone number into his mobile device.

'Please call me Cyril,' he responds whilst opening the front door for my departure. 'We'll be in touch.'

'Cyril Black?' I find myself inflecting whilst stepping out of the apartment block: I'm *certain* this is the name of a Celebrity; quite possibly a famous Rapper?

'Fabio?' a not wholly unfamiliar voice enquires.

'Yes?' I affirm to this unlisted person who's called my mobile.

'Please identify yourself in *full*?'

'This is Fabio A. Bordino, documentary film maker. Is that Mr. Strauss?'

'You can call me Mathew,' the voice replies in what sounds a strained attempt at affability. 'Are you still in the vicinity?'

'I'm not *so* very far away.' I'd repaired to a nearby café in an attempt to make sense of my baffling meeting; over the preceding hour I'd several times watched the footage shot with my "button-hole" camera but remain completely in the dark concerning this confusing situation.

'That's good. My original luncheon appointment had to be terminated so I'm hoping you are still available?'

'You won't see me…you *won't* see me!' Mathew Strauss is talking to somebody on his mobile. '*What* part of that don't you understand about the *fact* that *you will not see me?!*...Listen now, for the last time-*you will not see me!*' He cuts the call then hands the phone to Mr. Black who proceeds to smash it into small pieces with a hammer before evacuating the room. 'Sorry, *where* were we?' It takes me a few seconds to surmise Mathew is speaking to me.

'Roland?'

'Of course.' He's then frowning again. '*What* did you infer from that phone call?'

'Virtually nothing at all- it was ambiguous *at best.'*

'*Really?*' he replies brightly. 'Right, Roland- how is he?'

'*Still* in need of a *healthy* kidney!'

'Draw up a list of items that will make him more comfortable.'

'Do your businesses render you *too* preoccupied to do *any* of that yourself?' I ask with a forwardness which visibly surprises Mathew. 'Have you *not* made time to visit him *yourself*?'

'Perhaps you can help me consolidate my appointments, Fabio? By the way, *what* type of businesses do you think I run?'

'From what I've witnessed so far, I imagine some kind of staff recruitment?'

'Very astute, Fabio,' he beams back. 'I do *indeed* provide services that provide the right people for the right…service. I can help you.'

'*Help me?*' I bristle, '*How so?*'

'This documentary you're trying to do, of course,' he replies with a smile. 'It can be a *mutually* beneficial enterprise.'

'I'm not sure you know *what* type of film maker I am, Mr. Strauss,' I state firmly, 'but I will *not* be appropriated by you in the ways your brothers *attempted*.'

'They *did*?' Mathew's eyes light up. He then explains at length how his own burgeoning career as a film producer had been arrested, *literally*, by a "*misunderstanding*" which "*wrongfully*" linked him to several criminal Organizations he claims to have had no knowledge of. 'Excuse me?' He's breaking off to don a pair of spectacles to read the caller I.D. on his ringing landline: these eye glasses give him the appearance of a David Bailey-era Ronnie Kray. 'What *now*?!' Strauss barks into the phone, 'this *again*?!…Do you *know* what you are? You're just static, white noise, *bad* energy *driving out* the good!…Yeah? Well the same to *you*, Mum!' With this he slams down the phone. '*What* is it with the women in my life?!'

'Perhaps you can let me know *something* about your Mother?' I enquire.

'*Every* last one a nutter! You've got my ex-wife, the disloyal, grasping bitch. Then you got the daughter I lost-'

'She *died*?' I interject out of respect.

'She *might as well have* when she *chose* to turn her womb into a turd incubator,' he spits back with scorn. Just then Mr. Black re-enters the room: could this conversation be the reason for his scowl? 'And now *this* madness from my *own* Mother?! Women will always seek to undermine men-they're *always* on mad missions such as civil rights for pot plants, petitioning to give their pet cat the vote and trying to prove that if a tree falls down in a forest then it's the *man's* fault!'

'Boss,' Cyril says at the close of this tirade, 'it's time.'

'You *still* there?' Mathew, covering his mouth, is speaking into a new mobile phone helpfully provided by Cyril. 'I've got to be careful with that deaf woman across the road...I've seen her do sign language so she might be getting employed by the Enemy. Your car?'

'*Mine*?' I reply, once I realize he's speaking to me. 'Ok, this way.'

'To my mate, the film-maker,' Mathew flips back to the conversation on the phone, 'she does all the flapping of the arms they do...Yeah, that and the seal song...*Not* Seal the musician, you nob- it's the *way* that they talk... Yeah, say *what* you like about her...*You know it!*'

'I like nice things,' Mathew purrs whilst surveying a row of brand-new high performance vehicles. I'm furthermore confused by this scenario because I hadn't anticipated our frenzied journey here *merely* to browse a car showroom. 'I'm in the position to appreciate the *finer* things in Life. To acquire them. Let's face it-*everything* is a commodity to be bought and sold.' Strauss strolls along this pride of cars, each one more impressive than the previous. I take in the *full* implications of what's been said when he comes to the end of this prestigious selection to join a statuesque woman wearing a stylish business-suit that compliments her immaculate facial bone structure. They disappear together behind a door I presume to be an office to *seal* deals.

'It's one of the *greatest* aphrodisiacs!' Mathew startles me. I'd stepped out from the showroom to check my emails and had failed to hear his approach.

'*What* is?' I'm peeved after receiving a message *not* to my liking.

'The scent of a brand new car interior.' Strauss is lighting up a disturbingly phallic cigar. 'It goes straight to my prostate gland.' Suddenly I'm violently assailed by a horrific vision of Mathew's darkest, most disturbing depths. This terrifying image troubles me all the more by working in tandem with the email I've just been sent by "Agent Provost": 'You are playing a *dangerous* game!'

'Where was I?' We're currently in what *appears* to be a lap-dancing club. The reason for my uncertainty of *precise* location is because we'd entered this venue through a nondescript shop front, which I suspect be a secret entrance.

'Vermeer?'

'Ah yes!' Mathew's eyes become reignited. 'A painting by the Dutch Master is about to become available on the open market and I'm *very* keen to acquire it.'

'*You are?*' I splutter into my tomato juice: I've been taken aback two-fold here; my initial discomfort was due to the presence of a highly unlikely dancer performing on stage; fresh astonishment comes to me now with Mathew's revelation that he sees himself as a contender to own a truly unique and iconic Artwork whose value will be tens, if not *hundreds* of millions of pounds! '*What* appeals to you about Vermeer?'

'I'm drawn to the frozen, bloodless qualities of his human forms.' This is in ripe contrast to the topless Rubenesque torso gyrating behind him. 'Ironic, really.'

'*What's* ironic?' My attention is then morbidly drawn back to the dancer, and it's only now I surmise -gleaned from a grisly glimpse of this person's over-stuffed thong- that this is a man *rather* than a woman.

'The lurid machinations utilized by those ruthless merchants to be patrons for such beauty,' Mathew embellishes. 'And now, *despite* their feeble protests, the Artists of today *still* know what side their canvas is buttered on. Our own enterprise could be very good, Fabio, a bit like John Luke Goddard, only with *better* clothes and *proper* hairstyles.'

'The Big Cheese was in touch,' Mathew tells someone on his mobile phone. We're back in his apartment. 'He said that the Big Wheel is ready to be rolled by the Big Man and there will be *no* big problem because the Big Honcho gives his blessing…Good, I'll be in touch.'

'Big up, big Mathew!' Cyril whoops at the end of this phone call then performs a lively rap and dance routine which confirms it's likely he's a famous Rapper, *possibly* with ambitions to be an Actor? 'Don't forget the big banana for the big, *big* score-bigtime!'

'This is why I didn't want you filming anything *just* yet!' Mathew says, turning to me with a scowl upon his face: a terrible realization suddenly threatens to overwhelm me; Strauss has been oblivious to me filming *all* our time together on the tiny camera secreted to my person; I hold my nerve amply to remain silent about both this and future footage I'm *hoping* to capture.

'*Why* do I have to be in the back of your car, underneath your coats?'

'We're meeting some of my film production associates,' Mathew tells me from the front passenger seat, 'and they wish to remain anonymous.'

'*They know,*' remarks Mr. Black, at the wheel.

'*What's that?*' Dread fills me when I imagine that this unfathomable duo have been aware of my candid camera *all along.*

'They know their *film* stuff,' Mathew elaborates. 'They might *even* be able to pull some strings with your *own* projects.' Could this pair be playing tricks upon me?

'Welcome back after the commercial break!' I look up blinking into the daylight to discover I must have dozed off. My Subject enlightens me, 'Forgive us for taking so long but our producer friends insisted on a casting call *too*.'

'I'll have to log you out, gentleman,' a man in an official-looking uniform says, hailing down our vehicle as we're leaving this place which I only now surmise is a large expanse of land destined for redevelopment.

'But we didn't log *in*,' Mathew tells him.

'I'm sorry sir,' the man counters, 'but it's mandatory-*everything* has to be accountable. Name please?' He's addressing Cyril, who remains silent. 'What's up with your friend here?'

'His mum told him never to speak to strangers.' Strauss replies. 'Fabio, I think we might have dropped our ticket where we were parked so can you go look for it please?'

'Please co-operate, sir,' the man persists as I climb out of the car. 'I'm not here to make the rules, *only* to enforce them.'

'Ok, the part is yours,' Mathew tells this person, who now appears to be one of the actors auditioning here today.

'I couldn't find your ticket,' I tell my companions upon my return- not surprising since I'd been obscured from view and had *even* taken a nap during my stay here.

'No biggie,' I'm told whilst getting back into the car.

'What's that noise?' I enquire during the course of our journey. 'Is something rattling in the boot?'

'Probably just some film equipment having become dislodged,' Mathew replies. I find the Parking Attendant's hat alongside me on the back seat, which confirms it was *merely* a costume prop utilized by that Actor for his rehearsal. Just as we're arriving at our destination I ask again about the disturbances to the rear of the vehicle but Strauss and his colleague are still deeply engrossed in a business-speak which *continues* to elude me.

'Not *here!* I will call you office to office,' Mathew tells somebody on his mobile. 'I *know* you haven't *literally* got an office…No, not my *actual* office…Public call box to public call box, you numpty! Get with the Programme for fuck'sake!'

'Mathew,' I say, once this call has finished, 'do you suppose we were followed back here today?' At least one vehicle had trailed our journey.

'Of course we were,' he replies blankly, which once more throws me. 'Maybe you have a theory *why* we're being watched, and *by whom?'*

'I don't know, Mathew.' Is he implicating *me* in taking part in this surveillance upon him?

'So you know nothing *at all* about the criminal charge I was on several months ago?'

'I'm aware of a charge you were *acquitted* of.'

'From *where* exactly?' Mr. Black makes his presence known at my shoulder with this highly disconcerting question.

'From a deduction of sorts,' I hear myself quaver. I dare *not* reveal my Source.

'Go on then, Sherlock,' Mathew says with relish, 'enlighten me?'

'Even though there was no media attention on your case, there has been *much* speculation on the grapevine.'

'What type of grape?' Cecil demands.

'I dare say that might be the case. And there has obviously been *some* talk in *certain* circles but just *how well* connected are you, Fabio?' Mathew's tone becomes increasing chilly, 'So Mr. Bordino, *are* you privy to shop talk in certain places such as boxing gyms and drinking establishments of a *certain* persuasion?'

'And then there's the video you sent me, *of course*,' I illuminate, after having finally recalled something which *should* help me acquit myself.

'What *type* of video?' Cyril inquistions.

'Mr. Strauss's trailer for a proposed feature film- the very *same* one that his Legal Defense used to exonerate him, *of course.*'

'That's possible,' Mathew concedes though I'm furthermore flustered by what comes next, 'but it has *not* escaped me what has been happening to my family in the past few months, Fabio.'

'The interviews with your brothers concerning finding a suitable kidney donor among them for your sibling Roland, *you mean?*' I put in as innocuous a way as I can muster.

'Yes,' Mathew replies, grim-faced, 'those misfortunes that have befallen my poor brothers during, or perhaps *because of,* your filming.'

'Mr. Strauss,' I contest, 'my quest has been to *prolong* the life of your brother Roland so I can *hardly* be blamed for the irresponsible lifestyles of the rest of them. Forgive me for saying but they seem *hell-bent on self-destruction*, and I don't think pointing a…recording device at them would induce them to speed up *that* process!' I'm now *especially* self-conscious of the secret button-hole camera which has been my *constant* companion.

'Not a bad opening gambit,' Mathew smirks, 'but let's look at the evidence for the prosecution. Kevin and Billy have gone missing, Dougie is back to shitting his pants again and Robby has gone *right* off his pussy.'

'Prosecution?!' I implore. '*Is this a trial?!*'

'So Fabio,' Strauss continues, 'if indeed that is your *real* name, what *precisely* is going on? *What* have you been doing to my family? Are you, as I suspect, serving as some kind of *scourge* upon the brothers Strauss? Is it your objective to *wipe them out* to a man with this proverbial *curse* of yours?... Well – is *that* it?...*What are you doing to my family?!*'

'I… That…really *isn't*…the case.' This is *all* I can manage.

'Sayeth the guilty man,' Mathew retorts, seemingly staring into the very core of my being. What he declares next makes me grateful to be seated because I feel I'm about to faint, 'You've probably done me a *huge* favour with those brothers of mine.'

'But… I *don't* understand?' This is putting it mildly!

'They are one torrent of shit after another,' my current Subject helpfully explains in a brighter hue, 'take a *relatively* inoffensive one like Peter, whom you are fortunate enough *not* to have met.'

'As a Subject?' I remain perplexed as to *precisely* where this is leading.

'Peter joined the army *just because* I bet him he wouldn't! He's been a *constant* source of embarrassment to me. I had to take him off doing the door at a nightclub I had partnership in after a shameful cross-dressing incident – I really *can't* have somebody like that representing me.'

'Does that make him *such* a bad person?' I reason, hoping to get to the bottom of this bewildering exchange.

'If only it were *just* that,' Strauss continues, 'I then gave him a perfectly legal courier job which also turned into a humiliating experience for the *whole* family.'

'How so?'

'Then you've got that retard Robby, who you unfortunately *have* already met, running around on his perverted little projects – Dad really should *not* have hired him out for medical trials as a kid.'

'He *did*?!'

'Do you know Robby's mission statement recently imparted to me?' Mathew sighs. 'This is in response to me asking him if he had any profound theories on *the meaning of Life*, and how best to live it, and *here* was his reply – "Abolish soft porn because it is hated by both porn-lovers and porn-haters alike." *That* is his theory for world peace! Then you've got those other coprophiliac cowboys Douglas, Kevin and Billy, *all of those* pointless pricks poisoned by whatever *pus* is pissing through their scum-osphere. Thanks Fabio, you've *really* been providing a *useful* service for me there!'

I'm still dazed after having been chauffeured home that evening. This state of mental apoplexy remains even after I've several times watched the secretly-filmed footage shot earlier. I log onto the internet to discover I still have no further messages from my clandestine friend within the police constabulary: has this person tired of correspondence with me, *or worse still*, gotten wind of, and taken offence with my fraternization with Mathew Strauss?

I'm then compelled over the next few hours to examine my *own* motives for this uneasy new acquaintance. Having collated nothing more profound than wishing to progress with my project, and perhaps use *whatever* advantages my most recent Subject might be able to offer, I return to my internet device to compose an email. With the exception of Mathew I address *all* the brothers Strauss, including Peter (the sole sibling I've yet to meet) with the following message –

"Greetings Agent Provost – *what's new?!*"

'So can you match that?' Mathew is once more on the phone. Cyril, wearing yellow rubber gloves, is scrubbing plates and cutlery with a washing-up brush while his Boss, mobile pressed between shoulder and ear, dries these items with a tea-towel. I've been drawn back to the office again today by some strangely unfathomable gravity which defies *any* type of logical definition. We're in the kitchenette area. 'So can you match that?... Ali, just answer the question – *can you match that price?*...*I've got my phone rules too, such as bin the burners after a move and *never* speak on landlines or in cars but… Oh, it's *not* a code-name?... Your *real* name *is* Ali?!... Cover your *own* tracks then…So you *can't* match that then?... Ok, I'll go to the Pakis then – the Tooting Taliban don't haggle like this… *Too late now!*' With this Strauss drops the mobile into the soapy water.

'*New* move then?' Cyril asks while retrieving the phone from the sink and, possibly absent-mindedly, scrubs it with his washing-up brush.

'Mathew,' I remark once this baffling chore has been completed, 'may I address you about *something* I've noticed?' He nods to Cyril, who subsequently leaves the immediate vicinity. 'I've noticed you have used *certain* terminology that *should*, in our more enlightened era, be deemed *unacceptable*-I'm referring most specifically to his racist use of the word'-

'What you need to consider, Fabio,' Strauss cuts in whilst inducing me to join him sitting at what I assume to be his conference table, 'is that I *distinguish* myself from those around me by my ability to be objective and aware of *all* around.' I notice a plastic water bottle on the table to his side, which seems to have been adapted for some other use. 'That is the secret of my success.' He's still seemingly oblivious to this object which reminds me of something I can't *quite* define at this precise moment, 'Inasmuch as the measure of those lacking, and who subsequently fail and fall.'

"Fail and fall" how, and in *what* way precisely?' I remain distracted by the plastic container within reach of Mathew: it's covered not by a bottle top but instead by silver baking foil; a broad plastic straw protrudes from an incision just below this.

'Whilst the majority of people scramble about, imprisoned in the moment, I function *both* in *that* moment, and to shape the moment *to come*, cast within the image of my *own* choosing.'

'A *visualization* technique? A positive image you can forge within your mind's eye to achieve your goals?'

'I'm able to have an Objectivity to *everything* around me,' he continues, with referral neither to myself nor to the makeshift bottle just inches from him. 'It is *my* machine of industry manipulating events that *I alone* have fashioned. I am thus free from these machinations.' It's only now Strauss notices the object so very close to him. Without warning he lashes out, sending this plastic bottle flying across the room and causing it to spill its contents upon impact against the conference room floor: ash and discoloured water stain the previously-pristine carpet; the straw ricochets under a nearby two-seater settee.

'Someone must have left a *film* prop! Or perhaps the habit of one of those thespian types?!'

'Boss,' Cyril calls out across the room, causing me to jump. I've been helping tidy the room up. Mr. Black hands his employer yet another new mobile phone.

'Peter?' Strauss responds, '*How* did you get this number *so* soon?... But *who* gave it to you?!... Best you think *who* that might have been then...No Peter, I owe you *nothing*...not *even* for Mum-*this is goodbye!*' I'm suspecting that *this* Peter is likely to be his brother, the sole Strauss sibling I've yet to meet. 'This completely illustrates my point!' It seems I'm being addressed again at long last, 'People like *that* only serve to distract those who've *actually* got something worthwhile to do.'

'Perhaps *I* could approach him?'

'*Why* would you want to do *that*?!' Mathew is glaring at me as though I've said something deeply suspicious, offensive even.

'To be the donor for Roland.' I'm attempting to make this sound as innocuous as possible: perhaps stress, fatigue and frustration are getting the better of me? It seems reckless for me to continue to covertly film these meetings but I'm forced by some strange compulsion I remain unable to *fully* comprehend.

'Put your filming on hold for the time being.'

'*Time being?*'

'There *is* an alternative possibility.'

'*There is?*' Could he be aware I've been filming *all this?*

'A business associate has some potential donors from South America,' Strauss informs me. 'We might use Peter *only* as a last resort.'

'I've noticed that you are *very* hard on your brothers.' I'm aware my observation is trivial in comparison to the thrilling possibility that my Project may *additionally* cover the themes of migrant exploitation and the illicit traffic in human organs!

'It is likely this comes from our upbringing,' Mathew explains, 'our father was a very physical man, perhaps he was over-compensating for having virtually *no* personality of his *own*. He kept us in check with a *reasoned* regime of calculated brutality. This was *until* his physical strength began to wane.'

'That's when you and your brothers became more independent? More challenging of his authority?'

'Indeed, it was then down to *me* to restore Dad's physical form of order to squash Billy's woeful sporting embarrassments and Dougie's attempts to undermine and ultimately *destroy* the *whole* family with his singing.'

'Was that *really* your brother's intentions?' I splutter back.

'We *all* have our *own* ways of showing contempt, Fabio.' I'm sensing he's now scrupulously searching for some sign of this within *me*?

'Is your father at rest now, Mathew?' So far this specific information has *continued* to elude me.

'In Eastbourne,' he sighs, 'not *quite* as dead as my brothers might have probably told you. Dad is quite comfortable now thanks to me, and *in spite of* all my siblings.'

'Look, I'll help you track him down *myself*,' an athletic man of around thirty pleads in a Liverpudlian accent, 'it was *him* who's robbed ya' -*not me!*' He clings to a dancer's pole, wearing only an over-stuffed thong in a bizarre reprise of my previous visit to this lap-dance club: this person is *less* enthusiastic than the previous performer; his face is red and puffy; he appears to be showing signs of distress?

'Put a bit more effort into it,' Mathew induces, '*how* are you going to pay off debts with *such* a lacklustre approach?' This is too outlandish a situation for me to take seriously: the *only* explanation possible is that this is a strange *Actorly* exercise, or *another* pre-planned rehearsal like the one several days previously where I'd witnessed a hammy thespian doing a broad-take on a zany, bumbling car park attendant.

'And for your next scene,' Cyril sing-songs, which confirms my theory, 'a fancy dress party-you've come as a pin-ball!' Mr. Black proceeds to wrap this actor in a length of duct tape. Strauss urges me to join him for refreshment at a bar *elsewhere* within the club. Soon the music blasts yet louder from the area we've just left. It's both heavy and *irregular* on the percussion.

I wake up sweating and trembling. Unable to either get back to sleep or recall the *precise* anatomy of my nightmare, I log onto the internet to read emails I'd been too weary to check earlier. There's still no response from my Police contact but Robby Strauss - *of all people*- has replied to my group *"round-Robin"/"Agent Provost"* email. Equally surprising (considering our less than cordial last meeting) is the fact there's *no* trace of resentment or suspicion in his message back to me, *if anything* I sense gratitude! These sentiments would be best served in his own words-

Dearest Fabio,

Firstly I'd like to take the opportunity to thank you for your help in my growth as an Artist. Blooming under your *adoring* gaze I felt inspired to write my life story and before I knew it *I've only gone and got myself* an agent who connects me both to a *proper* documentary guy (no offence intended!) *and* a bidding war among publishers *desperate* for my autobiography! Because the working title is "Mammary-Speak!" I'm getting compared to some dead Ruski, Vlad the Nobokov (or *something* like that) but I wasn't too impressed after a Google search reveals his book called 'Latoya' is all about a *nonce*!

Another potential publisher tells me I could be the new Marco Proust, *not* the racing driver. This one had a bird called Madelaine and apparently he liked to eat little cakes out of her lady parts so *that certainly sounds a bit of me!*

I'm guessing you're on the brink of your *own* massive break so I'll sign off here.

All the best,

your friend Robby.

P.S. -you mentioned the name Agent Provost- any relation to the adult movie performer Pablo "Pecker-Power!" Provost?

Sensing *no* further light has been shed on this subject I retire for the night. It's only when back in bed am I *fully* revisited by the night terrors from earlier: here is something *even more* monstrous than my memory of Robby Strauss attempting to marshal a mob of masturbating maniacs; assailing *all* my senses within this nightmare, I'd been shrunken in size then placed deep within the darkest chasm of Mathew Strauss's prostate! Needless to say *no* further sleep was forthcoming this night.

'

'You won't see me...You *won't* see me!' I'm getting a sense of *deja vu:* drawn back to Mathew's apartment -*still* secretly filming him against my better judgment- I'm witness to a bizarre phone conversation which feels word for word like one that's *already* occurred.

The buzzer alerts us we have a visitor. I observe Strauss watching the entrance of the building on CCTV before casting my own glance. For a split-second I have the uncanny impression I witness *myself* standing there! After looking again - having rubbed my eyes- I realize there *must have* been a trick of the light because it's now plain to see that the man captured within the video-entry screen looks almost my *polar* opposite: he's got the physique of a rugby player, *no* spectacles, square of jaw and with casual-dress in *contrast* to my *own* appearance, which is *always* formal.

'Teddy!' Mathew greets this man after nodding to Mr. Black to open the front door. Upon entry this visitor remains silent and produces an A-3 sheet of paper which he presents to us: "*Azure*" is written in big, bold letters. Strauss looks confused so this person drops this sheet. Another message on a successive piece of paper underneath reads, *"That means this place is bugged!"*

'Fucking hell!' exclaims Cyril as he strolls off elsewhere within the apartment. 'Who invited Bob Dylan?!'

'Teddy Boy!' The two embrace like long-lost best friends. 'It's good to have you back.'

'It's good *to be* back!' Teddy enthuses. 'Grab your speedos, boss- let's do a sauna.'

'You just want to see me in my budgie-smugglers, you homer!' Strauss counters. Both men laugh as though sharing a private joke. 'I've got a *better* idea.'

'What's all that static from the macaroon?' Teddy asks Mathew. For some inexplicable reason we're currently inside a car wash. Tellingly, they are upfront while I occupy the back seat.

'I want you to deal with people who *won't* have it with him, and for him to see people you *wouldn't* want to know.' I have the impression they are discussing Cyril; it has not escaped me that "*macaroon*" is very probably a racist term; I shall at some point have to address my Subject with both this and his previous *bigoted* insistence that Asian people are likely to join the Taliban and other terrorist organizations.

'You're the boss, *boss*,' Teddy replies from the front passenger seat. With a backdrop of furious soapsuds gyrating against the wind-screen I study the younger man's finely-chiseled profile: there seems something familiar about his Classical good looks; in an *alternative* turn of events he could *quite possibly* have been a Movie Star! 'Thanks for the big break, boss, I *won't* be letting you down. I know how you were like a big brother to my *own* big brother.'

'I'm not doing this for him,' Mathew retorts. 'I'm doing it for *you* because I know you've got your head screwed on. You're dependable and are prepared to do *whatever* it takes.'

'My brother used to tell me all about your firm,' Teddy relays fondly, 'the Nutty Boys!'

'That was madness,' Strauss chuckles, 'then we evolved into *the Nutty Farmers*. Still, nostalgia ain't what it used to be.'

'You're right, before you know it mugs begin pining for "on the buses"!'

'Man about the house?' the older man counters as though this is another private joke.

'Needs eviction!'

'Eh?' I see Mathew frowning in the reflection of the sun visor. 'Is that another old pop reference?'

'Right up there with you, boss,' the younger man replies, 'I was referring to your tired, worn-out ancient mate- *"Love thy neighbour"!'* Both of them explode with laughter in another seemingly coded counter-point which continues to *completely* confound me. Eventually the mirth, together with the vigorous machinations of the carwash, subsides. I look up to see that Mathew is now studying me intently within his mirror.

'How's your mate?' Mr. Black says by way of greeting whilst I follow Mathew back into his apartment after having dropped Teddy home.

'Are you talking shit to me?!' Strauss suddenly roars. This is the *first* time I've heard him raise his voice. It appears to be a rare occurrence because Cyril looks shocked then turns to me with an expression somewhere between alarm, embarrassment and quite possibly resentment towards me for having witnessed *such* a furious outburst. Mathew is quieter in tone when he speaks again but no less commanding, 'Make yourself useful and give me that fucking new burner!' His Assistant obediently hands Strauss a mobile phone which he snatches before strutting away to make more calls. I find myself shadowing him, not least to escape the menacing glare of Mr. Black. 'Just keep the book of true crime stories by your phone,' my Subject instructs someone (likely to be a film production assistant) ,'You got it- you were telling a mate a story from the book…We're all covering our arses, mate…Yes, that we were discussing

the screenplay with that Producer we know…Yes, the C.P.S. will shit in their pants if you were to bring in *those* character witnesses…You know it!'

'He doesn't believe you for one minute so *don't* try to deceive yourself,' Mr. Black tells Teddy, who's just arrived with what looks like a metal detector, which he proceeds to hold aloft and pace up and down the living-room with. 'Bugging devices *which can turn themselves on and off when voice-activated?!* You're having a giraffe!'

'I don't know *what* you're talking about, pal,' Teddy calmly replies, 'I'm just doing some spring-cleaning.'

'*You fit?*' Mathew has reappeared after having completed his calls. Cyril rises from the settee but Strauss strolls past him to hand his car-keys to Teddy.

'Don't wait up', Teddy tells a glowering Mr. Black as we leave.

'Looks like my hooter after a big charlie session,' Teddy says as Mathew places a round red plastic nose upon him. We're parked near a hospital. I'm now a backseat witness to an even more peculiar scene: the younger man's face is pasty after having been heavily-applied with white foundation; he wears a shaggy green wig and this claret blob completes his transformation into a clown. 'Have you got one of those flowers that instead of squirting water, fires bullets?'

'*Very* funny!' Mathew cuts in. 'Remember to bust up the piece afterwards and drop it down a succession of drains.'

'Are you sure about this?' asks the now completely unrecognizable Entity, who'd look more at home under a big tent.

'As soon as he's out of hospital he'll be gunning for us,' Strauss is quick to reply, 'or at the very *least* will be going the wrong way concerning the Old Bill. Putting one in his nut is the *only* remedy.'

'No, I *meant* the outfit,' Teddy chuckles.

'Come on, *who'd* ever suspect a children's entertainer?'

'Part of your script?' I ask, after the younger man has made off towards the hospital.

'What's that?' It's likely Mathew had forgotten I'd been present: my "fly-on-the-wall' credentials remain intact. 'Oh yeah, *part* of the script. Sit up front with me?'

'A couple of your brothers mentioned clowns,' I remark, once we're back on the road.

'They did*!?*' My Subject suddenly looks pale. 'In *what* context?'

'Just in general.' For some inexplicable reason I've lost my nerve to enquire if the term *"agents of destruction"* (a phrase used by *several* of the Strauss siblings) might mean anything to him. 'Probably just a childhood thing?'

'Let me tell you something about childhood,' he counters with an abrupt change of demeanour, 'I wore spectacles.'

'And?' I retort with bemusement. 'So did *I*, and as you can *clearly* see, I *still* do!'

'No Fabio, you *don't* seem to understand. What you *need* to know is that my eyesight was 20:20 - perfect.'

'Why was *that*?' I'm forced to ask after comprehension continues to elude me.

'It was my Father's idea,' Mathew replies in a manner which could best be described as wistful. 'I can't explain *fully* but here's something on my device which might be more enlightening.' I'm then subjected to a song called "A boy named Sue" by somebody called Johnny Mash. 'You understand now?'

'Yes Mathew,' I respond as the music fades away, '*all* very understandable now.' The truth is, *however*, that I don't *even remotely* infer what message, *if any,* is being conveyed here. 'He looks very familiar,' I say in an attempt to change the subject, 'your friend Teddy.'

'Of course he does,' Strauss replies without a beat, 'he's the actor Tom Hardy'.

'The Movie Star?!' I splutter back. 'But *why* do you call him Teddy?'

'His character in the intended film we're making is called Teddy, and because Tom in a method-style actor he *insists* on getting called that both throughout pre-production and during actual filming. I *hope* you will keep that in your confidence and respect that integrity, Fabio?'

'Here's to a *very* special birthday boy,' Teddy/Tom says, raising a glass, 'a very happy birthday to my *dearest* friend and mentor, happy birthday Mathew.'

'Happy birthday Mathew,' a chorus of friends and associates chime in. Cyril's salutation is less enthusiastic. *None* of the other Strauss brothers are present, possibly for the reason they've *chosen* to celebrate elsewhere, in their *own* separate ways. Once more we're at the lap-dance club. *Thankfully* there are no nearly-nude male dancers present here tonight.

'Here Boss,' Teddy/Tom announces, 'a special surprise for you.' This is the cue for three other men to emerge from amidst the other party-goers then approach him and Mathew at the stage area. A jittery Mr. Black springs into action, breaking free from the throng to clutch at something inside his jacket breast pocket. 'Chill out, chief!' Teddy/Tom responds, 'just a little something we prepared earlier.' He's then joined by the trio to perform a slightly mistimed but spirited song and dance number compromising of many film references, including several gangster movie allusions I recognize *in spite of* my indifference and only limited knowledge of this particular genre. At the close of this -concluding with an outbreak of "jazz hands"- a polite amount of applause is elicited from those present. A single pair of hands supersedes this, albeit in a slow clap.

'That was the whitest thing I've *ever* seen!' Cyril calls out, alerting all of his *un*favourable response to this performance.

'It was just a bit of light-hearted fun,' Teddy/Tom replies, 'so *what* have you got?!'

'Behold, a fitting gift for a prince,' Cyril declares as he moves towards a tall, round, covered table. He pulls the fabric away to reveal a giant birthday cake. 'Happy birthday Boss!' There's a prolonged silence. Eventually Black looks awkward then projects *louder still* with his vocal tribute. Still nothing, which prompts him to kick the "*cake*", subsequently revealing it to be not a soft confection but some solid facsimile *posing* as one. A few titters escape from those present, which causes a grimacing Cyril to storm over to another area of the club. He then bursts into the ladies' toilet before emerging again a few seconds later with a scantily-clad blonde female, whom he grips by the hair. He drags this person, whose face is coated with a mass of white powder – perhaps she *too* has *overdone* it with the foundation?- to the area he'd made his premature announcement. 'Get in the cake!' he commands her, 'you are fucking this up – *get in the fucking cake!*' Several of the party-goers (mostly mature couples) display signs of disapproval. Some of these slip away to leave the premises.

'A slight misjudgement, would you admit?' Ted/Tom puts to Mr. Black. The party has whittled down to just these two, myself, Mathew and a *different* female, this time a brunette in a similar state of *un*dress. She's spent most of her time here at the apartment (where the soiree has reconvened) sniffing at some white substance splayed across the elegant marble kitchen surfaces. 'Is not the girl supposed to jump out of the cake *before* everybody sees her?'

'You're just another johnny-come-lately,' Cyril growls in response. 'I've seen off a dozen opportunist tramps like you!' I'm taken aback by this abrasive language: could this be some form of unconventional actors' workshop roleplay?

'The little fella hasn't got faith in you *anymore*,' Teddy/Tom counters, 'this is why he's now brought me onboard.' Is it possible these two Thespians are in competition for the *same* part in Mathew's film production? Colour-blind casting *would* be admirable, *if nothing else.*

'One wrong move chief,' Cyril emotes through a gritted, pearly beam punctuated by an occasional gold tooth, 'and you'll be in the ground. Prepare yourself to be land-fill!'

'Knock off the flirting, you two!' Mathew has reappeared. He's shadowed by the immodestly-attired female. She offers a rolled-up banknote to her fellow party guests together with an incline of her head towards a table laden with several long, thick lines of white powder. Whilst Strauss partakes of these I observe Cyril sidle alongside a series of kitchen drawers. He discreetly opens one and, in a flowing motion, removes a carving knife before spinning with the grace of a dancer to tuck it into the back waistband of his trousers. I imagine I'm the sole witness to this before looking over to see that Teddy/Tom has also noticed. With a smirk on his face the younger man approaches Black then pats his own pocket, in what could *possibly* be a message to convey he has his *own* party piece to perform *should* this occasion call for it? *All at once* I feel as though my nose has been *violently* assailed! I stagger back against the kitchen fittings. It takes me a few seconds to process the fact that the lone lady present has shoved a *considerable* amount of white powder -which I suspect to be drugs!- into both my (soon throbbing) nostrils.

'Get in the party spirit!' she tells me in a surprisingly cut-glass, upper-class accent.

'*Is that cocaine*?' I'm aware my question might make me appear a little naïve and unsophisticated.

'Oh, *my*!' She turns to the others, quaking with laughter. 'Where did you find *this one*?!' My next shock comes when I'm suddenly and all too distressingly aware that I'm desperately in need of a bowel movement- and so I dash off in haste to the nearest bathroom!

'*Such* a sensitive soul,' I hear the woman giggle as I slam and lock the door, wrestle with my underwear and place my posterior down upon the pan *just in time!* As what seems like everything I've consumed over the last few days -and much more besides- erupts from my lower orifice like distempered lava, I become aware of only *one certain, undeniable* fact: cocaine is an *extremely expensive* laxative! From my new throne, an extremely nicely designed toilet (see my observations on this *very* subject *earlier* in my transcript) I hear music blast out elsewhere within the apartment, and surmise that the party has stepped up a notch in my absence.

'*What's happened?!*' I ask upon my return, feeling several kilos lighter: our female guest is now sprawled out across the floor, blood is protruding from her nose, and there are traces of *other* wounds about her person; Mr. Black is attending to her; Teddy, seemingly oblivious to *all* this, is performing a peculiar dance.

'This was a mistake,' Mathew laments. 'I knew I *should* have supplied jelly and ice-cream.'

'Boss,' Cyril -failing to get a response from his lady friend- cries out in despair, 'I didn't sign up for *this*!'

'Who would win in a fight between library tramp and the smelly old bloke who lives in the park?' Mathew is *again* on the phone. I've made a morning visit to his office in accordance to him summoning me here. His Assistants –unusually- are nowhere to be seen. 'No, it's *not* code, it's a TV-pitch…I've got my film-maker mate here who's getting urged to make his documentaries *more* commercial.' This part of the transcript is a succinct way to economize explaining my *current* predicament! 'Ok, back to *why* I called you-they lifted Silly-bollocks from his *garage*…I know, and I thought they were going to do something that might *actually* affect or upset me?!' Strauss laughs. 'Here, does "you-know-who" have a healthy kidney?...Never mind, *just* curious- I'll be in touch.'

'Mathew,' I eventually enquire, 'does either the name *"Agent Provost"* or the term *"agents of destruction"* mean anything to you?'

'It's an internet glitch,' he replies, 'for all I know they are onto me there *too*.'

'Who is *"they"*?'

'Wait!' My Subject turns to glare at me from across his desk. It *only now* occurs to me that he'd already started *another* phone call, therefore had been responding to *somebody else*. 'Go on, the auction…Yes, *literally* the auction…It's *not* a euphemism- it's for the Vermeer coming up for sale…Vermeer, the Dutch master, you philistine!...How's *that*?!' I realize Strauss is *finally* addressing me. 'He reckons he's never been anywhere *near* Israel!' He returns to whoever is on the phone-line, 'Of course I'll get it. They *can't* stop me like last time…I'll be in touch.'

'What, *or who,* previously stopped you acquiring a Vermeer, Mathew?' I ask once he's terminated this conversation.

'The usual type of thing,' he sighs, 'redirected Governmental forces sticking an oar into the spokes of Trade and Industry, rivals using processes to discredit me, poor business advice, *Lord rest them*, and the trifle of a custodial sentence I happened to be serving at the time.'

'Let's hope nothing like that impedes you this time.' I'm hoping this sounds inspiring. Strauss's reaction is merely a long, silent stare that seems to peer into my very soul. It comes as a relief when he receives yet another phone call.

'Film *everything*,' Mathew tells me, *'don't miss a thing.'* This strikes me as *deeply* ironic because I've *already* been secretly documenting him for the past few weeks but it's only now he *gives* his consent -even encouragement- to be filmed. We're in a warehouse less than a mile from both his office and home. I pan along a line of around a dozen olive-skinned males, ages varying between late teens to early-mid 40s. The source of my bewilderment is due to the fact they've *all* been stripped to their briefs/undershorts. Strauss is seated at a desk, flanked by Mr. Black and Teddy/Tom. Each man *is in* turn summoned, processed with paperwork, issued with what looks like medication (a zoom-in with my camera reveals these to be laxatives) and a loo roll before told to join a new queue for a toilet. The most recent Applicant -this has all the appearance of *another* rehearsal- whispers something to Cyril who, looking confused, relates this message to Mathew, who subsequently is also visibly baffled. The man is compelled to go through a series of mimes before eventually the penny drops, resulting in Strauss producing a pair large of tongs which this performer eagerly *accepts* before moving onto the *next* part of his Casting process. Another man -who has expressed interest in my camera - gives me a silent yet histrionic greeting. Unlike most of the others waiting (several of whom cover their face for some reason) he chooses to show his stagy display ahead of processing, and so goes through a series of graceful movements culminating in him acting out a *"man-in-a-box"* routine, which he's *clearly* been rehearsing at length.

'I think I get it now, Mathew,' I call out once the last man has been processed.

'You *do*?'

'Yes,' I respond with modest though justified pride in my deduction, 'I would say these gentleman are attending the up-coming, World-famous London Mime Festival.'

'*Nothing* escapes you, Fabio,' Strauss replies with a chuckle. I then furnish him with the fact I'd attended last year's event, and had been especially impressed by the winner, who'd given a *very* poignant depiction of the oppressive regime currently afflicting his homeland, *all* within his chosen medium of voiceless performance.

'Anyone who persecutes Mimes can't be *all* bad,' Teddy/Tom remarks as I'm guided to the exit.

'Get that footage to me tomorrow please?' Mathew asks whilst walking me to my vehicle.

'*Which footage?*'

'This footage here today, *of course*,' he replies without expression. 'I need to finish up here so I'll be in touch.'

'Of course.' I'm curious about something recently much on my mind. 'Your friend Teddy…'

'*Yes?*' I can tell that my Subject is keen to get back to his business in hand.

'He's been saying a few things that have made me doubt his authenticity.'

'He *has?!*' Suddenly I have Strauss's undivided attention.

'What, you *mean* like he's a bubble, *a wrong 'un?!*'

'I'm not sure I'd *precisely* put it like *that*, Mathew.' I'm unfamiliar with his terminology, and so attempt to be more succinct, 'I was referring to his take on Strasberg and Stanislavsky.'

'Fabio, tell me now -*what the fuck are you on about?!*'

'Well, concerning Tom's, or *rather* Teddy's, approach…'

'Spit it out, Bordino, *before* we die of old age!'

'Well, is Teddy, *or rather* Tom… is he *his* character? Or is *he*, well, *him?* Precisely *how far* does this Method "thing" go? I mean, surely when he's walking up the red carpet at his latest film premiere he can't *still* be thinking that he's his film's *character?* Is "*he*" always *his* most recent role? Perhaps "he's" never really Tom, *at all?*'

'He's not really Tom at all,' Mathew confirms as he heads back to the warehouse, 'in reality he's that *other* actor, Jack O'Connell.'

'They're gone!'

'*Who*'s gone?' I'm hastily dragged inside Strauss's apartment.

'My boys,' Mathew replies once he's guided me to the settee in his front room.

'*Your* boys?' I confess to being confused: I'd heard him refer to a daughter, albeit in derogatory terms, but *never once* a son or sons.

'My boys, *of course!*' Only now do I realize he's referring to Teddy/Jack O'Connell, the actor, and Cyril, the rapper. It seems as though Strauss has become relaxed concerning his *usually* immaculate appearance: the suit has been replaced with a grubby bathrobe; he's red-eyed and unshaven; even his customary coiffure has degenerated into a tufted expanse of wire wool! 'You *won't* be seeing them…Just before I was going to join them at the pub I got a message to stay away.'

'They had a falling out with each other?' The toxic masculinity betwixt these two men had not gone *wholly* unnoticed.

'Worse,' Mathew replies grimly as he sinks into an armchair, 'apparently they bumped into a group of jokers, verbal banter had begun but soon went bad.'

'I take it this *wasn't* with the Mimes?'

'It seems Cyril and Ted turned on these people, and gone a *little bit* Old Testament on them unfortunately. It turns out these wankers they threw acid over were off-duty Coppers and so the CCTV coverage got seized *immediately*…Cameras, *eh*?'

'*Cameras*?' I'm beginning to suspect *Mathew's* claim that "*Teddy*" is the actor Jack O'Connell is *not entirely* reliable.

'They will be the end for *all* of us.' This sends a shiver down my spine. I observe Strauss closely and cautiously to see if he's insinuating anything concerning me personally but detect little of the cool, collected, calculating, often slightly menacing man I'd gotten to know over the preceding weeks: he looks vulnerable, raw, as though stripped of some *vital* veneer *essential* to his existence; I *almost* felt sorry for him.

'Mathew,' I venture, sensing the time is right to approach a *very* specific and pertinent point, 'considering the high-profile natural multiple birth, the fact that the Media were initially enamored with these highly rarified Sextuplets, *why* did the

Public Eye then close, *or be prevented from* seeing your collective developments?'

'*In plain and simple English please, Fabio?*' Strauss beseeches, as though in pain.

'*Why* did the cameras never come back to you as a family?' I flesh this out in the most direct way possible. '*Surely* the World would have wanted to know what was next for these six brothers *all born at the same time?* I *can't* believe the Public would *no longer* be curious about the way you might all *later differ*, or possibly even all develop in a *similar* way to your other siblings. So Mathew, why was there *never* a sequel to the original documentary about the birth of you and your brothers?'

'The sins of the Father,' he eventually murmurs.

'So it *was* something to do with your Dad?' My supposition is met merely with a sullen silence.

After leaving Mathew's apartment I log into my emails to check for further developments. At last another of the brothers Strauss (Robby's reply was of *no* use at all) has gotten back to my *"round-robin,"* in this case Peter, the *sole* sibling I've *yet* to meet in person: his refreshingly succinct response is thus:

"Any relation to Adrian Provost? Perhaps we can discuss sometime? Peter."

I begin to mentally compose a response whilst scrolling down the rest of my messages but my train of thought is halted, *wrecked even*, by a highly anticipated reply from my contact within the Police Force. There's an apology for the delay, citing preoccupation with a time-consuming criminal case. I then read I've been invited for a drink in Central London this very evening, an offer I *immediately* accept both by email and text message.

This Acquaintance is already comfortably installed within a booth at our arranged location when I arrive. After a warm greeting I am poured a glass of wine from an expensive looking bottle on the table. Even though I'm virtually teetotal I reason it would be churlish *not* to accept, and so I partake whilst catching up with news this friend has for me. He's fully informed about the movements of Mathew Strauss and his colleagues, more so even than I and proceeds to elaborate upon the finer, *more gruesome* details of the violent pub incident, which go far in excess of the *all-too-brief* account the Media had *merely* touched upon. He puts the correct names to these two men involved- *neither* of whom (as I'd previously been *led* to believe) is an actor or rapper! I'm expecting him to ask if *I myself* can contribute additional information but this enquiry is *not* forthcoming. Moreover, he seems happy to furnish me with *yet more* Intel, *possibly* as a result of feeling guilty for not having gotten in touch sooner. In such charming company I find myself responsive to more wine, and when another bottle is ordered -on *his* expense account- I feel *quite* powerless to resist. Another hour or so passes amiably enough but tiredness creeps up on me, therefore I ask to be excused to make my way home. I'm offered a taxi but since public transport would serve me most amply I decline. And so we leave together after exchanging a fond farewell and a promise from him to be provided with *more* data *very* soon.

It is only when I get home -after having dozed off on the train- that I discover my discreet surveillance camera (I'd still been wearing during my meeting) has been either lost or stolen. I admonish myself for such carelessness, and find scarce relief only *after* remembering I'd already downloaded most of the footage of Mathew. I remain remorseful however that the original material and device is *no longer* within my possession.

Having gone to bed, sleep strangely eludes me. I turn on the television to catch up on current affairs. A few minutes pass before a news item emerges which has *yet more* ramifications for Mathew Strauss.

'I felt I had to come,' I tell Mathew after receiving a surprisingly warm greeting upon arrival at his apartment.

'All ok?' he asks breezily as I take a seat in his living room. I'm suddenly dumb-stuck, not *least* because I'd expected to find him in the same dishevelled state I'd encountered only yesterday. The evidence before me *however* is of the *complete* restoration of immaculate hairstyle, characteristically expensive, *flawlessly-* tailored suit, crisp shirt and tasteful alligator loafers. Even his new spectacles give him less the Ronnie Kray-look, *more now in semblance to* a *respectable* investments banker.

'I've got some bad news for you, Mathew.'

'Why?' he responds with a sardonic smirk. 'Somebody *else* has snuffed it?'

'In a sense- you missed the Vermeer auction.'

'I know,' he retorts with a shrug, 'unfortunately I was preoccupied with a few things. Would you mind if I make a few calls?'

'Sure, while you do that I can help clear up?' But when I cast a glance around the apartment I see that it's been reinstated to the spotless, palatial majesty in which I'd *initially* encountered it.

'I said tidy up but that's taking the piss!' I turn back to observe that Strauss has already proceeded with his telephone communications. '*All* he had to do was wipe the dabs away so what's he want to burn the *whole* fucking place down for?!... Well, now there *will* be an arson charge-who did you give the job to?...*Arthur Brown?!*...Next time you need to cover some tracks try *not* to employ a notoriously psychotic fucking pyromaniac!'

'Just a bit of my own correspondence,' I announce to Mathew whilst going out onto the balcony. He's already preoccupied with another phone call. I email his brother Peter with a request for a hook-up in the near future. Then I see *renewed* interest from the Corporation I've called "Broadcaster A". I reply with a view for a meeting ASAP to discuss my potential commission.

'I've just got a text to say Brownie ain't been nicked,' Strauss tells yet another person on his mobile as I return, 'he's been ironed out!...Yep, already binned 'cos he was hardly gonna clear up after himself…*Of course* the Old Bill will try to pin that on me *too* so eradicate *all* connections we had with him- get the Bear to cover his manor, the Shark south of the River and have the Hammer coming in from the North in a pincer movement.' Much of this *clearly* coded conversation is lost to me *this time on account of* the peculiar odour I've detected. I then notice a familiar-looking bottle adapted for some other purpose on the table. A small amount of smoke whirls from the silver foil-covered top.

'Mathew,' I venture, working on a hunch, 'has somebody been smoking drugs in your home?' He is, *however*, busy with yet another Caller.

'Maybe it's *one* of your lot who's going to do a deal against me?!...You *ain't* off the hook...*Who else* could be calling me a wrong 'un?!' Then to my distress I see that Strauss has stood up, and is staring straight at me. I experience an escalating sense of anxiety as he marches towards me, after having tucked the mobile between his shoulder and the side of his head apparently to free up his hands for some *other* task. His arm juts out and I feel a sense of relief only *after* he reaches for something on the table. My Subject then puts a white pellet on top of the bottle, places his lips to the straw protruding from it and inhales after heating this pea-sized object with a lighter. Again I detect a smell not unlike burning plastic.

'Something medicinal, I trust?' I utter nervously in the absence of anything more constructive to say. Suddenly Mathew erupts in an explosion of smoke, and for a *split-second* I imagine he's suffering the *same* suspected fate of his brother, Billy, by succumbing to the phenomenon of spontaneous combustion! But when the haze clears I see that he'd *merely* exhaled this (probably) intoxicating emission. Then he blows up again, this time with a mirth which soon becomes untenable, hysterical, *seemingly insane!* This hilarity eventually gives way to a fit of coughing, which *in turn* leads to another seizure of sorts. This *also* looks to become uncontrollable, resulting in him clasping the left side of his chest and arm. Then Strauss is less steady of his feet. He begins to stagger, regains his footing by clutching the table but this is *not* enough to stop his legs buckling, resulting in him crashing to the floor. I rise to investigate and consequently learn he's fallen under the table, *or more likely* rolled there after the initial impact. Even the coughing has now stopped, which makes me speculate upon *what* might happen next.

Suddenly a ring tone sounds off. Relieved by this breaking of a painfully prolonged silence I check my phone but see that it's *not* me being called.

'Hello?' comes a muted response. Eventually a shaggy head bobs up, revealing to me that Mathew's attack had *not* been fatal *after all*. 'Hello?' he reiterates, sounding surprisingly *un*flustered considering his dramatic exit merely a minute or so previously. He then flinches on account of the fact his mobile *continues* to ring. Presently I observe he'd had the plastic bottle, or –as I now surmise – drug pipe, against his ear *in lieu of* his phone. Having *eventually* discovered this mistake for himself Strauss answers with more conviction- '*Hello*!?!'

'Well, if *certain* people's doors are going through I'm inclined to think they'll go the wrong way,' a terrifyingly-familiar voice replies!

Suddenly his attention is back upon me- slowly, as delayed as the anatomy of a nightmare, the horrifying realization dawns, or rather *crashes* down upon me that this person on the speakerphone is none other than Mathew *himself!*

'But how?!' I gasp.

'You *won't* see me,' this voice – *now clearly* belonging to the most recent Subject of my documentation – declares, *'you won't see me!'*

'What are you going to do now, Mathew?' I ask after he's smashed his phone into tiny pieces. I'm relieved he seems calmer now though remain fearful he might yet deduce the possibility that someone might have *somehow* acquired my secret footage to use against him.

'*What am I going to do?!*' he echoes contemptuously. He then retrieves the converted bottle/drug pipe, produces another -even larger- white pellet and proceeds to ignite another blast of this toxic substance. 'I know *who's* responsible for all this,' he mutters at last, presumably after the effects of the narcotic have worn off.

'*You do?!*' I quaver, desperate for alarm not to be detectable within my tone. '*Who*?!'

'The Great Clown- that terrible being who mocks *all* of Creation!' This grants me temporal exoneration. But unease and bewilderment remain on account of once more getting reminded of the bizarre concept of a malevolent Clown, which for some baffling reason is now *replacing* Mathew's prostate gland as *the very pinnacle* of images *most* troubling to me!

'Why would the Great Clown afflict *you* specifically?'

'Not just me,' he rationalizes, 'you've been aware it has stricken all my Kith and Kin? The sins of the Father, *and all that.*' I want to again question Mathew about his Father, and the *real* reason he and his siblings went unheeded by (or perhaps even shuffled away from) the Public Eye after the initial enamourment towards this *singular* phenomenon of Sextuplets. But he presses on with *his* take on the current situation. 'Regardless to what *nearly everyone* might be saying these days, some Biblical shit *does* still go on.'

'What, *like* the seven deadly sins?' I have to admit that theology is *not* my strong point.

'That's *exactly* what it is!' Strauss enthuses with an exhilaration as though he'd just taken *another* hit from his drug pipe, '*Seven* brothers, *Seven* Deadly Sins! Robby is obviously *Lust*, Kevin is *Envy*... But then *all* my brothers are guilty of that when it comes to *me*.'

'*Vanity*?' I put to him but receive merely a blank expression. 'What Sin is Roland guilty of?'

'*Slothe*, of course,' Mathew replies without pause, 'all that lazing about in hospitals, expecting *everyone else* to do *everything* for him. He needs to snap out of it! He's a greedy sod too so add *Gluttony* to his list!'

'And what of *Wrath*?' Has this man *no* self-insight *at all?!* My next thoughts are for some *inexplicable* reason verbalized *aloud*, 'I sense *Pride* within thee!'

'Pride?' He looks confused. 'Is that *even* on the list?'

'*How* on Earth will you be able to fix *all* this?! I'm relishing my temporal role of Inquisitor: it's currently my very own *"scent of new car interior."*

'A new Patent I'm about to process.' Strauss is attempting to bring order back to his hair. 'Or rather an expired copyright that is now ripe and ready to be appropriated by *I, myself*, to serve *my* future plans.'

'And what *precisely* is this Patent you are about to acquire?' I probe with skepticism.

'Why, *Reality* itself, *of course*. It will be recast *in mine own image.*'

'Like a self-improvement programme?' There is something of his brother Billy's Life- coaching schemes about this.

'Nothing so prosaic or petty,' Mathew smugly retorts. '"*Reality*" as you know it will become something else entirely. It will literally be transformed into something you and all your fellow minor players won't *even remotely* recognize, and *all to serve me* and the vision I have for the *whole* of Humanity.'

'That's *quite* some…plan,' I stammer, 'do you already have the suitable staff to help you implement all this?'

'There is *no* immediate position for you, Fabio.' He flashes me an apologetic smile. 'But I'll bear you in mind for the future.'

'The future *you alone* will fashion?' I gasp in exasperation.

'I'm glad you have such faith in me, Fabio,' he retorts, either oblivious or unheeding of my doubtful line of enquiry. 'Now if you don't mind, I'm about to commence a Board meeting with my various staff.'

'You are expecting your employees?' I'm trying to make sense of *all* this.

'Why, they are *already all* here, Fabio, can you *not* see?' Strauss casts a self-satisfied beam around the empty room. 'I have *all* my emissaries present, my agents, frequented at *strategic* positions, currently here amongst us to *re*-programme and reverse *every* process at odds with *my* will. This message comes to you from The Reality Re-imagined Corporation. Thanks for your time.'

'The doctor is not *presently* in residence,' a large, mature black lady wearing a maid's outfit announces in a broad African accent.

'The doctor?' I'm standing on the doorstep of the apartment Mathew had occupied only two weeks previously. 'Would that be Dr Strauss?'

'No, Dr Chrishala,' she informs me. 'Are you part of the courier service transporting his personal effects from Zambia?'

My next port of call is the office space I'd visited during my lengthy period spent with Mathew. Nobody is here. The place is empty. Even all the fittings have been stripped bare.

'Is it possible for us to meet sometime this week?'

'I'm currently doing the night shift,' Mr. Strauss replies over the phone, 'so some time after 2pm?'

'2pm?' I echo.

'Yes, that's when I get up.' This is Peter Strauss. Mathew's mobile and landline numbers had gone dead *just hours* after my *last* encounter with him.

'Have you been watching the news?' the voice on my mobile phone asks me.

'About Mathew Strauss?' I enquire, flipping on my television to catch only the tail end of this item very pertinent to me. 'Have they named him?'

'You'll have to look for *yourself*.'

'Why has he *only just now* been arrested?'

'He fell out of favour with certain people of influence. You can only play *that* sort of game with the *right* friends,' my Acquaintance on the Police Force replies, 'plus we were lucky enough to get hold of some *very* useful information.' There's a strange hue to this person's voice I hadn't previously been aware of: could he be gloating?

'*Who* were these influential friends of Mathew?' The phone-line goes dead.

I learn *a little more* when the relevant information is repeated onscreen. There is no mention of names, just an announcement of a large seizure of drugs and the arrest of "key members of a major criminal Organization". I then see images of Mathew's former offices, where I'd heard him discuss an intended fictional feature film dealing with themes *very similar* to these *factual* events.

Further coverage of this cordon captures something I hadn't noticed on my final visit: a message has been emblazoned in red paint across the -now sealed- entrance; M.S. is a grass!

Episode 6:

Peter, Security Operative.

'...a tale told by an idiot, full of sound and fury,
signifying nothing.'
Macbeth, William Shakespeare.

'I should employ this shmuck full-time,
just to slug him in the kisser!'
Allen Woodyman
(change of name for legal reasons.)

'I'll admit it's become a *bit* of a struggle paying the bills,' says the man I will identify as "*Security Guard 1.*" He's speaking to his colleague whom, for the purpose of this transcript shall be "*Security Guard 2.*"

'Can't the Missus go back to work?' Number 2 enquires.

'She already has- she's writing.' My ears suddenly prick up: amongst my production notes on Peter Strauss -my most recent, *intended* Subject- is data detailing that his (possibly estranged?) wife is an author.

'What?!' counters his Colleague. '*How long's* it take her to write down a shopping list?'

'It's a *book* she's writing,' Guard 1 retorts, 'Chick Lit.' This certainly *sounds like* the person we've come to visit.

'Chick *what?!*' Disdain is audible *thanks* to our sensitive recording equipment. I cannot see this person's face because my crew -consisting of Troy and Stan- is filming from a *considerable* distance (and with only *limited* light) but I imagine his expression is one of contorted befuddlement.

'Chick Lit, you know'…the first man bumbles, 'like, *Women's* Literature- she's aiming at getting a publishing deal for the novel she's writing.'

'What's *that* about?!' Security guard 2 retorts. His profile is now illuminated from some as yet unseen source. I trust Troy is zooming-in upon this.

'Y'know, female stuff,' comes the reply, 'trials, tribulations, and all that.'

'My question was rhetorical,' his Colleague grunts before casting a glance in our direction. For a disconcerting moment I suspect he's seen us!

'Come on, Paul,' the first man (whom has certain vocal traits which *could* possibly identify him as Peter Strauss) appeals, 'it will be of interest to both women and men, couples *especially*.'

'*Sexy, is it?*' this man we've heard identified as Paul asks before turning his torch towards us. This prompts me to dip lower and closer against the wall I'm concealing myself behind. I turn to see that Troy, *ever* resourceful, has found a new vantage point to continue filming. When I look to my left *however*, I witness Stan taking flight!

'It's about marriage and having children,' the man -we suspect to be *our* Peter- elaborates, 'the struggle for women to juggle *all* their roles.'

'For the love of *all* that is sane,' Paul beseeches, 'you've *got* to stop her!' He then turns back towards *us*, making me *all the more certain* we've been detected. The beam returns. I look to Troy. He makes a run for it. *I follow.*

'Did that conversation strike you as *somewhat* sexist?' I whisper, once we've found a more substantial hide-out to plan our next course of action.

'I suppose so,' Troy replies whilst adjusting something on his video camera. I'm *greatly* relieved to again be working with *such* a competent professional. This also frees me up to concentrate on content *rather* than the tiresome technical side. Stan, *not so proficient* a practitioner as *you may recall,* has been rehired for *another* purpose I shall reveal some time hence. Suddenly a flashlight fully envelops us.

'State your business!' someone barks out from the darkness. I then feel the full beam *directly* in my eyes!

'We're the film crew.' I turn to see that Troy has taken this verbal initiative.

'The call is *not* for another two hours,' our unseen interloper informs us, *'who* are you?'

'Peter?' I'm catching my first *full* view of this person with his approach. 'Peter Strauss?' He certainly has a similar bone structure and gait to his siblings.

'Who's asking?' he demands as the two other Security Guards - *so* vocal during our secret filming- sidle up beside him.

'Peter, it's *me*, Fabio- we've been in talks about the documentary project concerning your brother, Roland.'

'I've got this,' he tells his Colleagues, who exchange bemused glances before sauntering away. 'But you were *supposed* to come to my place later today- this afternoon?'

'Forgive us,' I reply, 'we thought no harm visiting you here at your night shift?'

'Is *this* for a feature film?' Troy's question is wisely chosen for it engages our new Subject with something he seems happy to reveal.

'Yes, I've got yesterday's shooting schedule around here somewhere.' Suddenly something else catches Strauss's attention, causing him to spring into action. He charges at this object or person just beyond my visual scrutiny. Troy films this trajectory whilst I pursue Peter. I then observe him dive at a darkly-clad figure, grabbing hold of this supposed intruder before wrestling them to the ground.

'*Whoah!*' a familiar high-pitch voice squawks. '*Only me!*' Once this person is allowed back upon their feet I see that it's my inept soundman, Stan.

'Is he with you?' Peter asks.

'No,' Troy hastily replies, 'we've *no* idea who he is!' I'm *rather* gratified with this quick-witted response from my *new* Cameraman.

'Still here?' Strauss asks after having escorted a protesting Stan away from the vicinity. 'The rest of the film unit will be here in an hour or so, and my shift ends when I get relieved by the day-shift about an hour after that so you can *either* hang around until I knock off or visit me at my place this afternoon?'

'I think we made the *best* decision,' I tell Troy after choosing the *latter* option for our meeting later today.

'In offloading Stan?' he jauntily responds whilst placing his camera inside my van before climbing into the passenger seat. I'm just about to drive away when there's a fierce banging noise outside. I peer out to see a pathetic-looking Stan rapping against the exterior.

'You're my ride home,' he bleats.

'Give me *one* good reason why I should help you after you ran off *like that?*' I demand.

'You'd *better* listen to the audio I picked up on,' he whimpers whilst wrestling with the door handle.

'*We'll* be in touch, Stan,' I say after pulling up outside his abode.

'Best I hang onto *this*.' He's clutching his audio equipment close to his bosom while climbing out from the back of my vehicle.

'As you *wish*,' I snort before accelerating away with *no* further offer for him. It's at this point the greatly expedient Troy informs me that he'd covertly filmed Stan playing us back his recording, thus making our *own* copy and making *that* tiresome clown superfluous for any *future* plans.

'The struggle for women to juggle *all* their roles.' This is the voice of the person we'd *initially* thought to be Peter Strauss.

'For the love *of*…you've *got* to stop her!' retorts Paul, his colleague. There's a pause in this soundtrack at the point we'd suspected our presence had been detected. The men resume their conversation, fully captured by Stan who'd not (we now surmise) fled the location but *instead* repositioned himself elsewhere to continue recording.

'Isn't that sexist?' At first I suspect this to be my *own* voice, having said *something to his effect* after having taken flight.

'Peter's missus was claiming to be writing a novel,' we hear Paul say, 'go ask him how *that* went!' There's then audible activity *likely* to be their approach towards our latest Subject. 'Straussy, tell him about your wife's writing *career*?'

'Glad to,' we hear the true Peter drone in a distinctive Strauss monotone, 'she's written a novel, and has a most *novel* way of writing this novel.'

'How's that then?'

'She'd make me stay out late in the evenings so as not to distract her work. That's how I got adjusted to the nightshift. I'd get home in the mornings to find her drained, or busy having a script meeting with her agent, Abdul, of which I allowed them their privacy for professional reasons. Then after the birth of our child, Abdul-'

'*Abdul?!*' Security Guard 1 (who as yet remains nameless) cuts in, incredulity evident in his voice.

'We liked the name,' Peter chirps with guileless embellishment, 'anyhow, I became a full-time dad for a while when the other half was away on her publicity tours.'

'*Did* she get published?' S. G. 1's tone is tremulous.

'Indeed *yes*, Terry, her books have been brought out by a company called Vanity Publishing. She's now working full-time from home, hence the little apartment I've rented for myself.'

'*Jesus Christ!*' S.G.1 (now identified as "Terry") sounds increasingly strangulated. 'I need to act *fast* to stop her!'

'What's that?' I imagine Strauss is about to question his Colleague's curiosity but the audio recording takes an *entirely different* turn. 'It looks like two blokes hiding by that alcove- is one of them *filming us?*'

'Peter,' I call out across the street, 'we have an appointment?' He's emerging from the front door of an address he'd given us, and is apparently strolling off somewhere?

'Just getting us some milk,' he yodels back. 'Right, *this* way,' he instructs upon returning from the nearby convenience store.

'This is *quite* a staircase,' Troy remarks as we ascend to the second floor.

'*Just* another flight,' Peter cheerfully announces.

'I imagine it helps you keep fit?' I mention as our host unlocks the door to his home. Suddenly we are assailed by a *very* unpleasant smell.

'What the hell?!' he exclaims. I look into this place earlier described as an "apartment" (even "*bedsit*" would be *too* grandiose a term for this *tiny* space *little more than* a broom cupboard) to observe a state of disarray *so* severe as to suggest a burglary has occurred! 'If I've told you once then I've told you a *thousand* times, Mr. Peterson, get off your lazy fat arse *and get yourself a job!*' I look about, expecting to see another person here but observe *only* the presence of an overfed ginger cat lazing within a frayed armchair.

'Do you live alone here, Peter?' Troy asks as he sets up his camera.

'Well, with the exception of Mr. Peterson,' he answers whilst attempting, and ultimately *failing* to dislodge the feline from the *only* visible piece of furniture. 'Here, let me give you the grand tour of the place. Well, this is clearly Mr. P.'s territory, and over there is the audio-visual observation maintenance.'

'That old, fat-back television?' Troy enquires. He's already filming.

'Moving along from that,' Strauss carries on regardless, 'is the dining room-stroke-socializing area.'

'It's a *very* small table,' I remark.

'*Aha*!' Our host reaches underneath it to produce a pair of tiny stools that look more suited for pre-school children.

'What's *that* in the corner?' Troy asks. I look over to see a pile of clothes, newspapers and other items of a *less* identifiable and sanitary nature.

'*Wank-sock corner!*' I look to the doorway, the location where this intrusive outburst had originated. To my astonishment I see Stan standing there! I turn to our host, whose expression is similar to how I imagine my *own* to be. Then his face cracks. A slow, deliberate smile creeps across his broad features.

'Stan,' he emits with no sign of disquiet or disapproval towards this *uninvited* interloper, 'I was about to ask these lads *where* you were.' I look to Troy but he merely remains impassively filming.

'Forgive me for being late,' Stan says whilst looking directly at me, a smirk upon his lips.

'No worries,' Peter cheerfully responds, 'pull up a pew?' Subsequently this *invader* picks up one of the paltry stools before positioning himself at the *centre* of the room. I'm confronted with the preposterous and *wholly* distracting sight of him perched midpoint at the place *intended* for my interview. 'Stan explained everything.'

'*He did?*'

'Oh yes, he told me how you like to play japes on him, as one *does* with junior work colleagues.'

'He must have sounded *very* convincing,' I manage at last. Justified, *righteous* anger towards my former Soundman is rising up from within me.

'More than that, Fabs,' Strauss continues, 'it was only after you fooled me into ejecting him from the location, and after your *own* exit, that I decided to do some detective work.'

'He's *no* slouch, our Peter,' Stan interjects, 'quite the Colombo, *in fact.'* My now *unwanted* ex-Employee's expression has transformed to one of *evident* hostility towards me.

'What *type* of detective work?' I'm loathe to ask after *no* further clue is given.

'I took a butcher's at your net pages,' Peter elaborates in the celebratory glow of his own sleuthing, 'and who do I see there but our *dear* pal Stanislav here, *bold as brass!* Nice snap, *by the way'*. It *only now* dawns upon me concerning this tenuous though *incriminating* link: several weeks previously I'd been forced to post a photo of Stan on my website; *partly* to secure his confidence with the *feigned* prospect of more work -to lull him into a false sense of security which *might* help him implicate himself *should* he be part of the internet conspiracy against me- but *also* to show my potential Broadcaster Commissioners I already have *several* staff at my disposal.

'Where's your sound recording stuff, Stan?' Troy asks curtly.

'He left it here when visiting earlier,' Strauss beams before producing the equipment from behind the armchair, which remains occupied by the torpid tom-cat. 'Right, where shall we start?'

'You were in the Army?' Stan enthuses in response to what he's just heard. 'Did you fight in the Falklands?'

'That was just before my time,' Peter replies, 'but I was out in the first Gulf war- got out a bit before the second one, thankfully.' We've relocated to a nearby café since four adults within so small a place as *that* "apartment" had proven inadequate- there had been insufficient space *even* to swing Mr. Peterson! 'It seemed the natural step after that to remain within the security trade and join the fraternity of door personnel.'

'You were a nightclub bouncer?' Stan elicits. 'What, like, *old-school?*'

'I did regulate the safety of patrons in a nocturnal venue for several years.' Despite the pomp of Peter's vocabulary his delivery is flat, and there's a paradoxical, near *pathological* modesty about him. 'It started off well but things soon reverted to violence on an *almost* daily basis.'

'You kicked some ass?' Stan emphasizes with an irksome wink and air karate-chop.

'Not *quite* what I've put on my C.V.,' Strauss shrugs, 'but what *could be* added is getting glassed several times, occasionally stabbed and on one bank holiday even shot at, something I *wasn't* keen to have installed as a custom.'

'You weren't *quite* Patrick Swayze then?' This tedious technician then looks startled by the glares he rightfully receives from Troy and I for this *deeply* inane comment. '*Come on,* I was referring to "Roadhouse"! I've *never* seen *nor* will *ever* watch "Dirty Dancing"!'

'The last straw was sustaining an appalling injury from a barstool utilized as a projectile,' Peter laments before draining his mug of tea.

'Thrown by a disgruntled patron?' My question is less from curiosity, more to pre-empt a *further* inappropriate comment from Stan.

'No, thrown by a work colleague- "*mental*" Mickey Baker. Apparently he had a terrible aim and was crap at cricket-fielding, *not* that anyone would *dare* coach his technique.'

'Better with the bat, *eh?*' Stan blurts back.

'You didn't think to get a *less* hazardous job?' I enquire.

'I did eventually,' Strauss replies. 'It was my good fortunate to attain a position at a different venue where gentler folk would frequent.'

'Your brother Mathew mentioned something to that effect.' I'm *specifically* thinking of a public cross-dressing incident his sibling had referred to.

'Oh, that!' A blush rouges Peter's cheeks. 'Yeah, he got me doing the door at a fetish venue he had a business interest in, *you know,* the whips and the chains, *and what-nots.*'

'Is *this* where you were stigmatized for wearing a sarong?' I enquire.

'Oh, you meant *that*?!' Strauss looks relieved, as though let off the hook concerning something even *more* incriminating. 'Did I say *Fetish* Club?! No, you wouldn't catch me going somewhere like *that*! What Mathew was referring to was a place where trendy Show-biz types would go. This is where the "Posh and Becks incident," or *scandal* to some, was to occur.'

'How about renaming it "Bosh-gate"?!' Stan excitedly interrupts once more. 'Sounds *more* dramatic- did you ever have to dress as a woman to go undercover to foil a blackmailing, *or even* kidnapping plot?'

'Not quite,' my Subject sighs, 'seeing as David Beckham had taken to wearing a sarong in public I thought *I'd* follow suit. Or rather *not* wear a suit by wearing *similar* dress to him, well, *almost* literally *a dress?*…whilst greeting and admitting club-goers.'

'Which *itself* did not *quite* get the reception you were expecting?'

'*Twat!*' Strauss exclaims, giving me the impression he's offended by my line of questioning. '*Complete tit!* And I was also called *"a massive wanker"* too, and all for *merely* keeping up with the fashions!'

'It came as a *surprise*?!' I splutter, having choked on my latte.

'*Who* could possibly have known?!' he replies. 'I'm loving this chat, but I need to get ready for work. Why not visit me on my shift later?'

'Same time? ' Stan intercepts. 'Same location?'

'There's been a change of plan,' I tell Stan over the 'phone, 'Peter won't have time to meet us on *this* occasion.' Troy and I have arrived at the location an hour earlier than our previous visit here.

'Funny,' he replies, 'that wasn't mentioned to me.'

'And *how* could *you* be *so* confident in him relaying *that* to you?!' I retort with undisguised irritation.

'Because I'm with him *now!*' I look over to a film unit vehicle (which had previously escaped my scrutiny due to scant lighting) to see my *former* sound-recordist standing alongside Strauss by a catering-size urn. 'How do you take your tea?'

'You're *already* filming?' Peter observes as we approach.

'What *precisely* has Stanley here been saying?' I demand.

'Not a great deal. Look- I don't know *what's* going on between you two but just let me *warn you both* that I'm a drama-free zone so *best* you leave your histrionics *outside* of this film location.'

'Agreed,' Stan smirks, 'blessed be the peace-makers.'

'As long as they keep *out* of the line of fire,' Troy murmurs, which involuntarily evokes a titter from me.

'Listen fellas,' Peter states as though drawing a conclusion, 'this could *well be* the *shortest* documentary in history.' This chills me: is he announcing he *won't* be cooperating, and therefore dismissing us from using him as a Subject for my film?! My mind continues to be in a state of flux when suddenly he springs into a sprint away from us. *'Here, mate!'*

'Where's he gone *now?!*' I ask Troy, who remains silent though continues to film something just beyond my field of vision.

'I knew him when he had fuck-all!' an insidious voice sounds out. I look over to see the two other Security Guards approaching. Peter re-emerges with a shabby-looking, bearded man, whom I now surmise was the subject of the negative comment made by one of the night staff.

'This is Oaksey,' Strauss chirps, as though this should explain *everything*.

'It's probably *his* old man?' Paul mutters to his co-worker Terry.

'I still *can't* believe it's you, Straussy!' the man identified as "Oaksey" gushes. 'What's happening here then?'

'Just a location for a feature film.'

'All about *you*?!' Oaksey's broad grin exposes infrequent, discoloured teeth.

'Sort of,' my Subject winces, 'here Oaksey, the catering staff left tea and a few sarnies so let's get some scran.'

'*Stanislav!*' Stan hisses at me as Peter leads his long-lost friend to the giant urn.

'*What?!*'

'My first name is *not* Stanley,' my now unwelcome sound-recordist insists, 'it's Stanislav! Don't you read *anybody's* C.V.?!'

'Thanks for *all* your help, Straussy,' Oaksey says as he's leaving. 'Keep up the therapy, and I'm *sure* they'll get your medication right *sometime soon.*'

'Old Army buddy?' Paul enquires as the dishevelled man disappears from view.

'Indeed so- you'd learn a good few things from the Military.'

'Such as?' Security guard 1 –who's been *more recently* identified as "*Terry*"- quizzes.

'Taking a bullet for a buddy,' Strauss shoots back without hesitation.

'Sounds painful!' Paul counters. 'Take a bullet *where* precisely?'

'Take it *in the line of fire*,' comes the patient explanation, 'take the impact of hostile fire *in place of* a fellow brother in your platoon.'

'Oh, a bit like *this*?' Terry splays his arms whilst diving across the space between Peter and Paul before wincing as though sustaining a bullet wound *in place of* his friend.

'A bit,' the former soldier sighs, 'but with better posture.'

'No Tel,' Paul caws, 'I absolutely *insist* I take this *particular* slug *for you!'* He accompanies this with a balletic leap.

'That's a negative, brother,' Terry, *in turn* exclaims, *'this* one's on *me!'* He then performs his own acrobatics.

'On the *contrary,* dear chap,' his co-worker guffaws, *'I've got this one well and truly covered!'* Strauss slips away from this jeering duo. His expression is unreadable.

'What initially attracted you to join the Armed forces?' I ask, once out of earshot of the others.

'It came in adolescence after getting a birthday present of some military badges from a maternal uncle,' Strauss clarifies. 'This awakened a collecting frenzy for me where I acquired a broad array of that specific type of insignia and paraphernalia. Then one day Dad sat me down to explain we were Jewish on his side of the family, which *sort of* scuppered my Nazi memorabilia so *generously* gifted from Mum's siblings.'

'Mathew told me…' I pause after Peter peers at me with a look *so* earnest it briefly interlopes my train of thought. *'What* precisely *did* happen when you were working for your brother at the Kit-Kat-Klub?'

'Nothing happened to *me!'* He suddenly looks anxiety-stricken.

'I wasn't insinuating anything happened *to you personally,'* I respond in as diplomatic a manner as I can muster, 'perhaps to a *work colleague?'*

'Working somewhere like *that* can have an effect on a man,' Strauss acknowledges after regaining his composure, *'not* myself, *you understand* but a colleague of mine who'd become *particularly* affected. Let's call him Mister…X, anyhow, my friend, *this Mr. X* was a regular sort of chap, nothing out of the ordinary. So anyhow, there he was greeting patrons at the door of this fetish club, overseeing the events inside, occasionally cautioning the Clientele with the *no* blood-letting, *no* permomarking policy, *alas* not with *complete* success. Anyway, events conspired where this *friend of mine* is one minute advising people to lay off the lash a little, to the *next* step where he finds himself hog-tied, face-down, getting rectally *intruded* by some high-tech contraption straight from Stuttgart! At least I *think* that's what it said on the manufacturers' packaging? Well, "*Versprung-durch–technick*" certainly *didn't* apply in *this* case! I, *erm*, my *friend,* this Mr X, was *never quite* the same again.'

'Peter,' I chance, feeling the moment is right, 'who is "*Agent Provost,*" and *what* do the "*agents of destruction*" mean to you?' Suddenly he appears very anxious, and is groping for something beneath his hi-viz vest. Eventually he pulls out an object resembling a weapon!

'We have a situation!' I fear a physical attack of some sort: have I unearthed something so secretive -so *harmful* to him- that he would resort to violence?! 'Come in, *over!*' I *only now* realize that the object brandished by him is *merely* a walkie-talkie! 'Come in, *over!*...Terry?...*Paul?!...Come in, over!*'

'What?!' a bleary voice eventually responds on the communication device. This person sounds as though they've just been woken. '*Whassup?!*'

'We have a code B-52 on our hands!' Peter dramatically declares.

'A *what?!*' I now recognize this exhausted voice as belonging to Paul.

'Ain't that a *plane?!*' an *equally* irritable Terry crackles from his own walkie-talkie.

'*Precisely!* A stealth action possibly *soon* to be deployed!'

'Is anybody *actually* nicking anything?!' Paul bristles across the line, 'Burning anything to the ground?!'

'*Worse!*' a grim-faced Strauss blazes back. 'I've spotted some culprits in the vicinity who *look likely* to be students!'

'*Students*?!' Paul chuckles. 'Just throw a bar of soap at them!'

'Gentlemen,' my Subject asserts whilst proceeding to march off in the direction to where the incident appears to be occurring, 'I need to impress the *gravity* of the existential threat that students steal road cones, *my* road cones! I have 42 cones *in total* so enforce the protocol of counting them, *each and every one* because *all of them* are *essential* for this work. And remember- some of these cones *even* have names! Make the *greatest* effort to protect *all* the road cones at *all* costs, gentlemen, *over!*' A lanky figure with one of these road cones crowned upon his head emerges from the darkness.

'I chased them off!' I now observe this is Stan. Peter is scowling. Hopefully this is a sign *even he* is tiring of this *most* vexing of individuals?

'Well, that's the whole film unit in,' Peter announces after admitting the last of a series of vehicles onto this location. 'What are your plans for today?'

'I have a meeting early this afternoon,' I reply, sensing that Stan is eavesdropping somewhere: subsequently I'll *not* disclose that my meeting is *specifically* with the Broadcaster I'm *most* anxious to acquire my Commission with. 'Any plans *yourself* before your night shift?'

'I'm visiting a farmer friend,' Strauss replies in a twist which confounds my expectations.

'I'll have to take a rain check,' Stan salivates at my shoulder. He's gorging on an overstuffed breakfast bap provided by the caterers. 'Allergic to sheep, innit. See you here tonight, fellas.'

'Do you take an interest in Agriculture, Peter?' I ask, once our Spy has thankfully left.

'A little,' he replies, 'but more because this friend has just had a litter of Collie pups- one of which *might* make a good guard dog.' I can't possibly *imagine* where he'd accommodate such a creature! 'Come along with me *if you want?*'

'What did you do *next*, Peter?' He's driving us in his own beaten-up vehicle. Troy films from the back seat. 'I mean, after the *clearly* traumatic episode working in the fetish club?'

'I tried to restore some dignity to my life.' The scenery is becoming pleasingly greener as we exit the M25. 'The writing was on the wall, *some* of it even true.'

'You *remained* working with your brother, Mathew?' I put this by way of a question although I've *already* received this *specific* information.

'He made me the Head of marketing, promotions and publicity,' my Subjects answers, devoid of curiosity *how* I'd been privy to such data: I refrain from mentioning I'm aware this job was *merely* handing out flyers in the street; I'm *even less* likely to make reference to a newspaper article from this period reporting of *"the all-singing, all-dancing leaflet eater!"'!*

'How did *that* go?'

'Not *so* well,' Strauss replies honestly, 'I'd been down-sized in just about *every* area of my life. I got some therapeutic help concerning my strange diet at the time, and what I was *later* diagnosed as having.'

'Which was?'

'Suppressed Anger Syndrome.' I'm *not* convinced this is even a *recognized* medical condition: I'll have to investigate *where* (and from *whom precisely*) he'd sought this help. 'Anyway, Mathew found me another gig.'

'Did this aid you *at all?*'

'Initially it gave me a sense of purpose. My brother entered me for body building contests but *unfortunately* that led to a lot of negativity amongst the door staff community.'

'*Jealousy*?' I'm not *completely* convinced concerning this claim since the photos of Peter in his prime reveal he'd had only the modest physique of a flyweight boxer (in a division he'd had *some* success in, and which I'm hoping to touch upon soon) but nothing to suggest he'd *ever* had the brawn to compete in the bulked-up world of body building.

'More like unadorned contempt,' Strauss grumbles, 'hatred even. You see, I was taking part in the *women's* heats.'

'But *why?*' I gasp. 'What could have possessed you to do *that?!*'

'What you need to understand,' he replies whilst crunching his gear stick, 'is that Mathew is a *very* persuasive person.' I'm tempted to enquire exactly how much he's aware of his brother's *current* situation but resist since it might open *yet another* digressive can of worms. 'And to be fair he reasoned I didn't stand a chance in the men's competitions so should give the women's one a go, and no disrespect intended but sometimes it *is* hard to tell.'

'So how did that go?'

'Not as well as *we'd* imaged- my humiliation had stepped up to a *whole new* level. Sensational newspaper headlines *aside*, I didn't even *make* it through to the finals! The only offer I got after that was a return to the boxing ring.'

'I'm hoping to touch upon your successful boxing career, Peter?'

'This comeback consisted of weight division-free, inter-gender bouts,' he winces, 'which put me *straight back* into Casualty. As for my *conventional* boxing career, well, I'm *not quite* ready to talk about that *just yet.*'

'*Surely* you've had enough time to take stock to address *everything* that has occurred in your Life?' I'm hoping my attempt at a tender tone is not betrayed by my compulsion for him to be *completely* transparent.

'I've certainly had enough time on my hands to think about the *bigger* questions in Life,' Peter responds whilst indicating to turn off into a country lane.

'Such as?'

'Who are we? Where do we come from? *What* are we? *Where* do we go to?...Who's that knocking at my door?... *Whatever next?...*'

'Where are we going, *indeed?!*' I sense Troy say under his breathe.

'It was during this period of contemplation that I fell victim to identity fraud.' This comment has thrown me what I've heard referred to as a *"curve-ball"!* 'Someone was attempting to get loans under my name. I only found out about it after my personal details were sent back to me post-marked *"pointless"*!

My humiliation was *complete* when my wife at the time left me for someone who actually *had* an identity.'

'Was that Margo, who's now with a wheelchair-bound bank clerk?' I ask, mentally shuffling through notes I'd made only a cursory study of.

'No, Margo was the one who during the course of our marriage decided she was a lesbian. The clue was that she was passive-aggressive, though in truth not *so* passive. Margo, or *Marco* as now known, is currently with a *non-gender-specific* person called Osama. I'm referring to Tilly, the one I have my oldest son with.'

'Do you ever get to see that son?'

'Sadly not but he's a bright one, so I've been told- he's now doing Media Studies.'

'Which university?' I'm hoping it's one *superior* to the dubious establishment that processes the likes of my former sound-recordist!

'It's a tailor-made course he can do from home, his mother tells me,' Peter proudly states. 'He does it from his *personalized* educational settee, and can *even* do his exams through T.V. remote control. I *can't* pretend to understand the technology but it's *all* itemized on the bills I receive. I'm hoping I'll be allowed to attend his graduation. Well, *here* we are.' We pull up outside a modest farm house. As we climb out of the vehicle a middle-aged woman emerges from the property.

'You got the message?' Her eyes are red, as though she's been crying. 'Thanks for coming.'

'No problem,' Peter replies, 'is he still available?...The one I had in mind?'

'*What?!*' The woman's face begins to contort, her expression a wasteland located somewhere between grief, confusion and anger.

'Where is the old sod then?' he chirps, apparently oblivious to *whatever* this situation entails. 'Off out with his shotgun?' It's at this point the woman bursts out into a fit of sobbing. A young man –quite possibly her son- rushes from the house to comfort her. 'Has something happened to the puppies?'

'Get the fuck out of *here!*' the teenager rages.

'Perhaps *I* should drive us back?' Troy offers.

'Believe it or not,' Peter croaks, sprawled out across the back seat, 'I do get a little down in myself sometimes. My therapist told me that many of my problems are likely to have come from what he describes as *"a brutal father."* But what he seems *not* to understand is what a *great* sense of humour Dad had. The times we'd sit down to dinner and he'd roar out that it tasted of excrement. Then he'd have us in stitches, *only* occasionally *literally* so, with his comedy Greek Waiter-impression where he'd get us boys jumping for cover like little Commandos. Mother would object to all those projectiles, or at least *until* he'd reassure her the crockery was a discount, faulty-item bulk buy. Cutlery would be thrown with *more* consideration however, hence the game we called "corridor of death." Bless Mother, she'd nurse us back to full health, and all *without* having to resort to *frivolous, depersonalizing medical conventions*. Life is brutal, she'd tell us, but *at least* it's short.'

'Peter…' I'm pausing to conjure the right approach, 'did your therapist ever mention the concept of denial?'

'What do you mean?'

'You touched earlier on something about suppressed anger?'

'It must be suppressed well,' he replies, 'because I *can't* for the life of me find it.'

'I suppose I can talk about it now, considering the law of double jeopardy,' Peter confides. We've sat down to an overpriced, *underwhelming* lunch at a motorway services.

'Your boxing career?'

'Give me time for *that*, Fabio,' he winces, 'I'm referring to the courier work I did for my brother Mathew.'

'All legal, *he claims?*'

'He *still* claims so,' Peter sighs. 'Anyhow, there I was at the airport on my way off out the country when I get pulled aside by Customs officers, *you know*, for the obligatory Security check. Perhaps they thought I was a Jihadist on account of me having a bit of a beard coming through due to a shaving allergy at the time? *Anyhow*, to cut a long story short, my luggage was subjected to a controlled explosion, and so you can *imagine* the hard time Mathew gave me considering that his *special* parcel was now delivered in the form of confetti! However, on a *positive* note I *did* get acquitted of smuggling cash, along with several other criminal charges such as conspiracy, drug trafficking and a *few* terrorist acts. In fact the *only* thing the C.P.S. *did* convict me of was for nonpayment of shaving balm from duty free, which I'd forgotten to pay for amidst *all that* confusion. Alas, my brother wasn't *too* forthcoming with giving me *additional* work after that. Do you suppose he's *still* annoyed with me?'

'When was Mathew last in touch?' I turn to Troy, dismayed by the unexpected intrusion of his question.

'It's been awhile.' He does not expand upon this, and so preserves the mystery of *just how* aware he is of his brother's *current* situation. Instead he regales us with a supplementary story about another situation experienced at an airport where he was bidding farewell to a woman he'd become romantically attached to.

'But isn't that the ending of the film "Casablanca"?' Troy asks once this tale comes to a conclusion.

'Yes, it *is* Casablanca, *now* that you mention it,' Peter sighs. 'Memory can play funny tricks on us.'

'How so?' I enquire.

'Well, I'd *gotten used to* women becoming lesbians during the course of our relationship but this *most recent one* chose to become an ISIS bride *rather* than date me!'

'Sheep allergy, *indeed!'* Troy remarks as we climb back into my vehicle. 'Bollocks!'

'Agreed,' I reply, 'he had shepherd's pie for lunch.'

'*Not* Peter,' Troy counters, 'I was referring to Stan's *sudden* departure. Do you suppose he *already* knew about the Farmer turning a shotgun on himself?'

'I thought we're cool *now*?!' Robby Strauss has finally gotten through to me: I'd had a dozen or so missed calls from him whilst occupied with a *most* productive meeting with my Broadcaster *of choice*, whom has now *confirmed financial commitment* to my film, and all *precisely* on the terms *I* had requested.

'We are,' I reply, '*as far as I'm aware?*'

'So *why* the *static*?!' His tone is agitated. 'It's *well out of order* to claim I'm sexist and racist, *come on,* Fabio- I've fucked *far too many* brown women to be accused of *either* of those charges!'

'*Why* would I even get involved with *such* a reductive situation?'

'Makes for a bit of juicy drama, *doesn't it!?*' Robby bristles back across the phone-line. 'And who the fuck is this *mate of yours,* Agent Provost?!'

'May I speak to Mrs. Mary Strauss please?'

'You're caught her just before her afternoon nap,' an androgynous voice -I assume belonging to be a Nurse at the old folks home- informs me, 'may I ask *who's* calling?'

'Tell her it's her *son,*' I reply in a sudden flash of inspiration.

'Is that Robert?' eventually a croaky tone emits, 'I *do* hope you've changed *that* answer phone message of yours?'

'Yes dear,' I reply, affecting a fair attempt at an Estuary accent.

'That's *not* my Robert!' Mrs. Strauss sternly replies- it appears my ruse has failed? 'Peter Paul Rubens!'

'*The Painter?!*' Perhaps she's suffering from Alzheimer's?

'*That's my boy!*' Mary replies more warmly. 'How are you, *son?*'

'I'm very well thanks…Mum.' I'm aware the ethics of this situation might seem dubious but I feel *justified* since I'm in search of an *essential* piece of the puzzle which hopefully should *make everything else* fall into place.

'Mathew called to say there's progress with Roland,' she continues, which opens *another* vista of possibilities for me, 'but I've not heard from the rest of your brothers-*have you?'*

'I'm sure they're all fine- probably just a bit busy right now. Mum, *may* I ask you something?'

'Of course!' Mary suddenly sounds many years younger than her *actual* age.

'Why did the TV companies and newspaper people stop coming to visit us? Why was there *never* a sequel to that documentary they made about our birth?'

'That was down to your father, *of course.'* Her response becomes chilly. 'You'd have to ask *him* that!'

'He's not been very well,' I relay from information received about John Gilbert Strauss. 'Perhaps *you* can speak to him for me?'

'Any child of mine would *know full-well* that me and him have *not* uttered a *word* to each other in *over* twenty years!' Mary Strauss furiously shoots back. *'Who* the fuck *are you?!'*

'Good evening,' Terry greets us at the entrance to the film location.

'Can we help you, gentlemen?' Paul asks after neither man shows any sign of allowing Troy and I admittance to the site we've become accustomed to visiting.

'I hope all is well with our mutual friend, Peter?' I enquire as an artifice to move onward.

'So it's for the well-being of our mate you are *primarily* concerned about?' Paul issues with evident sarcasm. 'Not *just* for your *own selfish* purposes?'

'Come on, guys,' Troy appeals, flashing them his charming smile, 'it's a non-binary thing.'

'*Who's* binary?!' Terry growls back. '*Beware* casting *aspergers!*'

'What my colleague means,' I sigh, 'is that this is *not* an either/or situation. It's *not* mutually exclusive to be *both* beneficial to Mr. Strauss *and to* make a satisfying film about him. May we see him please?'

'He's a bit busy right now,' Terry retorts. 'Can I let him know *precisely who* wants to see him?'

'We have the *same* employer,' I assert: this is wholly correct *now* that I have the *full support* and *financial backing* of the *same* Broadcaster, whom has also *condescended* to commission the frivolous *fictional* drama currently employing these *disposable* minions. 'I have my *full* production outline and *executive* contract too *if you insist upon seeing them?*'

'We're *just* looking out for our mate,' Terry sniffs, having browsed my paperwork. 'He's *no* stranger to getting stitched-up and exploited.'

'Where is he now?' I ask, once having gained access to the location.

'You'll find him round the back of the vehicles,' Paul replies, 'by the honey wagon.'

'The *what*?'

'*Follow your nose!*' cometh the curt response.

'*What's happening*, Peter?' I've been distressingly confronted with the unwholesome sight of my Subject struggling to redirect a pipe leaking dark waste matter from a mobile Portaloo toilet to a nearby drain.

'Just a *minor* hiccup.' He himself is covered in this *same* foul-smelling effluence!

'*Surely* this is a job for a qualified plumber?' I implore. 'Or at the very *least* those providing this faulty public convenience?'

'They're on their way, I expect,' he bumbles, 'I'm just attempting a bit of damage limitation before the *whole* site gets swamped.'

'What's been your experience with the film-stars you've met on set?' Troy asks. He's already filming.

'Up and down,' Strauss sighs, which also aptly describes the motion he is currently performing with his upper body, *lifting and dropping* the pipe he's holding to ensue the expulsion spray hits its target. Much of this filth *however* (visibly identifiable as faeces!) falls short, therefore impacting upon the area *around* the drain. 'Varying really, positive for the *most* part. Sly Stallone said some very wise things, *at least* according to his translator. Richard Gere was a very nice person, and I'm *happy* to scotch malicious rumours because during that shoot I saw *no* sign of *any* roving rodents. I found Johnny Depp a bit aloof *though-* don't waste your time asking *him* the football scores. And *of course*, some of these Hollywood types don't behave *quite* the way you'd expect them to.'

'Can you give any *specific* details?' I enquire.

'Vin Diesel likes his Brussel sprouts. And then there was one example where...I *shouldn't* really say...'

'You can tell *us*,' Troy coaxes, 'we can *always* edit it out.'

'Okay,' Peter agrees, 'I was once minding a *certain* writer-director-film actor- how can I refer to him?... Alan?...Woody... *man*? Anyway, between takes on this daytime London Street location, members of the public were trying to approach him for autographs. My job was to keep them at a distance from this diminutive, bespectacled award-winning New Yorker, allowing them to approach him *only once* there was a break in filming. Anyhow, after a succession of fans had met my *current* Client, up-rocks this *very* striking, busty young Actress in a *very* low-cut blouse. I *presume* she'd an acting background because she handed him some promotional pin-up style photos of herself. *Only then* did I observe that this Actress, *correction*, the *professional* term *now* is *Actor,* anyway, I then noticed that this scantily-clad, heavily-cosmetisized, large-breasted Actor was a carbon-copy of my first wife, with whom I'd had a daughter and who I hadn't seen in years but *was* aware would be of *similar* age to the young adult standing before me now! Initially dumbstruck, I'd eventually managed to wrench out the word… daughter? *"Daughter?!"* Mr. Woody-man then exploded, seemingly having *completely* misconstrued the situation, and so subsequently ranted "She was *not* my biological daughter!" It can't have been the highlight of *either* of our careers, the *one* consolation being that it took several minutes *after* filming had resumed to realize I'd been punched *full* in the face by the usually mild-mannered Mr. Woody Man…*alan.*'

'And what of the young woman you *thought* to be your daughter?'

'I doubt if it was *really* her,' Strauss laments with a shrug, 'she was *at pains to deny this* upon her *hasty* departure.'

'Peter,' I venture, having had my nostrils violently assailed *anew* by this stench which shows *no* sign of abatement, 'have you *ever* thought about finding some *alternative* form of employment?'

'*What?!*' he cries out in exasperation whilst attempting to wipe filth from his face with his soiled sleeve, 'and *leave* Show Business?!'

'I've eaten thanks,' I tell my Subject in response to the offer of a sandwich. He's been hosed down and loaned a change of dry, clean clothes but the foul odour remains. He then produces a box I presume is to store the food away for later consumption but when it's opened I'm met with a *most* unexpected sight.

'Your cat died?' Troy enquires whilst zooming his camera in upon the inert bundle of fur inside. 'You brought him here for burial?'

'*Not at all,*' Strauss protests, 'Mr. Peterson is in the *rudest* health. He decided he wanted to come to work with his daddy tonight, *didn't you!*' Troy and I exchange bemused glances, unconvinced by this still motionless moggy: it seems Peter is in denial concerning the passing of his pet. 'He'll soon be wide awake when he gets a scent of the big fat juicy rats scurrying about this place.' He then rattles the box before plunging his hand inside. This has the effect of suddenly reanimating the feline, who subsequently retaliates with *full* fury against his owner. 'It seems it's Mr. Peterson who's the one with the *barely* suppressed anger issues!' Strauss laments whilst removing his now clawed mitt. This pet prison is then tenderly placed down by the side of the catering table, allowing respite from further disturbance. Just then I notice another suitcase-sized container stored nearby, recognizing it as the casing that houses Stan's especially sensitive recording equipment. I gesticulate to Troy of its presence, and from his expression take it that *he too* surmises my former Soundman has planted it here for the purpose of attaining covert coverage. As Peter strolls off I rattle the cat container with my foot in the hope it will make Stan's recording unlistenable due to the distress of a noisome tom. But this plan backfires when the creature springs from his box to disappear off into the night.

'You made it then?' I spin round, suspecting Strauss had seen this but instead observe he's preoccupied in welcoming the return of his old Army buddy. 'I've kept some refreshments for you.'

'I hope you don't mind,' Oaksey replies, 'but is it alright a few mates grab a bite and share some tea to keep the cold out?' Before any form of invite is forthcoming four bedraggled homeless-types emerge from the shadows to make a hasty beeline for the sandwiches. The subsequent feeding frenzy prompts me to go in search of Strauss's work colleagues to see *why* they'd allowed a crowd of vagrants onto the location. Eventually I find both Terry and Paul fast asleep inside their vehicles.

'Take care of yourselves now,' my Subject calls out after the homeless men as they're leaving.

'That was a very kind gesture you did there, Peter,' I say, both to re-engage our dialogue and to distract him from the fact that one of the uninvited visitors is leaving with Stan's suitcase.

'Wait,' Strauss yells out to the ragged group just as they're exiting the gate, which makes me suspect he'd seen the theft *after all*, 'did any of you see my cat on your way out?'

'Peter,' I say after our lengthy though fruitless search for Mr. Peterson, 'I feel the time is right to show you something on my laptop'. I then play CCTV footage time-coded from two decades previously, which I'd received online from a *still* unknown Source the previous day. It depicts a person getting hit by a vehicle in what looks like a pub carpark. 'Can you either confirm or deny you are familiar with *this*?'

'It was a *long* time ago, Fabio,' he sighs, 'some things are *best* left in the past.'

'Where *you* the recipient of this incident?' I persist as the onscreen car drives away from this *obvious* crime scene without aiding, *or even checking upon* the injured Party.

'I'm just trying my best to build up my karmic credits, Mr. Bordino,' Strauss gloomily retorts, *'do* what you *have* to *do!'*

'Who, or *what*, is *the Great Clown?'*

'Oh, that's an *easy* one.' His demeanour has become surprisingly light. 'I've come to terms with him *long ago.'*

'You have?! You *don't* see him as the agent of *your* destruction?'

'I faced him full-on, Fabio,' comes another unexpected reply, 'he *no longer* holds dominion over me.'

'That must be very liberating for you, Peter?' I look back to my laptop to see something I *hadn't previously* noticed: a figure walks into shot to observe the aftermath: even though the picture quality is poor I can make out that this person is wearing an expensive-looking suit, horn-rim glasses and has a *familiar-looking,* immaculately-tended coiffure.

'I threw a rigged boxing match, Fabio- it was *hardly* Cain and Abel'. It *only now* makes sense to me *why* Harry the boxing trainer had refused to speak about Peter, *even insisting* that he was long dead!

'*Straight* out of "On the Waterfront"!' Troy gasps in awe.

'But *this* happened in *Hounslow*!' my Subject disputes. A caption then streams across the video: *K.O! – Billy "Boy" Strauss verses Peter Paul Rubens.* 'I'll be in my local café this afternoon if you need to ask me *anything* else?'

'We might be passing,' I reply, not *immediately* grasping the significance of what Peter is *trying* to tell us. By the gate I notice something in a puddle which compels me to pick it up. It's an I.D. pass, *possibly* stolen by one of the homeless men then discarded *once* they'd learned it to be of *no* value to them. I see a familiar photograph upon this laminated credential: and a name which will *eternally* be branded into my psyche; *Peter Paul Rubens Strauss.*

'You've *quite* made your mind up then, Peter?' We've met him at his local café.

'I was going to have the steak and kidney pie,' he replies, 'but it didn't seem right under the circumstances.'

'Liver and bacon,' the Waitress calls out before placing a plate down before Strauss.

'I *meant* your decision to be a donor for Roland?'

'As I told you *right* from the *very* beginning, Fabio- this is something I'd decided upon *quite some time ago.* '

'You *did?!*' I splutter into my latte.

'Yes Fabio,' he informs us between ingesting spoonfuls of mashed potato, 'don't you recall when I said way back that this *could be* the shortest documentary in history?'

'Oh, so *that's* what you meant *by that*,' Troy sighs. His own order of tuna salad sandwich remains untouched.

'So we could have saved ourselves those *many* visits to your night shift?' I ask, having had my *own* appetite arrested by this *unpalatable* disclosure.

'I thought you were *just* enjoying hanging out with me?' Strauss answers before piling into his main course. 'I know I've made the *right* decision- the therapy helped confirm *that*.'

'What *form* of therapy have you taken?' I enquire.

'The relaxation techniques certainly helped.' Peter proceeds to provide me with both the following information *and* an open-mouthed view of what he's currently masticating. 'I'd been advised to relax and float downstream- I realized this was *only* a metaphor *after* a distressing incident by my local canal. And I try to console myself that there is *always* someone worse off than myself. *Funny though*, because every time I ask my Therapist who *specifically* this person *worse off* than me *is*, this *particular* question *remains* unanswered. But I've learned to see my life *less* as a series of bitter disappointments, disastrously failing relationships, traumatic familial betrayals, tragically missed opportunities *and* a myriad of intense personal humiliations, and *more* as a way of changing myself *completely* out of *all* recognition.'

'Do you have *absolute* faith in this advice?'

'My previous Therapist was a lot *less* helpful, Fabio,' my Subject replies whilst picking at his teeth. 'He told me I *didn't* have an inferiority complex, merely that I simply *am* inferior. My *current* Practitioner consoles me that, with lots of hard work, dogged determination and perseverance, there's the chance I *might* one day be lucky enough to wake up to find myself *utterly transformed into a completely different person entirely*.'

'This current therapist of yours,' I venture, working on a hunch, 'would he happen to be your brother Billy?'

'He's making *something* of a name for himself,' Peter beams back, exposing a collation of unidentifiable food matter wedged between his teeth. 'I know I'm doing the *right* thing.'

'I see you do your bit for the environment,' Troy remarks. I look down to see a bleached, tatty plastic bag by our Subject's feet.' No blowing away to get stuck in trees on your shift, *eh*?'

'Oh, *this*?' Strauss replies. 'I did have a smart ox-blood, initialed leather suitcase but can't seem to find it *right* now.' It then dawns upon me that he's just described the case I'd witnessed one of the homeless men steal, which I'd *presumed* to have belonged to Stan! 'Oh well, best I get my head down for a few hours. I'll be at the West Middlesex hospital at 5pm this afternoon if you want to meet me there?' I confirm these plans. Peter then rises from the table, shakes both Troy and I by the hand before turning to leave. Just before he reaches the door his "bag-*for-life*" splits and spills its contents- some most *personal* personal effects- out across the café floor.

'I remember it well as a fledgling journalist,' the voice on my phone-line tells me. 'Sextuplets conceived at the *cusp* of colour television- it should have run and run.'

'So *why* didn't it?'

'All to do with the father, *of course*,' confirms the *Chief* Commissioning Editor of the Broadcast Corporation which *now* employs me. 'He was already nuts deep in some *heavy duty* political shit.'

'My research on John Gilbert Strauss didn't pick up upon anything *overtly* political.'

'Of course it *wouldn't* have because those he helped out *became* too big to fail. They were experts at covering their tracks. Time might be ripe for you, *however*.'

'How do you mean?'

'A deathbed confession from the old man *may* reveal where all the bodies are buried, *quite possibly literally!* Get yourself down to Eastbourne *sometime soon* and you might *well* make yourself our newest, *hottest* property.'

This conversation -which *I'm aware* had *never* happened!- opens up a *whole new* vista of possibilities for me, creating a symmetrical narrative arc to *suitably* shape the fall of the house of Strauss. This could, *one might argue*, be a case of the *sins of the Father* but these siblings had free will to *defy* becoming misogynist, homophobic racists. Instead *however* they *chose* to busy themselves with sexist abuses, selfish gratifications and criminal endeavours to exploit, *rather than help* their fellow human beings. It now becomes clear there is *no* place for such toxic, Trump-like *deplorables* in Society, and it is *only* right that they *should* be stricken, smited , cuckolded, excluded, *made* obsolete and *replaced*. Their genes have *not* earned the right to be perpetuated, and so my *secular scourge* upon them has been *righteous and just!*

Peter, however, is *nothing at all* like his brothers. I shall have to devise a *different* approach for him.

'Thanks for coming,' Peter tells us, 'I *really* appreciate the support.'

'You look a *little* nervous,' I tell him. We're standing outside the hospital.

'A little,' he replies whilst straightening his collar and tie, '*who* wouldn't?'

'Did you *not* get the message?' Troy is filming in medium-to-long shot.

'*Message*? *What* message?'

'There's *no* need for you to be a donor, Peter.'

'Don't be silly,' he retorts, 'I've been for *all* the tests and proved I'm healthy enough to help Roland.'

'*Everything* has changed, Peter,' I inform him, 'you are *no longer* required as a donor.'

'Yeah, nice joke,' he replies, his features hardening. Two security guards emerge from the hospital entrance. 'I'll tell you how it all went- bye *now!*'

'They will tell you the same thing, Peter.' He halts upon noticing these men barring his entrance. Then he turns back to us, frowning.

'So you are going to claim he *never* really needed help!?'

'Oh, he's *very* much in need of help, Peter,' I state clearly, 'only it *won't be you* helping him.' On cue a police car pulls up nearby. Two officers spill from this vehicle.

'So *who* is going to be helping him then?!' His tone is displaying agitation.

'That's a *non*-issue right now,' I calmly relay. 'It could be *me* for all you're *now* entitled to know.'

'*Why* would you want to take *even this* away from me?!' Then Strauss's beseeching becomes belligerence. 'I *knew* the Great Clown would eventually take *some new form*, you bastard- is *this* what you had planned *all along?!*' It would seem my Subject has *finally* located his deeply suppressed anger issues.

'Go home, Peter.' This appears to antagonize him further, *probably* on account of him *having no real home* to return to: you might recall my observations *earlier* where I'd stated that you can judge a man by the state of his toilet; in Peter's case it's dirty, damaged, shared and in easy access of *any* passing vagrant stumbling in from the street.

'I'll break your fucking neck!' he rants whilst making a lunge at me but the two security guards intervene. The police officers then move in to help wrestle him down to the ground before handcuffing and arresting him.

'I don't understand,' Strauss whimpers after he's been read his Legal rights.

'What don't you understand, Peter?' I'm prepared for him to furnish me with something poignant, pitiful and *possibly even profound* though it's *more likely* I'll be subjected to *yet more* vitriol.

'When I'm seeking to concentrate or focus on something,' he replies -amazingly calmly- as though his sin of Wrath has *already* burnt itself out, 'I'll dab cold water upon my face. I won't dry it- just let it dwell there damply to seek clarity. And yet the first thing I do upon getting out of the shower is...*to dry my face...What* can possibly explain *that?*'

I'm re-watching the hospital footage shot the previous day when I receive a most curious email: *"Art thou certain ye hath yet known Wrath?"* This comes from someone identifying as *"The Great Terrible Clown"*!

Furthermore to my bemusement just moments later I'm sent a Skype request from the shadowy Source going by the name of *"Agent Provost"*! I immediately press the accept option then glare transfixed at my computer screen in fevered anticipation of whoever -or *whatever*- I'm about to be presented with. My initial glimpse is of nothing more dramatic than a drab, dim room. The sole source of illumination seeps in through a mostly concealed window in the corner. Eventually my eyes become accustomed to this, allowing me to make out a form that is little more than a silhouette.

'Can you hear me?' I call out. *'Kindly identify yourself?'* This shape appears to shrug, only now impressing upon me that it possesses life rather than being a *mere* mannequin. '*Who are you?!*'

'You *should* know,' a familiar voice eventually rings out. The curtain in this room is cast aside to confront me with a pasty, pimply visage which comes not as a *complete* surprise to me.

'I've long known you've had a part in this, Stan,' I tell my former employee, 'but *who* put you up to this?'

'Why would it have taken *someone else* to put me up to this, Fabio?' he goads from this mystery location. 'Perhaps you've *just* underestimated me?'

'I gave you *every* chance to flourish, Stan,' I inform him, 'it's hardly *my* fault you were inept *in everything* expected of you.'

'Projection, much?' he sneers back, which strikes me as childishly reductive. 'I *did* have a little bit of help, *however*.'

'From *whom*?' I demand. 'From *another* disgruntled loser who wants to blame somebody else, *anybody else* but themselves for the countless failures within their *own* wretched excuse for an existence?'

'We did leave you several clues, Fabio- for an investigative journalist you *aren't* very observant. So, *how* did yesterday's hospital footage turn out?' A chill suddenly assails my spine, my mouth goes dry and my heartrate begins to race. 'Not *so many* shots of your Subject, *eh*?' Disturbingly, most of what had been filmed was footage of me and my reactions *rather* than those of Peter Strauss: my *only* hope now for a suitably dramatic denouement is to acquire CCTV coverage from the hospital. 'And somebody *we both know very well* did a *very* effective job of second-guessing *everything* you were attempting to do!' My stomach lurches as the webcam is shifted over to the *other* person sitting within the room.

'Call it karma!' Troy issues a smile I *no longer* find *even remotely* charming. I'm then subjected to a lengthy, secretly-filmed montage *misrepresenting* me, and which is in *complete* contrast to my *actual* abilities as a *professional* Documentarian. This audio-visual travesty proves wholly distorting and devoid of *any* form of context, and has all-too-obviously been engineered to make me *wrongfully* appear to be an unscrupulous, cynical manipulator!

'This is on its way to your new boss as we speak,' Stan smirks.

'You're a shit,' I tell him, 'a duplicitous, *ungrateful*, conniving, *calculating little shit!*'

'I had a *very* effective mentor,' he replies, which extracts a guffaw from Troy. 'Now if you'll excuse us we need to attend to our *own* documentary, which *you* yourself *so kindly* helped us with. And just to show we're *not* ungrateful we'll be sending you an invite to the premiere- 'be seeing *you*, Mr. Fabio A. Bordino!' The screen goes blank, leaving me alone with my own baffled reflection.

My bewilderment shows no sign of abating when, a few minutes later, I receive *another* email, this time from an *"Adrian Provost (*children's entertainer*) AKA Agent Destruction!"!* I open it to see a still of what *seems* to be a children's party. To the rear of this photograph is a banner inscribed with the words *"Happy 8th birthday Christ Killers."* In the foreground are six near identical young boys expressing *varying* signs of distress. I look to the likeliest Source of this alarm to see a strange creature *-clearly this is "Agent Destruction"-* who, *very much of his time*, appears to be a peculiar hybrid of clown and punk rocker! All the children look justifiably terrified. *All* with the exception of one, who is wearing thick spectacles. He seems immune to this horror *so clearly* afflicting his siblings. Instead, this boy is succumbing to a *different* form of hysteria, *in his case* one of untenable, *insoluble* hilarity.

EvePress

Back to the Farm

The further investigations of documentary film-maker Fabio A. Bordino, who goes in search of a reclusive Showbiz personality who has retreated to his childhood home.

Crown of Wenceslas

Conclusion to the Fabio A. Bordino trilogy, where he documents the suitably Grand decline of a legendary Figure from European Cinema.

The Fugitive's guide to going on the run!

Edited by Fabio A. Bordino

and Rob Harman.

EvePress

Coming soon

Three colours dead

A suspenseful thriller featuring a hapless Critic falling foul of a megalomaniac Artist, who in turn devises increasingly elaborate ways to persecute his prey!

A satirical retelling of the Story of Job set amidst the Contemporary Art Scene.

The Poachers of Stratford

A historical romp explaining how a modest country lad named William Shakespeare was transformed into the greatest playwright in History.

Witness how, after a spell as a fugitive, the teenage William is forced to become a spy, infiltrating powerful and dangerous conspirators, first as a servant then as a fledgling actor within a theatrical troupe.

Marvel at how Shakespeare served an apprenticeship under Queen Elizabeth's "pet witch" John Dee.

Thrill at how the young Will helped foil the Babington Plot, a diabolical scheme to murder the Monarch.

Genre: Young Adults

Part of a trilogy

EvePress

Coming soon…

Night of the Succubus

A beautiful female demon wreaks havoc upon evil-doers.

The Cruse of Kali

Ruthless fortune hunters incur the wrath of a vengeful Hindu Goddess.

Shadow of the Cat

A sequel to Algernon Blackwood's 'Ancient Sorceries'.

They return!

The cast and crew of a film production in Southern Spain find themselves reluctantly re-enacting gruesome myths and historical events.

Wak-wak

After relocating to her husband's home in the Philippines an American newly-wed fears for her unborn child after a series of inexplicable events.

Redcap

An amnesiac former soldier returns to the now desolate place of his youth in the hope of unravelling a traumatic mystery.

Iron Dragon

A WWII tank crew encounter a series of most unexpected adversaries.

Reverend Roberts investigates!

A Victorian-era Vicar enlists the help of an unlikely ally to combat an ageless, destructive deity.

The plays

The Secret love lives of the Saints

An ensemble Cast participates in a frenetic farce scored with a series of witty songs.

The further Adventures of Oliver Reed

In a Celestial pub, staff and patrons induce the Screen Icon to give a suitably entertaining final performance.

Old Mother Tudor

The playwright William Shakespeare is haunted by the ghost of Elizabeth of York for the purpose of persuading him to portray her within a play.

Panto-maim!

The Archetypal figure of the Harlequin convinces a captive theatre audience that he's anything but the harmless character of myth.

Interactive!

Printed in Great
Britain
by Amazon